HONEY KO

(A Novel)

William C. Pennington

Honey Ko

(A Novel)

Published by William Charles Pennington
Copyright © 2020 William Charles Pennington

Cover design by Kyla Brichetto

All rights reserved. In accordance with the U.S. Copyright Act of 1976, the scanning, uploading, and electronic sharing of any part of this book without the permission of the publisher constitute unlawful piracy and theft of the author's intellectual property. If you would like to use material from the book (other than for review purposes), prior written permission must be obtained by contacting the publisher at william.c.pennington@writersenvy.com.
Thank you for your support of the author's rights.

This is a work of fiction. Names, characters, places, and incidents either are the products of the author's imagination or used fictitiously. Any resemblance to actual events, locales, or persons, living or dead, is entirely coincidental.

ISBN 9798628851043

1. Love and grief (Psychology)—Fiction. 2. Naval Aviation—Fiction.
3. Self-realization—Fiction. 4. Sailors—Fiction.
5. The Philippines and Thailand—Fiction.

Acknowledgments

My writing journey would not have reached the published novel point without Writers World admin Randall Andrews. His four-word critique of my first writing group submission gave me the confidence I needed to continue: "You have good pace." Colleen Aune's fifteen-hundred-word critique of the same submission deflated my ego and gave me the humility to take critique. Stephanie Vichinsky demanded I dig deep, rip my heart out, and bleed on paper what was buried in the unplumbed recesses of my soul. Stephanie's own writing soars like the classics we read in school. Writing group members who influenced me through their own incredible talent include Lauren Gregory; Jackie Stewart Collins; Ginette Paquette-Gadbois; Anna Dobritt; Kimberly Murphy Wilbanks; Frank Darbe; folk-singer, writer, and poet Jackson Ahearn; Angela L. Lindseth, whose chilling tales rival those of Stephen King; Mary Knuckles; R. L. Andrews; Elizabeth H. Prybylski; Sherry Antonetti; Kelly McLaughlin; Joyce A. Scott; Belinda Jordan Kinnari; Denise Robinson; Ireland poet Stephen McGuinness; Ani Alexander; Lyndi Scott; Kerry Elizabeth Blickenderfer Black, and many others. Beta readers include Michelle Wolfe, Jen Morio, and Jane Velde, all of whom provided insight that significantly improved *Honey Ko*. I can't thank my editor and biggest cheerleader of all, Laura Brichetto, enough for her support and encouragement. Most of all, I thank my wife, Jayne Michiko Ono Pennington, for her patience, love, and understanding.

Invocation

Susanna plucked a shrimp from the paper cone clutched in my hand and held it over my head like a seal trainer. She laughed as I leaned back and opened my mouth and wagged my tongue while struggling not to laugh. She brought the shrimp to my mouth, and I captured her long, graceful fingers between my lips. She hesitated and gazed at me, and her laugh turned into a smile. Oh, my heart beat fast, and I marveled at this beautiful Spanish woman and sucked her fingers into my mouth, and my tongue savored the flavor of Spain's greatest treasure. I was faintly aware of the seagull circling overhead, crying with anger at the meal it had missed.

We bought the quarter pound of fresh shrimp from the fish market on the plaza and then walked under an umbrella along the cobblestones of the waterfront of old El Puerto de Santa Maria. The rain stopped after a while, and we sat on the quay overlooking the ancient harbor where Christopher Columbus provisioned ships for his voyage of discovery. The sun came out, and steam rose from the puddles of water dotting the quay. I lay back, knees bent, on the old wall of crushed shells as Susanna leaned over me, shielding my eyes from the bright sun. She smelled of orange blossoms. Susanna always smelled of orange blossoms. I breathed deeply in the fragrant hollow behind her ear before the musty odor of decaying sea wrack intruded, and the salty fragrance of the vast great ocean, the granite-like permanence of the old city, the brilliance of the deep blue dome of sky overhead, the whole of the world spread before us.

Susanna. Our life together lay ahead. I swallowed the shrimp and reveled in the beauty of her green eyes as she slowly slipped her fingers from my lips. Her long, black hair framed her snow-white face and fell onto my chest. I sat up then, and we sat cheek to cheek, wordless, the closeness of her tiny, frail body a comfort.

I tightened my arm around her slender waist. My pulse throbbed as love for this beautiful woman raced through my veins.

"Come, Susanna. Let's walk along the beach. Give me your hand."

I helped Susanna down, and we walked onto the sandy beach. The wind tore at the frothy crests of the waves, and I tasted sea salt on my lips. The sea salt stuck to my skin in the humidity, and I took my shirt off and carried it in my hand. I paused while Susanna took her sandals off and dug her toes into the fine, warm sand. I carried Susanna's sandals as she dipped her toes in the water of the bay.

"Oh, Tomás," she cried with a laugh. "Dance with me, my love."

Susanna held my fingers in hers and danced around me on the beach between the sea wall and the sea, in front of a dozen other people walking along the shore. I dipped my head as I shook it and smiled. Oh, she was lovely in her gaiety. The wrap billowed from her body in the wind, and her black hair whipped about her white face that glowed with joy as she twirled and danced about me. I held her hand high, and she dipped beneath my arm and spun around and around and around, laughing. I spun Susanna into my arms, and I held her close as we danced together in the white sand of the beach beneath the bright yellow sun of a Spanish summer afternoon.

"I want to live forever, Tomás!" She was so happy.

I kissed her and let go of her hand and ran away up the beach. She laughed aloud as she ran for me, but I eluded her. Then I stopped and turned and flung the remaining shrimp as high into the sky as I could, and a cloud of seagulls converged above Susanna and plucked the shrimp from the sky. Susanna raced for me under the cloud of crying sea birds, her face bright and her lovely laugh ringing in the salty air as waves crashed upon the beach behind her and the sea gulls dipped and flew around her. I caught Susanna as she leapt into my arms, and we fell into the sand. We laughed as we fell, and we fell silent as our eyes fastened upon one another, and we breathed hard in our excitement, and Susanna pressed her hands into my chest and her lips onto mine. Oh, the lovely softness of the flesh of Susanna's lips. I feel them now, and I feel her feather-soft flesh pressing upon mine as though the years have not intervened between reality and memory.

Time passes, and grinds mountains into rubble and erases history into dimly recalled, tentative tales of memory, but it cannot erase the memory of the love a man and a woman feel but once, the love of a lifetime, the love of the ages. The love for which the heart burgeons into a breathless burst of yearning and passion and tenderness and fulfillment. The human love.

As we lay together in the fine, warm sand, Susanna's body pressing into mine, I held her in my arms, and her life beat in her chest and her life beat in my chest, and I knew how wonderful she was, and how fortunate I was, and I wanted this moment in the fine, warm sand beneath the bright yellow sun of a Spanish summer afternoon to last forever. I was so happy.

Book One

Olongapo, Philippines

1991

Chapter One

Tom Nelson

It's funny how the heart aches the same way in grief and love. It's as if the heart refuses to distinguish between the two most intense of human emotions. The only real difference between them is that one makes you cry while the other makes you smile. But that isn't always true. I've cried when in love and smiled while grieving.

I once asked Aida what love was.
"What is love, Aida?"
"Waking you when breakfast is ready."
"Love is waking me?"
"You work hard, honey ko. Sometimes I know you will wake up tired, so I turn off your alarm clock and let you sleep until breakfast is ready."

We were lying in the dark. She couldn't see my tears. The ache in my heart gave it a fullness my chest could barely contain.

The grief in my heart when Susanna died filled my chest the same way. I never thought I would love again. How do you tuck away the memory of a love so deep your spine tingled when she touched you? How do you forget the woman for whom all the love stories ever told were written? How do you put the pieces of heart back together? You never forget her, but you leave the pieces of heart where they fall and move on. You must move on. It may seem impossible, but you will love again.

I used to think love wasn't all it's cracked up to be. I tried to force love, but found disappointment. Like many people, I never made it far enough into a relationship to find out. I wanted true love instantly, the same way I wanted everything in life. But that isn't how love works. Love requires patience, a desire to be together forever, and commitment. Most people flee commitment when it becomes hard work. They expect it to be as easy as it was when infatuation ruled their emotions. Those who give up don't understand that infatuation is like a dream where all your attention is focused on one person with nothing to distract you.

The dangerous part of a new relationship is when infatuation fades and you notice the other person's flaws. You don't see your own, but measure the other person's flaws against your standards of what is acceptable. Flaws can be anything—physical, spiritual, emotional. When you accept that person, flaws and all, love stands a chance of lasting a lifetime.

What I missed for the longest time is that love has two characteristics: love can't exist in a vacuum, and love seeks its own level. Unrequited love is not love; it's desire that stabs the heart over and over and over. Love shared gains breadth and depth over time. When love stops growing, it dies. A heart breaks in response to something. Maybe your lover fell out of love. Perhaps love withered away because it wasn't returned. Maybe your lover died. Whatever the reason, one heart breaks when the other stops returning love.

Not long before she died, Susanna asked me why I loved her. We were in Barcelona, her hometown, to announce our engagement to her family. She lay with her head on my chest, her face illuminated by the moon rising above the Mediterranean. A warm breeze whispered across the balcony, stirring the scent of orange blossoms that filled the room.

Why do you love me, Tomás?
Because you're beautiful, Susanna.
Is that the only reason?
Because you're a perfect fit in my arms.
What else?
Because you give yourself to me completely.
Because you put me first in all things.
Because my heart aches when you leave the room.
Because I can't fall asleep without you beside me.
Because I miss your voice while you sleep.
Because I feel you even when I can't see you.
Because you make me whole.
Because you are my soul.
Because you're beautiful.
You said that already.
Did I?
Yes.

*Well, saying it twice means it's doubly true.
Can a person be doubly beautiful, Tomás?
Only you, Susanna.
Can a truth be doubly true, Tomás?
Only true love, Susanna.
How so?
Two people must be truly in love.
How do they know they are truly in love?
Because they have given themselves completely, one to the other.
How do they do that, Tomás?
Because they understand that true love is the gift of giving one's self unreservedly to another, that the giving of love is also the receiving of love, and that the spiritual renewal from the physical act is possible only after the giving up of self for one another.
I love you, Tomás.
I love you, Susanna.*

 I hadn't begun to move on from Susanna's death when my relationship with Aida began. Susanna's hands still held my heart while Aida's sought to peel away and replace them. I wasn't sure it could be done. I wasn't sure I wanted it done.

 She died of pneumonia three days before our wedding. Three years later, I met Aida in the Philippines, where the Navy had deployed my aircraft squadron. The struggle between the two women began at a small table in a crowded, dingy nightclub in Olongapo. One night, after I had frequented Rufadora Bar for several weeks, Aida asked if she could join me. Aida was soft-spoken and never asked for anything. I wondered how she came to work as a bartender. We met at the bar that way for a while until, one night, she asked if I wanted to walk her home. That night, for the first time since Susanna's death, I felt the first brush of love when Aida brought my emotions to life again. Maybe Susanna had receded enough into the past, or I had had enough of living with a heavy heart. Whatever the reason, Aida brought back all the passion I sent to the grave with Susanna. Which made me wonder if marrying Aida meant betraying Susanna.

 But why Aida? Why not another of the women with whom I eased my loneliness? I had not proposed to any of them, but I had placed them between myself and Susanna. I had used them to push away Susanna, to forget her, to stem the tidal wave of heart pain that swept through me when I let the frail wall between us fall. Wasn't sleeping with other women as much a betrayal as marrying Aida would mean betraying Susanna? If I were to carry Susanna with me for the rest of my life (and eternity?), shouldn't I at least pretend to be faithful to her?

In some strange way, though, I seemed to have placed myself between Susanna and Aida as if forcing them to fight over me. Was I too weak to choose for myself or too afraid to say goodbye to Susanna? Had I doomed her as if she were a ghost to walk Earth forever while I refused to let her go to her grave in peace? She filled my thoughts and dreams, but I had never considered she might haunt them. I sometimes spoke to her aloud as though we were having dinner together or sipping sangria on the terrace of our bungalow overlooking the Gulf of Cadiz. There were times I heard her voice as clearly as though she were whispering her decision in my ear. Somewhere deep inside, I must have wished Susanna would choose for me.

How long would I have to wait? If time heals all wounds, how long would it take to heal the gash in my heart? How long before I was free of …. I couldn't bear to think it. I didn't want to be free of Susanna. I wanted to move on, but couldn't. I was tied to Susanna like a drowning man gripping a lifeline.

Chapter Two

Tom

The balut man's quavering voice penetrated my sleep-filled head, and I squinted at the clock. My brain read zero-dark-early, but six a.m. glowed bright and cheery in the dark. He called out again as he wobbled away, pushing his creaking handcart.

"Baluuut. Baluuut."

Aida peeked at me from behind the edge of the bedsheet. She scratched the side of her nose and closed her eyes, her upper lip dotted with moonsweat glistening in the light from the window. Next to the bed, an old, brown fan blew the humid air around. Aida bunched the bedsheet around her neck and exhaled in exasperation.

"You tossing and turning all night, Tommy. I barely sleeping."

"Sorry, Aida. You stay in bed while I make breakfast for you."

I ran to the bathroom and splashed water on my face, then raced to the street to catch the balut man, flip-flops slapping my heels. I returned five pesos poorer with two balut wrapped in newspaper.

Aida loved balut, fermented duck embryo, seventeen days ripe and sold in the shell, a delicacy in the Philippines, but I couldn't stomach them. Sailors ate them when dared or offered free beer, or when too drunk to care.

I leaned over the bed and brushed my lips across her cheek and whispered. "Aida."

Her long black hair splayed across the pillow like a dark flower around her head. Her warm, lovely brown eyes had followed me from the door to the bed. Worry wrinkled her forehead as she reached over and touched my cheek.

"Do you sleep okay, Tommy? You look tired."

"I slept like a rock, Aida."

She put her arms around me and closed her eyes as I kissed her forehead. We lay together for a long moment before I untangled myself and left to shower, opening the bathroom window so the mirror wouldn't fog. While the water warmed, I leaned against the sink and stared at my reflection in the mirror. I pursed my lips at my thinning crown, inherited from my maternal grandfather.

I tested the shower water. Cold. I had forgotten to change the gas bottle, but wasn't about to run out to the shed for another. Steeling myself for the shock, I stepped into the stream of cold water. I could take a hot shower at the barracks, but it wouldn't do much good since I'd break into a sweat as soon as I left my room. But that was the PI, where the weather was always hot and damp, except during the monsoon when it was hot and wet.

I had almost finished showering when Aida peeked around the shower curtain. "Honey ko," she purred. She stepped in to join me and pressed her warm body against mine.

Aida's touch elicited the natural response, and I moved hard against her, the ache of desire intense. I put my arms around her waist, and her nipples pressed against my chest. I leaned down and drew my lips along her neck and across her cheek, tracing the line of her ear. A soft cry fell from her lips, and she turned to me with her eyes closed, and our mouths came together in a long, slow sigh. The flowing water glistened as it ran along her skin. I knelt and brushed my lips along the small of her back, caressed her calves and thighs and the curve of her hips, and inhaled the scent of her belly. Aida was impatient and urged me up, and I stood and let her move against me. She reached down and pressed my hand. The feel of her wet hair between my fingers aroused me.

"Oh, honey ko," she whispered. "You make me so happy."

I held Aida until her legs stopped trembling, then soaped her and rubbed her with a washcloth. She didn't open her eyes again until I took her hand and helped her from the shower. I dried her with a thick, heavy bath towel, moving slowly and massaging her body. When I finished, she leaned against my chest, and I dried her hair while avoiding her wandering hands.

"Here, Aida. Let me," I said when she reached for her hairbrush.

Any man who has never brushed a woman's hair has missed something tender and beautiful. I ran my fingers through Aida's black hair. The fine, silky tresses slipped over my skin like a whisper of breath. My fingertips traced through her scalp, behind her ears, down her neck, skimmed her spine, and stopped on the small of her back. She shivered under my touch, and goose bumps rose on her skin, and she pressed against me. The intimacy brought us closer, silent, the hum of the vent fan the only sound. My heart pounded as I drew the bristles through her hair.

The morning ritual stirred me with a peculiar sensation, a sexual feeling that took me to the brink but stopped short, my toes gripping the edge. The urge to brush through the strands of hair grew more intense with each stroke. Awareness of the surrounding room faded as passion consumed me. I wanted to take Aida to the same brink she took me. The soft bunches of hair slid between my fingers, caressing my skin and slipping away. I reached for more and drew the brush through again and again until my arm shook and I let it rest at my side. I leaned my forehead against her shoulder, and she reached behind and caressed me. When I placed the brush on the table, Aida winked at me and said, "Tommy, why your face is so red?"

I held her hand as she walked away, her fingers slipping from mine. She paused in the doorway to tie the towel around her hips. My throat tightened at the silhouette of her pointed breasts against the bedroom light.

The aroma of Aida's cooking reached the bedroom, and I hurried to the kitchen. I put my arms around her and peered over her shoulder.

"Mmm, smells so good. What is it?"

"Your favorite: sweet and sour fish with celery, carrot, red bell pepper, and snow peas, all in my world-famous red sauce." She stirred the dish and lowered the heat.

"And rice too?"

"Oh, Tommy. You're so funny. Of course, we have rice. This is Pilipino breakfast."

I checked a smile. Aida's occasional transposing of P's for F's embarrassed her. She was sensitive about it and would correct herself when among my friends from the base.

She pecked my cheek and said, "Thank you for the balut, honey ko. You're so thoughtful. I like when you do little things for me."

"I do them, Aida, because you make me so happy."

"My food makes you happy too. Hand me your plate, Tommy, and sit."

My taste buds watered as she brought breakfast to the table.

Yoshi, Aida's stray mutt, a Lab and Great Dane mix, ran his tongue around his mouth as I stirred the dish to release the aroma. Without warning, he barked. Aida jumped, then jumped again at a loud banging on the door.

"I'll get it, Tommy," she said.

I tossed Yoshi a last piece of fish as Phil Bryant's voice rose from the foyer. He ran up the stairs, his flight deck boots thundering with each step. He ran to the table and leaned over, hands on his knees as he caught his breath.

"Tom," he gasped. "You'll never guess what happened."

"Kenny transferred to Alaska?"

"Hah. Don't you wish. Jeff broke his leg. Master Chief Thomas called the barracks and told me to find you. You're taking his place on the detachment to Thailand. You leave Tuesday on the C-130 carrying the equipment. Pre-flight starts at 0400. The other crews take off Monday. You need to go to the hangar today and put together your pack-out kit of tools and supplies. They'll load the aircraft Monday morning."

I held my happiness in check. It wasn't my turn in the rotation for Thailand. What luck!

"I have to get back to base," Phil said. "You coming?"

"Oh, Tommy," Aida cried.

I grabbed my backpack and slung it over my shoulder. "I'm sorry, Aida. I'll make it up to you when I get back."

"Do you have to go? When will you return?"

"We'll be there at least a week. I won't know for sure until I get to the hangar."

"A week is so long, Tommy."

"I know, Aida, and I'm sorry." Her eyes were watering, and her face looked so sad. My heart ached as I caressed her cheek and kissed her. "I have to run now, sweetheart. I'll be back this afternoon."

The neighbor's chickens scattered as Phil and I hurried across the courtyard. Aida called from the bedroom window.

"Honey ko."

"Yes?"

"You forget your wallet."

I dashed into the house and swung around the end post of the stairwell. The newel cap wobbled but stayed put. Aida met me at the top of the stairs.

"Don't look so sad, Tommy."

"Oh, Aida. You know how much I love Thailand. I'll take you there someday."

"Promises, promises." She handed me my wallet. "You'd better hurry, Tommy, or they gonna send someone else."

"Not a chance, Aida!" I ran down the stairs, avoided tumbling the newel cap and called goodbye as the door closed behind me.

"Honey kooo."

"Ye-es?"

"Prop the door open so it won't jam shut if there's an earthquake, okay?"

"Okay."

I ran back and propped the door ajar between two bricks. Yoshi squeezed through the opening and ran to the gate, his tail wagging as he waited for me.

"Sorry, fella. You can't go this time."

The gate screeched on dry hinges as it swung open. I made a mental note to bring home a can of oil. A distant rumble from Mount Pinatubo reached my ears as I walked away.

I worried about leaving Aida alone.

Chapter Three

Tom

The sun rose blood-red through the ash drifting from Mount Pinatubo's smoking crater. Enough moisture filled the air to quench a dying man's thirst. The wind pushed the sun's heat against my face like a second skin. I turned away when the river's stench hit me, but it was no use. Whatever the official name for the vile smelling, lumpy sliver of waste that separated naval base and town, the Sailor's crude nickname stuck: Shit River. I shielded my eyes against the sun's glare, took a deep breath, and held it while I crossed the bridge to Subic Bay Naval Station.

I reached the guard shack, thankful I didn't have to breathe the river's fetid odor all day. The Filipino sentry gave my ID card a cursory look and waved me on. I checked the schedule at the bus queue but took a taxi rather than wait. We sped away for the barracks, driving along the shipyard packed with visiting warships. We drove past the airfield and the runway and into the jungle and up Sky Club Hill. Near the top, the view opened to reveal the deep blue water of Subic Bay backed by the lush green foliage of the Zambales Mountains reaching high into the hazy morning sky. The South China Sea beckoned in the distance. As we rounded the curve to the barracks, the cabbie mashed the brakes to avoid a monitor lizard sunning itself on the hot pavement. We inched closer. The cabbie honked the horn until the eight-foot lizard lifted itself on short, powerful legs, and sauntered away, flicking its long tongue in defiance. We arrived at the barracks next to the jungle survival school compound. I paid the driver and ran up the stairs to my room on the fifth deck. Sweat rolled off me as I caught my breath and peeled away my damp clothes and donned my uniform. I took a soda from the refrigerator and ate a cold slice of pizza leftover from the Sky Club.

A short bus ride later, I walked into the hangar aboard Cubi Point Naval Air Station, the aviation side of the giant American Navy base. Two P-3 Orion anti-submarine aircraft parked nose to nose filled the hangar. The cavernous structure echoed with the sounds of mechanics replacing a propeller on one P-3 while structural mechanics repaired a fuel cell in the starboard wing of the other. Good-natured voices and colorful language rose above the echoing clang of tools and roar of ground support equipment engines.

Fuel fumes enveloped me like Saran Wrap covering a bowl of potato salad as I walked across the hangar deck. I took the stairs to the coffee mess on the second deck and filled my mug to the brim with the lifeblood of the Navy. The cashier, a plain, cross-eyed Filipina in her mid-twenties with acne-scarred cheeks, returned my smile as she made change for me. Outside, I hurried for the air-conditioned comfort of the Airframes shop in the Quonset hut behind the hangar.

Kenny, the shift supervisor, walked in as I scanned the aircraft status board, jotting down maintenance notes for the detachment. His high-pitched Alabama nasal twang grated in my ears. I turned the radio volume up, but it didn't help. His voice rose to the pitch of an untuned violin in the hands of a tone deaf sixth-grader.

"Well, if it ain't my buddy, Admiral Nelson. Hey admiral, I heard you were whining to Master Chief about not going on the Thailand detachment. It wasn't your turn, you know."

"I'm not your buddy, and I'm not related to Admiral Nelson."

"So, you admit you were sucking up to him and got him to change his mind?"

"Whatever you say, Kenny."

"Now, why would you want to go to Thailand? What would your wife say? You just want to see that Thai chick you used to screw over there."

"She's not my wife. And her name is Aida, like the opera. You know what opera is, don't you?"

"Isn't that where fat ladies dress like Vikings and sing? I don't like opera."

"I didn't think you would."

"What?"

"Nothing. Screw you, Kenny."

"Screw you, Admiral. Won't your wife get mad if you go to Thailand?"

"You're such a jerk, Kenny."

"What?"

"You heard me."

He sniffed and pushed his glasses up with his index finger.

"I'm not a jerk."

"Yeah? People say otherwise."

Kenny flipped me off, but I ignored him. I picked up my coffee mug and notebook and left to join Phil in the First-Class Petty Officer's Mess.

"Kenny giving you a hard time about Aida again?"

"Like always. He calls her my wife and gives me hell about our relationship. He claims the only thing Filipino women want is a ticket to the States and says the guys who marry them are losers."

"Well, he's the loser: he cheats on his wife. Have you seen the girl he hooks up with at the Brown Fox? Good Lord, she looks like a water buffalo. How she gets guys to buy her drinks is beyond me."

"The real question is, how does that skinny, bug-eyed bastard get girls to go out with him? I'd scream and run if he leered at me. I'd lose my lunch from last week."

The light flashed on the massive, stainless steel, 65-cup coffee maker we called the Viking. I poured a cup for Phil, then filled my own.

"I've never met Kenny's wife. She must be a winner."

"I saw her at the terminal before we left Hawaii."

"What does she look like?"

"She's too good for him."

"A worm is too good for him."

"She could be a model."

"Get out."

"I'm serious. Unbelievable, huh?"

"Holy crap. I wonder what's wrong with her?"

Phil and I had been best friends since boot camp and roomed together when deployed overseas. Neither of us had any compunction about calling the other out for various sins and failings. Phil had a great liking for Aida and worried over what I might do if I went to Thailand. But I didn't expect a finger in my chest.

"Why do you want to see that girl in Thailand?"

I pushed his hand away and snapped at him.

"Don't put your finger in my chest, Phil, and don't question me like that. I'm not a child."

I sat on the edge of the sofa and squeezed the bridge of my nose. After chilling out for a minute, I leaned forward with my elbows on my knees, massaging the back of my neck.

"I'm sorry, Phil. I know you mean well. What makes you think I want to see Lek?"

Lek was an acquaintance from Thailand. We had had what people would call a torrid relationship with long nights of dancing and drinking away loneliness, desperate passion, violent arguments, and orgiastic make-up sex. She helped me forget what it was like to feel dead inside. We parted each time without commitment or promise. I wasn't in love with her, but her imprint on my heart remained deeply stamped as did my desire for the freedom I had felt with her. The freedom from love that came after mourning the loss of Susanna for so long.

"Why else go to Thailand?"

"Trained elephants. The food. The temples. What else is there?"

"You going to marry Aida?"

"What?"

"Are you going to marry Aida?"

"That appears to be her expectation."

"You're crazy, Tom."

"Why do you say that?"

"You think you can resist temptation long enough to make it back to PI?"

"Hey, I didn't ask to go to Thailand. Anyway, I only want to tell Lek it's over."

"Why do you need to tell her anything?"

"I don't want her hanging on to something that will never happen."

"You seem to believe she's sitting at home crying and waiting for you to come back. She's not, you know."

"We had a pretty serious fling. She might think I'll come back and marry her."

"Newsflash, Tom: Lek works in a nightclub on the Pattaya Beach strip. She's not waiting for you."

"She might be."

Phil shook his head. "If—and that's a mighty big if—she's waiting for you, I hope she doesn't find out about Aida. If she does, she'll have a butterfly knife when you see her. You think a woman threatening to cut off your happiness is funny just wait until the knife flashes in the moonlight. You'll sing falsetto."

"I just can't walk away without saying goodbye."

"Saying goodbye is the nice thing to do, but there's less danger in staying away from Lek and letting time erase you from her memory."

"I thought I was being altruistic by telling her."

"There's nothing altruistic about having your nuts cut off."

"Thanks for the visual, Phil."

"Keep the image in mind when you see her."

"I'll wing it."

"Good luck with that," he said. "By the way, I'm taking Lucy to dinner tonight. Why don't you and Aida join us?"

"Thanks, but not tonight. I'm going to take her to Grande Island for a picnic tomorrow. Why don't you and Lucy join us?"

"We're going to Manila. I promised to take her to the zoo."

"You don't need to go to Manila for that. Just bring her down here for the day. That'll entertain her."

Phil laughed. "No kidding. I'll catch you later."

We split up. Phil headed to his shop, I to mine. As I ducked under the aft fuselage of the fuel leak aircraft, I overheard two of the mechanics on the wing. One of them was donning a respirator mask.

"Bryan. Hey, Bryan."

"What?"

"I'll kill you if you let anyone near the fresh air intake. Beer farts make me gag."

Sailors.

Chapter Four

Tom

Aida, sweet and lovely like the opera, searched for treasure among the debris washed ashore by the latest storm of the monsoon. Her breasts filled her top as she leaned over to examine a bright and colorful smorgasbord of seashells, pebbles, smooth-worn glass, and curious shapes of driftwood. Breath caught in my throat as she turned, and I followed the long line of her legs as they curved with the round of her bottom and the straight line of her back that flowed beneath the hair that fell below her shoulders. This beautiful woman of twenty-one made every move a display of feminine eroticism, and she was entirely unconscious of the fact. I told her often how beautiful she was, and she blushed each time and replied, "Oh, thank you, honey ko."

Aida collected her treasure in a net bag that let sand fall away. She'd add the shells to jars lining the sill of the window over the kitchen sink of her apartment. The mix of colors, shapes, and textures would look pretty in the bright afternoon sunlight filling the window of the tiny kitchen. I thought of a similar kitchen I had known several years before and how Susanna had arranged seashells on the sill of the window of our bungalow in Rota, Spain.

Susanna was as real to me as though she were not dead. She often returned to my thoughts when I questioned whether I could love Aida with only half of my heart, for Susanna held the other. Aida knew of Susanna. I had spoken of her so Aida would not have to ask questions later. She thought I was carrying grief too long and too far, but Susanna was not just an image brought about by a misfiring synapse in my brain. The love between Susanna and me predated all other human love and was always meant to be. Our lives before finding each other were years spent waiting to find each other. We both knew it. When God created love, he created it from a perfect form. The love between Susanna and me was that form. All other love was a copy of the love we shared. When Susanna died, our love remained, for you can't kill love. Once given, once reciprocated, love is eternal.

Holding the bag in both hands behind her back as she crept along, Aida scanned the beach for those simple touches that bring the outdoors indoors and render a home warm and cozy. A glint of reflected sunlight in the sand drew her attention. She stepped across a rivulet running across the beach from the jungle to the sea. She stooped to turn over a fist-sized rock and screamed. Yoshi dashed over, sniffing and barking at the rock. Aida laughed, and the wind blew away her tinkling laughter as she fell onto her bottom.

"Are you okay, Aida?"

"Yes, Tommy. I'm okay." She shooed Yoshi away, and he ran into the jungle, thrashing through the underbrush and barking.

I stifled a laugh as Aida stood and brushed sand away. The gesture aroused me, and I pressed my hand to her bottom and spoke close to her ear. "Are you sure you're okay?"

"Oh, Tommy. Not now, honey ko. So many people might see us." She laughed again as she moved away from me and said, "A crab surprise me when I am turning over a rock. He looks so funny snapping his claw to me. Maybe he's thinking I'm going to eat him."

"It would take a bucketful of those little guys to make a meal. Why don't we buy crabs at the market on the way home?"

"If you like, honey ko, I will buy the crabs fresh tomorrow and make the soup for your supper."

"Okay. Buy crackers too, oyster crackers. You can't have crab soup without oyster crackers."

"Oh, they don't sell those at the market."

"I'll stop at the commissary after work and buy them. Do you need me to pick up anything else?"

"Yes. Napkins."

"There's a whole case of napkins in the hall closet, Aida."

"Not that kind of napkin, Tommy."

"Ohhh. Okay. Too bad you can't come with me."

"You're so shy, Tommy. Nobody noticing when men buying napkins for their wives. If they do, they thinking like the man is helping his wife and how sweet of him."

The earlier storm had washed away the brown haze of smog

and left behind a brilliant, deep blue sky. The sun was past high noon. I put on my shirt, and we continued our treasure hunt. A gust of wind peppered my cheek with sand and sea spray, and I turned away. The wind folded back the brim of Aida's hat. She laughed as she held the hat to keep it from flying off, and the graceful curve of her arm and the outline of her happy face reminded me of Susanna. Aida's brown eyes crinkled when she laughed and pierced my heart the same way Susanna's eyes had done. My throat tightened and I looked away.

As so often occurred when Susanna returned to my thoughts, my adoptive father's words rang in my ears. "Never find yourself having to choose between two women. You'll hurt one of them, Tom, and hurting a woman lowers a man."

I loved Aida, but I loved Susanna too. But Susanna died. What reason had I to choose? I wanted to let go of Susanna. I wanted to love Aida with a clear conscience, one free of ties to another woman. But I couldn't forget that Susanna died alone, without me by her side. I couldn't forget I was the cause of her death. I wiped my eyes with a knuckle and took a deep breath. I pretended not to notice Aida's curious look and kicked at a clump of seaweed. The kick loosened an odor that mingled with the fragrance of tropical flowers growing in the sunlight along the fringe of the jungle. As I leaned over to examine a seashell knocked loose from the clump, the medallion swung against my chin. Two flaws in the ruby set in the medallion blinked like red eyes in the sunlight. I replaced it inside my shirt and picked up the shell and dropped it in the red plastic cup that smelled of San Miguel. Moving along the beach, I nearly stepped on a sand dollar, its edges unbroken.

"Here you go, Aida. Look what I found."

"Ooh, that's a big one, honey ko. Don't break the edge." She squatted on her heels and leaned over her knees, turning the wet sand with her fingers, and picking out several tiny shells the size of a thumbnail.

"Honey ko, if we find enough of these little shells, I will make a soup for you instead of crab soup."

"How many does it take, Aida?"

"Two cups, Tommy. I tell you last time we come here. You are so forgetful."

I grinned and placed the sand dollar in the cup. I was forgetful, but Aida's iron-clad memory could recall what I had for dinner any night of the week months ago. I moved along the shoreline, turning away from breaking waves and sifting the sand with my toes.

Near the narrow causeway to Banana Island, several palm trees heavy with coconuts leaned over the water. I tried in vain to dislodge coconuts by throwing rocks at them.

"Climb up the trunk, Tommy. That's what my brothers do. Walk up the tree bent over like you are going to touch your toes. See? Watch me."

Aida bent over and stretched her arms toward her toes and took a few awkward steps.

"See? It's easy. Go ahead, Tommy. I catch you if you fall."

She looked like a monkey walking on all fours, and I had to try hard not to laugh.

"If it's so easy, you climb up, and I'll catch you if you fall."

"Oh, Tommy. You can do it."

"No way, Aida. I'm not your brothers. If you crave a coconut that much, we'll stop by the commissary and buy some on the way home."

Leaving the coconuts free to taunt others, we returned to the hunt, but I was hungry.

"Aida, my hands are full. Let's go back to the cottage. It's past lunchtime and I'm starving."

"You always starving, honey ko. Why you aren't fat?"

"It must be all the sex you force on me. It's great exercise."

Aida put her arm through mine and pulled me along the trail. We left the bags of treasure at the cottage and carried lunch to the pavilion. I grilled hot dogs and hamburgers and reheated the fried lumpia Aida had prepared at home. We sat close together and made small talk. Sometimes we didn't talk at all. We were closest in quiet moments and could almost read each other's thoughts. Often, I would find her hand clasped in mine and not remember reaching for her.

The breeze was cooler under the pavilion, and Aida rested her head on my shoulder as we gazed across the water at the warships and freighters dotting the bay at anchor. She stirred and yawned, then hugged her knees while her gaze carried her across the mountains to Bataan Province and her home on the shores of Manila Bay.

"I miss my family, Tommy." Her wistful voice carried a yearning that differed from the other yearning, the one where she worried that I would never propose.

"I know, sweetheart. I miss mine too. Why don't you go home for a visit?"

"Maybe. I thinking tomorrow I will ask Cora to go home with me. She's not visiting her family there for longer time than me."

Near dusk, we packed the remains of the picnic. We showered at the beach house and changed into street clothes. After depositing our bags on the ferry pier, we strolled along the trail to the seawall overlooking the dark blue water of the bay. A warm, salt-laden breeze carried the scent of seaweed through palm trees above the high-tide mark. We kicked off our flip-flops, and I helped Aida onto the seawall. I sat next to her while we waited for the ferry to Fleet Landing. Yoshi barked to join us, so I lifted him onto the seawall.

We dangled our legs above the waves lapping below. The setting sun's golden rays changed from orange to purple to red through the filter of ash drifting from Mount Pinatubo. For miles around the bay, strings of colored lights winked on at the clubs and resorts dotting the shoreline. F-14 Tomcats roared overhead, the orange-blue flame of their dual afterburners splitting the twilit sky. The warm night air wrapped around us like a soft, cozy blanket, and the tranquility of the evening pushed the sound of the aircraft into the background. I slipped my arm around Aida's waist.

"Oh, Tommy. You make me so happy. I'm glad you bring me here. This is where you tell me you love me for true the first time, remember?"

"I remember. Not much has changed."

"Change comes slow in the Philippines." She turned to look at me, her face curious. "Does change come slow in America?"

"No. Everything happens fast back home. People are impatient and want things now-now-now before they change their minds and want something else just as quickly."

"Are Americans impatient for love?"

"Most of them."

"Why?"

"Because just like having things now, they think love should happen fast too. They rush into a relationship because they think they're in love. They don't give love a chance to grow first. Sometimes, I think people believe it's all about sex. They think they're in love while the sex is fresh and exciting. But, just like everything else, they become disillusioned when the excitement and mystery wear off."

"Love with you will never become boring, honey ko."

"I love when you call me honey ko."

"That's because you are my sweetheart."

She rubbed her cheek against the stubble of my five o'clock shadow. "I love the scratch of your beard and the sound it makes against my cheek."

"I remember one night, Aida, as you lay with your head on my chest, you said you loved the sound of me made intimate by my closeness and the warmth of my body."

"I remember," she whispered. She pressed her nose to the hollow behind my earlobe. "I love also the smell of you, masculine and gentle. I like to breathe in your scent. When it fills my lungs, it's like you are filling me inside." She moved against me. "Hug me so I feel you."

I put my arms around Aida because she wanted to feel the muscles of my body. We sat close, so close that our hearts beat as one. After a while, her body ceased to be separate from mine, and I moved away and back again.

Aida wasn't voluptuous but possessed a perfect figure. She wasn't a striking beauty but was beautiful. Her voice wasn't high-pitched or low-pitched but seductive. Her accent wasn't awkward but endearing. Some women made themselves alluring or attractive. They puffed up their breasts, preened their feathers, and strutted their stuff. Not Aida. She had no need to present herself. She attracted men naturally, like hummingbirds to nectar. Men hovered about, hoping for a lick of Aida.

The flicker of lights along the arc of the shoreline to Subic City snapped me from my reverie. The rising moon with the mountains in silhouette, the soft lapping of the waves, the warm night, all induced a languidness I didn't want to disturb. Satisfaction with the moment, the weekend, the treasure hunt with Aida all combined to lift my spirit, and for a moment, my constant companion, the pain of loss that never left my side for long, fell away.

Aida caressed my cheek. "Are you sleepy, honey ko? The ferry will be here soon. You can sleep on the ride back."

"Um hmm," I said behind half-open eyes. "I love to sleep on the boat, but I'm not sleepy, just relaxed. It's been a wonderful day; I wish it didn't have to end."

"Me too."

"We should come here more often."

"Yes, we should, but you always want to visit Manila. I like Manila too, but we run around taking so many photos we don't have a chance to relax. Someday, we'll see if you enjoy Manila without a viewfinder as your guide. I will be your guide, honey ko."

"There's so much to see in Manila, though, especially Rizal Park and the zoo, and the national palace. And my favorite place in all the world to watch the sunset is from the seawall along Manila Bay. The colors are so vivid and run through the whole rainbow of colors."

"That's because the air is dirty with smog."

"Aida. Where's your sense of the romantic?"

"There's nothing romantic about inhaling Manila air. All that smog makes it hard to breathe and I cough too much."

"Well, maybe I'll bring you a gas mask from the base."

"Honey ko, I gonna tickle you if you keep joking to me."

"All right, I'll be a good boy."

"I don't believe you."

I laughed. "Okay, Aida, I promise."

I caught myself fingering the medallion through my shirt the way people drum their fingertips together or sit with their hands behind their head lost in thought. I'd heard the medallion held a curse but never paid it much attention. Family stories were full of oral history, some of which may have held a kernel of truth. My thoughts turned to Aida, and my breathing softened as the sounds of the evening faded. I loved Aida, but what would Susanna think? How could I betray Susanna's memory by marrying another as if she were a stand-in, a substitute for the woman I had loved at first sight?

Sam and Susanna McBride, my birth parents, had fallen in love at first sight while he was stationed in Spain. The intimate connection they made at their first, brief encounter, over an apple, of all things, blossomed into love during their second encounter later that day. Sam proposed to Susanna on the third day of their acquaintance, and they married three months later. They remained inseparable until Susanna died giving birth to me in the sixth year of their short life together. Six months later, Sam gave me up for adoption. He couldn't bear to raise me without Susanna. Six months after that, he died in Vietnam.

I had often wondered if my mother and Susanna could be

related. But I figured it was just coincidence that father and son had met such similar women with the same name, in the same town, doing the same type of work, halfway around the world. The similarities ended with their deaths, though. My Susanna's death had brought an end to everything we had planned. Our wedding, the chapel, the priest, the flowers, the dinner with friends and her family, the honeymoon in Barcelona. Our future. Except the ring. The wedding ring that had not touched her finger.

I walked beside her casket from the chapel to the cemetery under a clear, bright blue sky, then helped lift her into the vault, three rows up and two rows from the end. They hadn't wanted me to help, but I wouldn't be denied. Birds chirped in the landscaped shrubs, taunting me with their joyful songs as I stared misty-eyed under a heavy brow as the mason cemented each brick into place to close the opening. I closed my eyes and whispered a prayer as the mason sealed the vault, the tap-tap-tap of his hammer forever echoing in my mind as he set the final brick. After the mourners left, after the mason packed up his tools and left, I opened my fist and placed Susanna's wedding ring on the necklace. Next to my mother's medallion. It had felt right.

It had felt right, but it was so wrong, and seemed so unfair. Maybe it had to be though, since not only had magic struck twice in bringing both Susannas to us, but it also struck them down too soon, too young, too unfairly. Why had God chosen Sam and Susanna, and Susanna and me, to suffer his whims? I never had the chance to know my parents, and I never had the chance to know my Susanna. I didn't hate God, but I didn't understand Him.

I knew my birth parents only by what my adoptive parents told me, through letters between Sam and Susanna, and essays Sam had written after Susanna's death. The letters and essays told me theirs was a fairy tale romance, the kind others dream of, writers write books about, and parents hope their children find. The kind that comes once in a thousand years.

Twice in two decades. Susanna and I had had that kind of love. Did it run in the family? Would my son find that kind of love? No, that kind of magic was rare if it existed at all. Lightning doesn't strike twice in one place, does it? But magic wasn't lightning, and magic had struck twice in the same place for my father and me. I thought that if Sam were alive, if my father were alive, I would ask him if he believed in magic and if he believed in God.

Aida straddled the seawall with her back against mine.

"What do you see, Tommy?"

I leaned my head against hers and closed my eyes. A lifetime passed before me as hopes and wishes, dreams lost and dreams gained, filled my mind. I wondered where we would be in forty years, if we would be happy and content, rich or poor, if we would be successful, if Aida would always greet me at the door with a kiss.

"Us. With gray hair, crow's feet around our eyes, and wrinkled hands."

"Are we happy?"

"Yes."

I turned and Aida turned too. The moon shone bright over her shoulder, and I wondered if she could see it reflected in my eyes. *Magic didn't strike a second time for me, though.* I pressed my lips to her fingers. *It wasn't love at first sight with Aida. Our love took time to develop.* Her face and neck flushed red. *Two years have passed since we met, and we spent one of those years apart, carrying on our relationship through phone calls and letters without committing to one another.* Aida's emotional state changed and I could feel her rapid heartbeat. *Our passion has grown with my return to the Philippines. I haven't gotten over Susanna, I never will, but I no longer mourn for her. Or do I?* I held Aida's hands in front of my lips. Her eyes widened in expectation of more than finger kisses. *Susanna will always be a part of me, and I will always wear her ring next to my mother's medallion. It feels right.*

In a burst of emotion, I whispered, "I love you, Aida. Will you marry me?"

Chapter Five

Tom

Romance and a sexual tension made the air surrounding us buzz with expectation and fulfillment of some deep-seated desire or need. Holding her suddenly seemed so much more than just an embrace between two people. I saw Aida now as a necessary part of me, an essential element in what made me who I was.

At the time, I didn't realize what had happened. Only later did I come to see we had passed a stage in our relationship that left infatuation and passion behind as we entered the stage of commitment. It sounded almost clinical when I thought about it, but it was the only way to describe the change that affected both of us that night on the seawall.

What is love, Aida?
Watching for you through the window.
Love is watching for me?
I would die, Tommy, if you went away and didn't return to me.

I pressed my lips into Aida's black hair. She reached up and pulled my head to her, and we kissed until we were out of breath and her breast heaved against my chest.

I brushed the tears away when she pressed her hands to my face.

"Oh, Tommy. Of course, I will marry you. I love you so much, honey ko. I love you so much."

She gripped me in a vise-like hug when the earthquake struck. The ground rolled beneath us like the swell of a wave lifting a swimmer treading water. We were lucky this time; too often the movement came with the jarring motion of a decrepit bus driving over a pot-holed road. She relaxed her grip when calm returned.

"That scared me, Tommy. The volcano will erupt and what will happen to Olongapo? What will happen to us? What will happen to my family in Bataan?"

"We'll be okay, Aida. We're far enough away to be safe when it erupts, and your family is further away than we are."

"I hope so. But it still worries me."

She looked up as the sounds of the jungle returned. "It's always so quiet after the earthquakes stop, then the jungle noises begin again."

Another couple strolled along the path behind us, apparently unperturbed by the earth's movement. Their whispered conversation carried away on the warm breeze. The flowered wrap around the girl's hips and the poinsettia-like flower in her hair reminded me of Hawaii. The girl's bubbly laugh faded as they passed out of sight beyond the boathouse.

Aida snuggled closer. She squeezed my hands between hers and leaned towards me, her eyes glistening in the moonlight. But she grew silent, and a faraway look in her eyes reflected concern.

"What's the matter, Aida?"

"I'm afraid for how much you miss her."

"Aida, her name is Susanna. You can say her name; you won't hurt me."

"You say her name, Tommy, when you're sleeping. Sometimes it hurts me, but I don't say anything because I don't want to hurt you. But I worry you love her still."

"You don't have to worry. She died a long time ago. I've put the pain behind me. It's only natural that I think about her. You never forget the people you loved."

"Four years isn't a long time."

"It seems like yesterday. It seems like forever too."

She didn't say anything, but kept my hands in hers. She trusted me, and I knew I would never betray that trust. When she leaned against me and relaxed, I realized the tension that had gripped her over worry that I would never propose had flown away with my words. At that moment, I understood just how much Aida meant to me and how much I had worried about committing my future to her. My worries had flown too.

There had been many moments when she seemed a siren, but her song alone hadn't lured me into the dangerous waters around her heart. Her eyes, her beauty, her spirit. Her simple, uncomplicated manner. All those qualities made me speak the words she wanted to hear. She woke something inside me like a dormant volcano rumbling to explosive life. Aida had *it*, whatever *it* was. *It* smoldered in her eyes, glowed in her smile, burned in her touch. *It* burned me. Like candlelight to a moth, I couldn't resist the attraction to Aida, and I couldn't pull my finger out of the flame.

Before Aida, I had tried too hard to rediscover the love my parents had, the love I found with Susanna. Twice I had made the same mistake. Each time, I hoped the latest woman would be the one. My heart told me she was the one, but my head told me otherwise. My head told me the woman was no Susanna, that she wasn't as beautiful as Susanna, that she could never love me the way Susanna had loved me. But I never noticed my mistake. Not even when the woman told me she would not compete with a dead woman. So, the women walked away because no man can love two women the way a man and woman must love each other.

I thought it would be different with Aida. No woman since Susanna pulled at my heart the way Aida did, and she needed me as much as I needed her. But I had proposed on impulse in a tender, romantic moment when I was most vulnerable. I had spoken the words while telling myself I would always love Susanna, thus leaving Aida the loving cup for second place.

Something in the back of my mind had told me, or hoped, Aida would laugh my words off as a joke. She believed me, though, when the words floated from my lips like music taking wing and trilling into her ears. She had earnestly wanted to hear them. I could almost feel her heart flutter as joy spread like a warm smile inside her breast. Aida would have believed anything I said if it included the breathlessly beautiful words, "I love you, Aida. Will you marry me?" Had she read my mind, she would have read, *I love you Aida, but I love Susanna first.*

Another voice had slipped into my head, the voice that whispered cynically to most Sailors who visited Olongapo and fell for the treasures of that city. What if going to America were Aida's sole reason for being with me? What if Aida were using me for a one-way ticket to the States so she could send for the rest of her family?

The ferry whistled, and we walked to the pier, Yoshi beside us. We chose seats along the stern where the deck canopy wouldn't obstruct our view of the night sky. I leaned back and let the stars draw me away. The rhythmic motion of the boat and the lapping of waves against the hull was hypnotizing. Yoshi lay with his head on my lap while Aida dozed against my shoulder. She woke when the boat bumped against the dock at Officers Landing. I hailed a taxi for the main gate and then flagged down a jeepney for the short ride home.

Back in the apartment, I put away the picnic supplies while Aida unpacked and put away the clothes, a quantity of clothing since she had taken advantage of the laundromat at the cottage rather than wash them by hand at the cement sink in the courtyard. After we were settled on the sofa, she nestled against me and watched television while I read. Soon, her eyes closed and her breathing grew soft. She fell asleep with her head in my lap. I stretched and yawned, then gently picked her up and carried her to bed and undressed her, then undressed myself. I slipped under the bed sheet and stared at the ceiling, my hands behind my head. The medallion lay heavy on my chest, a constant reminder of love, pain, and hope. The heavy jewel linked me to another person, my father, who had suffered love, pain, and hope. I leaned over and withdrew a blue silk pouch and my old, leather-bound journal from the drawer of the nightstand. I set the pouch aside and leafed through the journal, stopping at a bookmark. The memories returned as I read:

I trembled as I reached for Susanna, my Spanish Madonna, and touched her hip. I pressed my palm against her smooth, white flesh and her warmth spread through me until my face flushed and the burn of rising excitement engulfed me. I rubbed my hand across her shoulder and trilled my fingertips along her spine, raising goosebumps from her skin, and a shiver. I caressed along her side to her hip and pressed my hand to the small of her back, bringing her body close, so close her bones ground against mine and her scent mingled with mine. She trembled and breathed out, her warm, fresh breath billowing into my face and nostrils, pulsing through the veins in my head until my temples throbbed. I inhaled her skin's fragrance of orange blossoms, and the hairs on my neck lifted as a wave of sobbing, intense passion shook my body and overwhelmed me.

Aida moved against me, and I rested my hand on her hip. She slept on, her face retaining a radiance of happiness.

I shivered as I brushed my fingers across her lips and she kissed them as they wiped away tiny beads of moonsweat. My angel's eyes, framed by her perfect oval white face and raven-black hair that reflected a billion midnight stars, held mine, unwavering, unblinking, penetrating. I pressed my lips to her silk-black eyebrows. Her fingers brushed along my chest and tickled my belly, and she held me. The smooth roundness of her body filled my hands as her breasts pressed into my flesh. I pressed my fingers between her buttocks and pulled her to me, and a cloud of intense, animal desire washed over me for this fragile, elfin-like sprite of a woman.

I shuddered and she shuddered and our lips met in a passionate expression of yearning, pressing hard together as we gave in to the desire to possess each other, to become each other, to be inside one another, to become one person. A trembling Susanna surrounded me as I became entwined within her, and our souls met as our hearts had met, and two spirits of pure love enmeshed one in the other as physical love bound us together and a simultaneous coming together transformed. I gave her all of me, and she gave me all of her.

Later, as we lay side by side in a nest of warmth cuddled between Heaven and Earth, Susanna turned onto her side then she moved on top of me. She brushed her fingers across my cheeks. Her eyes burned into mine and then they softened and a smile worked at the corners of her mouth and I knew she was going to be silly. She sang lines from a song she loved. "Kiss my lips and kiss my eyes, then I'll give you a great surprise. Kiss my nose and kiss my toes, what you'll get only heaven knows."

I blushed at the intimacy every time I read the letter. Sometimes the memories were so strong I couldn't continue and put the journal away, but always within reach. Ours, like my mother's and father's, was an extraordinary love, a wished-for love. Oh, how I longed to love like that again. The love I had shared with Susanna before losing her. Love with Aida was different, but comparing Aida with Susanna was unfair. No two people were exactly alike. No matter how much I wanted with Aida what Susanna and I shared, no two loves could be the same. Maybe love depends on one's state of mind. If I weren't grieving for Susanna, would I still love Aida? Did love come to me to fill the void left by Susanna's death? Had loneliness made me weak and susceptible, open to advances from the first woman to show an interest in me? I hadn't been lonely when I met Susanna. I hadn't been grieving for a lost lover. But my heart was still bleeding for Susanna when Aida came into my life.

I had been desperately sad and lonely when we met. At the

time, only three years had passed since Susanna's death. Only three years since I begged orders transferring me away from Spain. Away from the pain and the constant reminders. The Navy obliged by transferring me to Hawaii, where I found myself in a paradise limned in sorrow.

I put the journal away and took off the necklace. The necklace and letters were among the few belongings of my parents I possessed. My adoptive parents gave them to me when I enlisted in the Navy. They said my mother believed the medallion was cursed and the bearer would suffer her greatest fear. Her greatest fear was that she would die young.

I sat on the edge of the bed and held the necklace up. The medallion and wedding ring dangled side by side. The ring gave off a soft, golden glow in the light of the lamp. The reflections in the medallion's jewel filled me with an uneasy feeling. Could the curse be real?

What was my greatest fear? Snakes. I was afraid of snakes. That wouldn't be the point of the curse, though. The medallion's curse was for things that turned your heart inside out, strangled it. Things that made you weep and cry out during nightmares. Curses were spat from the black mouths of evil, soulless hags hunchbacked under the weight of the hate they stoked with the memories of spurned love, a bitten hand, a perceived slight from a well-meaning person. Curses were evil promised on a pure soul to the tenth generation of the tenth generation. Curses were jealousy, envy, lust, greed all bound into one oath and hurled at the hapless victim by a she-devil with a face twisted with hate. Those who feared you hurled curses to hurt you. Who had feared my mother, and why? Or my how-many-times-removed grandmother?

So, what was my greatest fear? That I would never again find Susanna's love? Yes. That I would never again find a love like Susanna's, one that bound a man and woman together in a holy bond of spiritual unity. If that were so, I always had the memory of her love to sustain me, to carry me through life. I had Aida's love too, but in some way, it wasn't the same. I fell asleep with the medallion gripped in my hand.

Chapter Six

Tom

I edged the gate open with a gentle push, but the squeal of the rusty hinges gave me away. I uttered a silent oath when Aida poked her head out the window.

"Oh, Tommy," she cried. "You forget again the oil."

"I'll bring the oil home tomorrow, Aida. I promise." Yoshi had run ahead, barking at the chickens, but stopped in the middle of the courtyard, his eyes following the action between Aida and me.

"You are leaving for Thailand tomorrow."

"Well, when I get back then."

She rolled her eyes and ducked back in the window. I sprinted across the sunlit, flower-lined courtyard, avoided clucking chickens, ducked under the crowded clothesline, and ran into the house. I reached for the newel-cap but caught myself, skipping on my toes until regaining my balance. I dropped my fly-away bag and stowed the groceries I had picked up in the pantry.

"Hey, Aida," I called. "Let's go out tonight."

Aida dashed in from the kitchen. "Oh, Tommy! Where are we going? To Rufadora? What time do we leave? I'm so hungry. Can we go to Wimpy's? I need to change my clothes. Does my hair look okay? Oh, the stove is on. Will you be okay to sleep tonight? You leave so early tomorrow."

"I'll be fine, Aida."

She raced for the kitchen, removed the whistling tea kettle, and turned off the stove, then ran for the bedroom to change. I caught her and drew her into my arms.

"Whoa, slow down, sweetheart, you're making me tired." I leaned back to look at her. She radiated a joyful beauty. "Your hair is beautiful, and so are you. Don't change a thing."

"Oh, Tommy. You always saying the sweetest things."

She hummed as she changed clothes. Drawers slid open and closed, closet doors rattled in their tracks, and her shoes clack-clacked across the floor. Then silence, as though she were looking herself over in the mirror.

"You can come in and change if you need to," she said.

"I changed at the barracks."

My stomach grumbled. I went into the kitchen and ate a handful of pork and rice, then washed my hands. "I'm ready when you are, Aida."

She walked into the kitchen and spun around on her toes. "How do I look?"

The white slacks and lime-green pullover complemented her skin tone. If the perfect female form existed, Aida had it. She was a woman all right, and she knew how to show it.

"You are so beautiful, Aida."

She looked down, smiling under long eyelashes. "Remember this look while you are in Thailand. It will be waiting for your return."

"I'm having second thoughts about leaving you," I said. "But I love our reunions."

She smiled and drew her fingers across my chin. "Not as much as me. I love when you come to me."

We left, Aida leading the way. I hurried to keep up with her. She looked back and frowned when the gate squealed but pushed on. The streets around the vast city market were busy with cars and trucks, and jeepneys lurching along as they stopped and started again to load and offload passengers. We caught a jeepney at the crosswalk to the city market. Aida couldn't sit still and danced in her seat to the amusement of the only other passenger, an older woman sitting across from us.

We had just rounded the traffic circle onto Magsaysay Drive when the earthquake struck. The jeepney lurched as the road lifted. A telephone pole snapped with the crack of a whip and crashed to the ground, narrowly missing another jeepney. I gripped the handrail and held onto Aida. The jeepney rocked side to side. The driver braked hard but couldn't hold them. Terror filled Aida's eyes; she held my arm in a death grip. The jeepney lurched again, and she slipped from the seat. I planted my feet to enough to see stars through the pain and tears. When my head cleared, I was eye to eye with the older woman. She strained to hold herself on the bench seat with her arms wrapped around another hand rail. Her lips were a thin, tight line. I nodded to reassure her. She reached up without releasing her hold on the pole and crossed herself before clutching her crucifix and praying.

"Put your arms around me, Aida," I yelled without taking my eyes off the woman. "Hold on tight. Don't let go."

"Oh, Tommy. Don't let go. Hold me."

"I've got you, Aida."

"Tommy!"

My chest turned cold at her cry. *Hold on. Don't let go of her.* She slipped from the seat again, and again I hauled her back.

"Plant your feet hard against the floor, Aida."

"I can't."

My legs ached. I was losing my grip. Aida was slipping away. I couldn't hold her.

Not again.

I was helpless, as helpless as I had been when Susanna died.

No. No.

"Tommy!"

The jeepney jumped the sidewalk and lurched to a stop. The ground was still again.

"Aida, are you okay?"

"Yes, I think so."

I helped her out of the jeepney, then gave a hand to the old woman who patted my shoulder and thanked me. She hurried away in the direction we had come. The earthquake lasted barely thirty seconds, but left Aida's nerves strained. She chattered away as we helped free people from an overturned jeepney. Except for one broken arm, there were only bumps and bruises to contend with and three young kids Aida corralled while their mother and I collected her belongings.

We headed for Rufadora after doing all we could for others. As we turned the corner to the side street, Grace and Luz, Aida's former roommates, screamed from the balcony above Rufadora when they saw her. Aida's pace quickened, and I held the door open and walked in after her.

The bar held a warm, intimate atmosphere, a far cry from the seedy, dingy joint it used to be. There was no real damage other than some crumbled plaster and fallen roof tiles and pool cues that spilled from their wall racks.

"Say hello to Mama-san, Tommy. I'm going to help Grace and Luz clean up."

The attractive, cultured woman didn't fit the mama-san image. She would not have looked out of place sitting at the head of a corporate boardroom table.

"Hello, Mama-san."

"Hello, Tom. How is it outside?"

"Not too bad from what I could see. Some downed telephone poles and store signs. Most of the injuries are from jeepneys; those things are deathtraps. I have a headache from banging around on the ride over."

"Oh, dear, let me get you an aspirin." Mama-san dug through her purse, pulling things out and setting them on the bar. She pulled out a coin purse and a blue clutch and, with a triumphant smile, a bottle of aspirin. "Here you are. And here is some water too. I'm glad it was not worse. I do believe the worst is yet to come, though. Mount Pinatubo seems to vent with more violence every day."

I swallowed the aspirin and squeezed my eyes closed. The bar's old jukebox was playing a screaming guitar song that didn't help my head. Mama-san clucked her tongue.

"Someone is playing that horrid machine. I detest that jarring noise. If it would not prove bad for business, I would change that music for opera. Do you like opera, Tom?"

"I love opera. My favorite is Aida."

"Oh, Tom. I would groan if you were a comedian." She shook her head and laughed, her white teeth flashing in her beautiful face.

On the wall behind the bar hung a photo of a red-bearded Sailor in dungarees, combat helmet, and flak jacket, and wearing blue-lens sunglasses and a wide grin. It was too far away to see clearly, but the Sailor was familiar in some way.

"Who is that in the photo behind you, Mama-san?"

"A dear, dear friend from a long time ago."

She paused and gazed at me for a moment before taking my hands. "How nice it is to see you again. Why do you and Aida not come more often?"

"My rotating work schedule makes it difficult to get into a routine."

"You are always welcome here, Tom. You know that. And Aida is so much fun to have around."

"She misses her friends. I think she'd like to come back and work here."

Mama-san stopped cleaning up and stood with her hands folded on top of the bar. "By the way, Tom. I hear you are off to Thailand. I hope you enjoy yourself, but not too much."

"Yes. It's a last-minute change. I'm replacing someone."

"How fortunate for you. I love Thailand. I have visited Pattaya several times and find it an alluring resort. Will you stay in a hotel or is there a barracks at the airfield?"

"We'll stay in a hotel. We have a van to carry us back and forth."

"I see," she said with what sounded like skepticism. "And what do Sailors do in Pattaya when they are not working?" Her eyebrows arched. "Will you window shop?"

"I manage to find good deals."

"There are good deals on every corner in Thailand."

"Yes, it would almost be a crime not to buy the wares they display."

"You make paying for it sound virtuous."

"Everyone has to make a living."

"Even if it hurts someone?"

"I'm talking about buying trinkets and gifts, Mama-san. What are you talking about?"

The slightest smile lifted the corners of her mouth.

"Jewels. What every woman wants."

"I buy from Ben's. He displays his wares behind glass too."

"I'm sure he gets his cut."

"I'm certain of it."

I didn't like the direction of the conversation and excused myself.

Her smile followed me as I joined Aida and her friends.

"Hey, ladies, how are you?"

"Fine, Tom," said Grace.

"Hello, Tommy." Luz smiled at me like a coy sweetheart.

The seat next to Luz was empty, but I pulled up a chair and sat next to Aida. I had spent my first night in Olongapo with Luz. I hadn't known she and Aida were roommates until Luz came to the apartment while Aida and I were there. Luz moved out soon after.

Aida was having fun reminiscing with her friends and making plans to get together, but I was bored, and hungry too. Aida was sharing from her friends' plates, so I left after a few minutes and walked to Mariposa's. I returned with a hamburger and fries, and with Phil, who had come from the base. We took a table to ourselves and ordered beers.

"So, how's Jeff? How did he break his leg?"

"He fell off a jeepney."

"How do you fall off a jeepney?"

"Yeah, that's what I asked. He was coming back from Subic City and thought it would be fun to hang off the back of the jeepney. The jeepney veered into a monstrous pothole, bounced around and threw Jeff off. He landed with his leg under him. Roger and Ed said they heard the bone snap. Compound fracture. It was sticking out of his leg and everything."

"God, that sounds painful. Where is he?"

"In the hospital. He's doing all right. He was so drunk he won't remember what happened."

"Well, I guess that's a good thing. He'll remember me taking his place in Thailand, though."

One, maybe two weeks in Pattaya Beach. Long days flying out of U-Tapao airfield and long nights barhopping. I loved the buzzing excitement of the nightlife, the beautiful women, sidewalk vendors, even the street urchins begging for handouts. I'd have to find Lek too.

"Tom. Tom!"

"Hmm? What?"

"I've only been talking to you for five minutes."

"Sorry. I was thinking."

"About Thailand, no doubt."

"Yeah. Wondering what to do about Lek."

"You'd better be careful, brother. You'll be in a world of trouble if you do anything more than say goodbye to her."

"We've been over this, Phil."

"I'm just hoping it sinks into that thick skull of yours."

My headache returned. I rubbed my temples. "You know what, Phil? It just doesn't matter. I love Aida. That's all that counts."

"All right, Tom. But I hope you don't hurt her."

"I won't."

I wasn't sure if Phil believed me or not. He didn't speak right away, but seemed to consider me for a moment. Finally, he said,

"You know what? I believe you," and left to join Mama-san at the bar.

I finished my burger and joined Aida, who was alone while Grace and Luz took their turns serving customers.

"Are you having a good time?"

"Yes. I'm glad we came. I've missed seeing everyone. There's so much to catch up on. I told Grace I will go to Manila with her next week to see her sister."

"What's her sister doing in Manila?"

"She studies teaching at the Normal School."

I caught Aida's smile as she spoke.

"Let's play pool," she said.

I couldn't beat Aida at pool. She had learned to play from the best pool players in the Pacific Fleet and could hold her own against most guys who challenged her.

"Why not? Just try not to bloody me too badly. I have to fly tomorrow."

She laughed and pressed her head against my chest. "I will rack, then clean up after you break."

"That hurt, Aida."

"Ohhh, so sorry, honey ko."

"Quarters?"

"Not tonight, Sailor. I'm going to make you want to go to Thailand to recover."

She gave me a beating for the ages. When it was over, you couldn't tell me from the black and purple cue balls. At least I got a kiss out of it.

It was late. I had to get some sleep if I was going to make my flight on time. Aida made her goodbyes while I joined Phil at the bar.

"Look after Aida while I'm away, will you, Phil?"

"What do you mean?"

"Check on her, especially if the earthquakes get worse. The volcano, too. They keep saying it could blow any time. I don't know what I'd do if anything happened to Aida while I'm away."

"Don't worry. Lucy and I will keep tabs on her. I'll let you know if anything happens. I won't leave her without knowing she's safe."

We said goodbye to Mama-san, who wished me luck in Thailand, and left, choosing to walk home rather than take a jeepney. The apartment door had opened in the earthquake. Inside, a thin layer of dust covered everything, and some plates had fallen off the counter. We cleaned up the mess, showered, and went to bed.

We made love the way people do when they want to avoid thinking. Aida couldn't bear the thought of my being away, and I found that, despite my eagerness to see Thailand again, I didn't want to leave Aida. We made love to hold on, to message each other that no matter what happened, this was it: we were committed to a lifetime together.

Aida, born in a poor fishing village on Manila Bay, in a hut with sand for a floor, palm fronds for a carpet, and a raised bamboo platform for sleeping, could be tough as nails. But she was also tender, kindhearted, and sensitive. She held onto me that night like I was a crucifix, and I held onto her like the answer to a prayer.

I woke during the night to find her watching me. There were tears in her eyes.

"What's wrong, Aida?"

"Nothing's wrong, Tommy. Go back to sleep."

As I crossed the courtyard early the next morning, Aida called from the window.

"Honey ko."

"Yes, Aida?"

"What is love?"

"Coming home knowing you'll be watching for me from the window."

"I love you, Tommy."

"I love you, Aida."

Book Two

Olongapo, Philippines

1968

Chapter Seven

Frank Bailey

The sun set on another blistering day in the Philippines as our C-130 touched down at Cubi Point Naval Air Station. The war in Vietnam was nine-hundred miles in the past. I could finally relax and put the horror of that last, bloody attack behind me. For the next week at least, I wouldn't have to look for a foxhole to dive into every time a Jeep backfired.

The Hercules taxied off the runway and parked in front of the air terminal. Once we cleared Customs, I gave Petty Officer Sam McBride his orders and told him to report to squadron admin the following morning.

After a short taxi ride past the destroyer and submarine piers, I checked into my room at the CPO barracks. Master Chief Franklin, "Chip" to his close friends and "The Master Chief" to everyone else, had asked me to meet him at Rufadora Bar at eight. I had time for a shower and a quick letter to my folks in Annapolis before heading into town.

Refreshed but hungry, I held my breath and crossed Shit River. I stopped at the corner of Gordon Avenue and Magsaysay Drive and bought several skewers of monkey meat from a street vendor. A scroungy black and white mutt ran across the street and sat next to me with a paw raised. He was pitifully thin, so I fed him a few pieces of meat and contemplated the scene before me.

Testosterone Alley would have been a more fitting name for the zone of pleasure up and down both sides of Magsaysay Drive to Rizal Avenue. Pheromones floated like moths around the little brown foxes clustering in front of every bar and intensified the burning urge for sexual release of young Sailors.

The vendor, a friendly, moon-faced old woman with few teeth

and a fixture on "her" corner for decades, joined me.

"Many Sailor out tonight, yis, yis? Many more soon when aircraft carrier arrives, yis?"

The old woman, known as Mumbles for her lack of teeth, leered at me. "How many babies you tink Sailor and bargirl make? Sailor only tinking about beer and sex when dey awake, yis? All day dey tinking sex with bargirl, and beer. Make good for business for me." She rubbed her fingers together.

"Look." She pointed toward a group of Sailors standing on the corner looking up at the bargirls on the balcony of Daisy Mae's Bar. "Dey looking for girls. Dey want to make babies. Maybe dey marry bargirl and take dem to America, yis?"

"Maybe," I said.

"What about you? You looking for girlfriend?"

"Not me. I'm thinking the same thing you are about Sailors. About young men in general. Food, beer, and sex. That's what drives the world, right?"

"Yis, I tink you are right."

Sailors would spend hours reconnoitering the perimeter of Magsaysay Drive, drinking beer, and looking out for willing young Filipinas ready to help them obey the irresistible urge to couple. In Olongapo, there were no boundaries to hold one back from finding love, planting one's seed, and fertilizing that seed. That release offered hope to the girl and her family. Hope that the seed would grow and bloom and pave a golden road to opportunity and comfort. The girl could bid farewell to poverty. She could forget her fear that one day, a failure at love, she would live out her years as a dry, wrinkled, bitter mama-san watching over a nursery of young barmaids clamoring for their turn to suckle at the teat of the American Dream.

After finishing the last skewer, I wiped my hands on a towel and tipped the white-headed, tiny old woman who rewarded me with a toothless smile. I left her still smiling and walked up Magsaysay, passing Wimpy's Burgers and Apple Disco, a club Sam and I had frequented in the past. I turned the corner at Mariposa's Restaurant, jammed with Sailors and Marines sitting at sidewalk tables, and walked up the hot, dusty side street to Rufadora Bar. A jukebox blasted Jimi Hendrix's "Purple Haze" and several women danced on the balcony above the bar. One of them called out to me. "Hey, handsome, you come see me?"

"I'm sorry, beautiful lady. I'm coming to see Chip, a friend of mine."

"Ohhh, you a benny-boy?"

"No, no, I'm afraid not."

She laughed and blew me a kiss and disappeared into the bar. Another woman, tall and slender, leaned on the balcony railing while observing my approach. Her beauty was striking. She turned to a call from someone out of sight, looked back my way, and walked into the bar.

Rufadora was new to me. I usually frequented Daisy Mae's, Slim's, or VP Alley bar, the patrol squadron's home-base in town. Every bar had its loyal patrons. Helicopter crews claimed Rufadora as their own. Not much differed between the bars, anyway. Every bar offered three things in abundance: cheap beer, cheap love, and loud music. I didn't care much for cheap love.

I paused in the doorway while my eyes adjusted to the dark. My lungs recoiled from the thick cloud of cigarette smoke wafting around the interior. Entering the bar was like crossing the threshold to another world, quite possibly Dante's Inferno. Here dwelt at least eight of the nine circles of Hell. I wasn't sure about heresy, but Sailors could do just about anything they set their minds to.

Tables covered in spilled beer and cigarette burns, nicotine-stained ceiling and walls, and the ground-in dirt of the floor tiles gave Rufadora a shabby patina. Framed photos of grinning American boys holding girls on their laps decorated the walls, along with dozens of squadron plaques given to the bar's mama-san in appreciation of the fun and memories of their R&R, or I&I as it was sometimes called: intercourse and intoxication.

Sailors and Marines in various stages of drunkenness crowded the bar. The dark interior and stale air gave the room a close, dingy, seedy feeling. The upright piano against the wall had seen better days; beer bottles and ashtrays covered the top, and the ivory keys had yellowed with age. Or was it cigarette smoke? A roar of laughter and loud cheers erupted across the room as a drunk Marine swallowed the contents of a beer bong to chants of encouragement. He wiped his lips, then fell out of his chair where he lay senseless. He didn't look old enough to shave. Two women in bikinis danced on tables on either side of the jukebox while Aretha Franklin belted out R-E-S-P-E-C-T. Several couples made out at nearby tables. I shook my head at the irony. The pretty woman from the balcony was speaking with an older woman, presumably the mama-san, sitting at the bar stretching along the back wall. She threaded her way through the maze of tables.

"Hello, Chip's friend. Have you found him?"

"Not yet, but it's dark in here."

"What does he look like?"

"He's a big man with a crew cut. He'll be chewing a cigar."

"Oh, Master Chief. He's in the back room."

"You know him?"

"Everybody knows Goody-Goody."

"Goody-Goody?"

"Yes. He's a good boy. He never bothers the servers but always buys them drinks." She leaned towards me and whispered in a conspiratorial voice. "And he's married. His wife lives on base." Her eyes and a smile gave away her humor. "Are you a good boy too?"

"My mother believes so."

"My mother believes I'm a good girl."

"I'm not married."

"I am not married either."

"I didn't think you were."

Her eyes narrowed. "Oh? Why not?"

"No ring."

She smiled under arched eyebrows. "You're a smart boy."

"I'm more careful than smart. May I join Goody…the Master Chief?"

"Come. I will take you to him."

I followed her like a puppy through the tangled knot of Sailors and Marines to a door at the near end of the bar. The mama-san cast a thoughtful look our way before turning her smile on me.

"Hello, Sailor. I've never seen you here before. Your first time?"

"What? Oh, uh, yes ma'am. Well, it's my first time in Rufadora."

"Will you come back again?"

I glanced at the pretty girl. "I just might, ma'am."

She smiled and said, "Good. We'll be waiting for you. Come see me if anything pleases you."

"Yes, ma'am. I will. Thank you."

The pretty girl's eyes turned my cheeks warm while I spoke with mama-san. She seemed to be sizing me up, placing me among the dozens of men who frequented the bar every night to see where I fit in.

She took my arm and pointed me toward the back room. "That was Helen, the mama-san. She owns Rufadora."

"She's quite forward. I didn't know what to say. I'm afraid I stammered like a little boy."

"You were fine. She always has that effect on the unprepared. She's observed human nature from that end of the bar for years. Her snap judgments of people are usually accurate. And she likes you."

"How can you tell?"

"She replied after you told her you might come back. She ignores those she does not like."

I had liked my guide right away and was keen to know more about her. "I'd better not let her down then. I'll make sure to come back often."

"Was there a purpose in your glance at me when you answered her?"

I ran a finger along the side of my nose, to both hide my blush and buy time while I wondered what to say next. This extraordinary woman was clearly enjoying my discomfort, if her smile were any indication. "Helen had me flustered. I think I was looking for help. She's a strong woman."

"Helen is not afraid of anyone. The police look out for her, and Shore Patrol comes by often to check on the military boys."

"Doesn't that make them stay away?"

"Does the bar look empty?"

She had me there. "Touché. What's your name?"

"Marie."

"Hello, Marie. I'm Frank."

"Hello, Frank." I took her hand when she offered it. Soft with a firm grip. Warm, too. "Your friend is Chip Franklin; that's amusing."

"I've heard that before."

Marie knocked on the door and opened it. "You will find Goody-Goody in here, Frank."

I was tempted to make a crack about not being goody-goody like Chip, but thought better of it. At six three, I towered over

Marie, but the hard gleam in her eyes and her straight back intimidated me for some reason. "Thank you, Marie. Will you be here long? Will you join me for a drink later?"

"No." She turned and walked away with the sensuous grace of a ballet dancer. Her long, jet black hair and light brown skin stood out against her white blouse. She was a glimmer of sunlight in the dark cavern of the bar.

Chapter Eight

Frank

Chip's iron grip dug into my shoulder while his other hand crushed mine in a handshake.

"Hey, Frank, great to see you, buddy. Come on in and join the party."

I lingered for a moment as I considered returning to Marie, but Chip was having none of it.

"Come on, come on," he said, tugging my arm. "Don't be shy. You know everyone here, don't you?"

His southern Georgia accent reminded me of home as he led me into a sea of Chief Petty Officers. I waded through the crowd, shaking hands, and exchanging greetings, and took a seat next to Chip at the head table.

"It's so good to see you," he said. "How you been? We've missed you something fierce. Hey, someone get Frank a San Miguel, will you? Stan, be a good fella for once and sound the bell. Thank you, shipmate."

Stan tugged a line dangling from the ceiling, and the ship's bell at the bar clanged four times. A few moments later, the door opened, and Marie entered carrying a tray and a beer. The room fell silent as Marie set the beer in front of me. Our eyes met.

A slight smile danced across her lips. "I thought the beer might be for you."

I reached for the beer, but jerked my hand back at the touch of Marie's fingers.

She set the beer on the table. "Jumpy, Frank?"

"Yes." The touch of her fingers reawakened a longing I had suppressed in Vietnam.

"Maybe you should go to bed. You look tired."

"Yes. Maybe I should," I said, not taking my eyes off hers. "Thank you for the beer."

"You are welcome." She gave me a smile, her eyes holding mine until she turned and walked out, closing the door behind her. She wasn't shy, that's for sure.

"Jesus Christ," a voice murmured. "Marie never serves anyone."

Someone else said, "Yeah, what'd you do to her, Frank?"

I leaned back in my chair and hooked my thumbs in imaginary suspenders. "Well, boys, some men have it, others don't. Try not to be too jealous."

Something bothered me after I spoke, though. It was cheap to speak of Marie that way. Maybe I had been in Vietnam too long, exposed to the crudeness of men who knew they might die at any moment. But that wasn't it. Marie was different. She was too mature, too cultured, too sophisticated. She wasn't a poor girl from the provinces seeing the big city for the first time. No, that wasn't it either. It was cheap to speak of anyone that way.

Another guy, Senior Chief Kelly, sneered. "Well, you must have done something. She's always so arrogant."

"She was pretty nice to me."

"You don't get out much, do you, boy?"

That got my hackles up, but I didn't say anything.

The loudmouth continued. "She'll sit all night and let Sailors buy her watered-down drinks, but she never goes home with anyone."

"Yeah," said Chief O'Brien. "She's as pure as they come."

There was an oily quality about the Senior Chief, an easy vulgarity in his manner that screamed creep.

"Didn't you ever see a drop-dead gorgeous woman you wanted to take out, buy her drinks all night, and get nowhere? God knows, I have."

"I can't say I have, Senior Chief. I generally treat women as companions, not conquests. But then, what do I know? I've been in 'Nam since we left Hawaii, so maybe you've pushed the bar a little lower. Now that I'm back in PI, I want to make the best of the time I have left. I'd rather get out into the provinces than spend all my time drunk or hungover or buying a piece of action."

"Well, war hero, you'll hit the bars in the provinces, won't you? Or do you plan to present yourself as the All-American Hero and impress the Flips with your boyish charm. Maybe you'll take photos with the pretty little Filipinas just waiting to grow up so they can move to Olongapo where they can shanghai Sailors into taking them home to their mommies. She'll probably tell him she's pregnant, so he does the honorable thing like any hick from the sticks."

"You make me sick, Senior Chief. I've been in and out of PI for twenty years and have never been treated with anything but kindness and respect. Do you look at all people the same way, or just the women who turn your drunk ass down?"

My nerves, still on edge from Vietnam, made my voice quiver with anger. I wasn't afraid of the prick, he was a scrawny bastard, but I didn't want to lose my cool and do something I'd regret later.

"No, Senior Chief, I won't hit the bars in the provinces. The people I meet welcome me into their homes. In fact, when I volunteer to help at the Catholic orphanage in the Barrio tomorrow, a bunch of Flips, as you call them, will be there working alongside other Sailors too stupid to realize they could be in town getting drunk. Wait, I can read their letters home now: Dear Mom and Dad, I could have helped repair an orphanage in Barrio Baretto today, but I thought it would be better to hang out in a bar and get drunk. Heck, I may never have another chance to travel overseas again, so I'd better make the most of it. Love, Chucky."

"Well, ain't you cute," the Senior Chief said. "Looks like I struck a nerve. What, you don't like it when I call 'em Flips? Are you a Flip lover, boy?"

"All right, Senior, that's enough." Chip glared at the Senior Chief. "How you talk in private is your own business. I expect your conversation to be civil and respectful in the Chief's Mess, wherever it happens to be." He looked around the room, his hands on his hips.

Chip was a big man, crew cut, steely-eyed, and imposing. Thirty-five years of service backed him up. "That goes for all of you. We're Chief Petty Officers, not thugs. Is that understood?"

No one said a word.

"All right then, meeting adjourned. Fall out. The smoking lamp is lit. Where's my cigar?"

O'Brien smiled and ran his finger across his temple. "In your mouth, Chip."

"Oh. Yeah. Someone ring the bell for more beer. My mouth is dry. And if Marie brings the beers to Frank instead of me, we'll have to have a long talk. Who's the President of this Mess, anyway?"

The meeting broke up. Most of the chiefs left for the base or other bars. A few gathered around a table to play cards. Senior Chief Kelly, red-faced and drunk, dominated a table of Chiefs who appeared annoyed by his presence. Ignored by the others, he eventually left.

Chip and I were the only ones left at our table. I downed the rest of my beer as I watched the door close behind the Senior Chief. "What's the deal with him? Is he always that way?"

"Paul? Not always. He quit flying last year after his helicopter crashed at sea. He was the only one to make it out. It was ugly. An engine caught fire and spread to the cockpit before they could do anything. The helo spun out of control and dropped like a rock. The pilot was on fire when they hit the water. It's the last thing Paul remembers."

"Poor guy. That's awful. I might not have said what I did had I known."

"Yeah. I knew the pilot. Taught him the ropes during his first tour of duty. He was a fine man, a hell of an officer. Family man, too." He brought the beer to his lips and took a long drink.

"Paul's working with us until he receives orders. I've tried to get him transferred early, but Washington tells me the only available billets are in Vietnam. That's no place for a man in his shape."

"Why is he such an ass?"

"Whatever goodwill people felt for him after the crash evaporated soon after he came here. He was different before the crash: easygoing, cheerful, happy. Not now. He's arrogant and cocky, talks too much, drinks too much, and resents authority. I sympathize with him, of course, but you can only do so much for someone in Paul's state. We've got him working in Operations, a job he's familiar with, but the Ops yeoman wants to kill him. If he doesn't get orders soon…"

"I'm glad you told me. I wanted to punch him after what he said."

A server entered the room and brought fresh beers and peanuts.

"Well, hello there, young lady," said Chip. "Now, why is a pretty girl like you working in a place like this?"

"Oh, Master Chief," said Amy, a pretty young woman of about eighteen. "You know I only work here so I see you."

"Well, it's nice of you to say that, sweetheart. Thank you for the beer."

"Do you want some food? Mama-san asked me to tell you she bought adobo and pancit."

"No, I have to get home soon. I have a busy day tomorrow."

"Ok. Bye-bye, Goody-Goody."

"Bye, now."

Chip puffed his cigar, blowing smoke rings toward the ceiling. "Nice girl, Amy. Too bad she has to work in a place like this. But where else can she hope to find the answer to her dreams? She's well-paid, supports her family back home, and looks for her hero in every Sailor who walks in the door."

Amy walked from table to table serving the remaining beers, the edge of the serving tray between her hip and arm. As she walked through the doorway, she swung her hips around in a smooth dancing move to make room for the tray. Conversation slowed as the Sailors stared, her white short-shorts holding their attention like boys watching cheerleaders practicing.

I cleared my throat and answered. "The same thing happens in countries all over the world, Chip."

"Yeah, but it's so in-your-face here. Poor third-world people looking for a first-world ticket out."

"The grass isn't always greener in the Promised Land."

"No, but the options are plentiful; she just has to get there. I just hope Amy does okay. I hope her Sailor is good to her." He chuckled. "If she's lucky, her Sailor will work for me."

"That would scare any Sailor."

"Darn straight it would, Frank. Someone's got to look out for those young knuckleheads. Hey, speaking of knuckleheads, what did you mean when you said you want to make the best of the time you have left? That sounded ominous. Is there something going on with you I should know about?"

I hadn't expected the question. It brought Vietnam back all too vividly in my mind. I rolled the beer bottle between my palms while I took a moment to figure out how to answer.

"Chip, you don't know how relieved I was to leave Vietnam. I don't mean the normal kind of relief where you get excited to go back to PI and sleep in a normal bed in a normal barracks. No. I mean the kind of relief…. Chip, I cried. I cried like a baby. I sat on the edge of my rack and cried into my arms. I walked around for months with a target on my back. When I got your message, a ton of worry and fear lifted from my shoulders. I feel safe here, but if I go back to Vietnam, I won't make it out alive. I won't, Chip. I won't."

He looked at me for a long moment without blinking. Then he stood, and I stood with him. He took my hand and gripped it. "I know it was bad, Frank, and I know what you felt. I had that target on my back just as you did. But it took a bullet to get me out."

He raised my hand to his chest, just below his left shoulder.

"Feel that?"

"Yes, Chip."

"That's where the bullet came out. Feel the other side."

I pressed my fingers to his back.

"Feel it?"

"Yes, Chip."

He stuck his cigar in his mouth and puffed until it glowed.

"That's why some men behave the way they do when they go home, or to Olongapo, or the Gut, Subic, Wan Chai, Phuket, BC Street, Whisper Alley, wherever they go to recover. To get the target off their backs. That's why the Senior Chief is an ass. Me? I don't know why I was the lucky one. I went home to Barbara. She was what I needed. Most men go home and live what appear to be normal lives, but under the surface, in the back of the mind, where the heart is missing a piece, is where the faces live. The faces of all the buddies who didn't make it out, and the faces of all the ones who came out wounded inside. You'll always see their faces. I guess in a way, that's how we honor them. But some men can't deal with the faces. They need someone to help them, but they look in the wrong places. Marie is interested in you. That much was obvious to the entire Mess. I needed Barbara and went home to her. She saved me."

He stubbed his cigar into the ashtray. "That's why I pulled you out, Chief. I didn't want to see your face the way I see the others. You need someone to save you. Maybe Marie. Maybe Marie will save you."

I had nothing to say in the silence that followed.

The Master Chief let go of my hand and strode toward the door like a wedge-shaped giant.

"Now, go talk to Marie. That's an order."

Chapter Nine

Frank

The silence pounded in my ears. I wanted to sit and think, but my knees were locked. All I could do was stare at the door that had both opened and closed a moment before. I had learned something about Chip and something about myself. I had often noticed the purple heart among his many decorations but never asked for what action he earned it. Those questions weren't asked; the answers were volunteered. Chip was one of those men you didn't question but accepted as invincible, courageous, impervious to harm and fear.

I had learned too that I needed a woman's understanding and strength, her gift of love for a deeply injured man carrying a heart full of scars. I needed a woman's tender touch to smooth away the creases and ridges of worry and fear that life flays a man with, and temper the thoughtless exploration of the dark side of the soul with soothing words and caresses. All women are nurses and all men are flawed, and both come together to love and be loved. How many words had I exchanged with Marie that night? A dozen? Two dozen? Something wonderful had shaken me, and Marie too, I was certain, when our fingers touched. She had felt it. Maybe Marie will save me. Would she? Could she? Did I need saving? I needed nursing. I needed a nurse.

I wasn't in Vietnam, however. It was over. I was safe. For now. But, still, something told me it wasn't over. Thinking about it raised the hairs on the back of my neck. My head filled with the faces of friends who died over there. I remembered them and regretted their eternal absence. Did the faces come to stay right away? Or did something trigger them to show up unbidden later as nightmares? Did I need saving now or later? I had never thought I needed saving, and never sought a woman because I needed her.

But now. Was now different? Was I falling for Marie because I needed her?

I wanted to talk to her, but her refusal to have a drink with me made me gun shy. Some servers had come into the back room after Chip left and invited me to play pool with them. My heart wasn't in it, though, and I went into the bar after a few games and sipped a warm beer while deflecting playful propositions from the servers on duty. I reminded myself that I hadn't had a girlfriend in several years. Maybe I hadn't been needy enough. I had been lonely, though.

The girls feared Marie. That much I gathered as they spoke openly about her while we played pool. She wasn't one of them and didn't try to know them. She didn't hustle guys for drinks, didn't dance, and always went home alone. She might let a guy buy her a watered-down drink, but he never made it past, "Thank you. Goodbye." Mystery surrounded her; no one knew where she was from, how she made her living, or why she worked at Rufadora. She drove a luxury car, wore nice clothes, and didn't smell of cheap perfume. Her jewelry was real, and she drove to Manila to have her hair done. Besides Helen, only Amy could engage Marie in conversation, joke with her, draw a smile from her. Now, for the first time in anyone's memory, she had revealed herself to be a woman: she was interested in a man. The last was said with a glance at me.

The bartender brought another beer and took away the empty. Warm again. On busy nights, beer sold faster than it could chill. I considered asking for a glass with ice, but it was laborious picking out the bits of rust and occasional fly embedded in the ice. Marie was sitting with a stocky Marine, the type who probably had *Mother* tattooed across his chest. The guy guzzled his beer and belched. He laughed and guzzled more and belched again, this time sitting up and concentrating. The belch rolled across the bar, catching the silence between songs from the jukebox and wringing applause from the crowd. The look of disgust on Marie's face spoke volumes. She pushed the glass away with her fingertips and walked from the table. He took another swig and picked up and finished Marie's drink. He wavered on his feet but steadied himself and joined a group of Marines at another table. They looked Marie's way and laughed.

She stood at the far end of the bar with her back to me, apparently unaware of my presence. I was disappointed; I had hoped to press my luck and have a drink with her despite the earlier brush-off. I decided to leave for the base. I had a long day ahead of me and looked forward to a quiet night's sleep without the constant worry of the odd mortar blowing up my hutch. I swept the loose change into the bar tray and downed my beer. I wanted to say goodbye but didn't relish another rejection. My self-esteem was solid, but women could make me feel small with a glance. I shrugged and walked to the door, weaving around tables and couples. I had just stepped through the doorway when a voice stopped me.

"Leaving so soon?"

She stood a few steps away, a blue clutch in her hand. She must have hurried to catch me.

"Pardon me?"

"I asked if you were leaving so soon."

"Yes. Tomorrow is a busy day. I need to get some sleep." My next words were a desperate attempt for sympathy, but I had nothing to lose. "I'm going back to Vietnam in a few days and don't have much time. I'd hoped to relax and chat with you and forget the war for a while." I motioned toward the blue clutch. "Are you leaving?"

"I had considered it. Did you not ask earlier if I wanted to have a drink with you?"

"Yes, but you didn't seem interested."

"That was then."

"Oh? What changed your mind?"

"You. You are not like other Sailors. Are you a loner?"

"I wouldn't say that. I'm not afraid to be alone. Solitude gives me time to think."

"What do you think about in your solitude?"

"Let's get that drink." I called for drinks and paid for them, wondering if Marie would get a cut. I regretted the thought immediately.

"Shall we sit at the bar, or would you prefer a table?" I handed Marie her drink, a Cosmopolitan. "I thought barmaids' drinks were mostly water."

Marie's eyes blazed like red-hot spikes. "I am not a barmaid." Her voice could have chilled a volcano.

"I spoke without thinking. I'm sorry."

"I thought you were a smart boy."

"I said more careful than smart. I was neither this time."

"You're forgiven." She turned toward the back room. "Come, it's quieter in the back; all the Chiefs have gone."

We sat at a table circled by the yellow light of a bare bulb dangling from the ceiling. Piano music poured through the door when two barmaids entered, laughing and giggling. They stopped short when they saw Marie, one bumping into the other. They backed out quietly, shutting the door behind them and silencing the music.

"So, if you're not a barmaid, what is it you do here? The other Chiefs call you pure."

"Pure? Is that what you men discuss at your meetings? Are there not more important topics to discuss than my purity? War, peace, wives?"

"The meetings are usually about work. I came out tonight to see Chip, an old friend. Everything stopped, though, when you brought my beer. One of the Chiefs pointed out that you never serve anyone. Am I special?"

"Special? Hmm." She tilted her head as she considered my question. Her chin rested on her hand, fingers folded against her palm. Her hair fell away to bare the breathtakingly perfect curve of her neck and shoulder, the delicate filigree of her ear. I yearned to press my lips to the hollow behind her ear and trace with my fingertips the smooth, pure line of her neck. Such skin. Not a blemish. She was carrying me away and breaking my heart. Danger signals should have flared up, but instead I just stared.

"No," she said, "just different."

"Is that good?"

"It's attractive."

"You're attractive."

"Am I?" She smiled, revealing perfect, white teeth.

"Yes. And intriguing."

"Oh? In what way?"

"You don't fit the pattern of the women in a town like Olongapo. You don't appear to be after a husband, or a Sailor's money." The words had barely left my lips when I realized my mistake.

"Do you know how insulting that is?"

"I don't mean it to be. Looks like I've stepped in it again."

"Yes, you have. Not all barmaids are gold diggers, Frank. Most of the girls here send money home to support their families."

Marie leaned forward, her eyes intent. "You seem to think the only thing barmaids want is money."

"That isn't what I think."

Marie ignored me and went on.

"Do you believe every Filipino thinks all Americans are rich? That the way Sailors throw their money around getting drunk and paying for women to sleep with them proves that they are smarter than everyone else? That they have so much money to spend, all they have to do when they empty their wallets is go to the bank and get more?"

"No, of course not. Don't put words in my mouth, Marie."

"Filipinos are not naive, Frank, and most women are smart enough to look with disdain on Sailors who care so little for their hard-earned pay."

"Marie, I'm not questioning the virtue of the girls who come to Olongapo seeking work. What concerns me is the disillusion that awaits them when they don't find the life of luxury they expect to find in the States. I see it all the time. Sometimes I think they would be happier staying here and marrying a boy from their village."

"How do you know what will make a Filipina happy? Why do you assume that a woman does not truly love the Sailor she marries? For that matter, why do you assume the Sailor does not love her?"

"I never said that, Marie."

"Tell me, how many Filipino-American marriages end in divorce? How many Filipinos return to the Philippines when they become disillusioned?"

"I couldn't tell you."

"I haven't met a barmaid yet, Frank, who returned from America because she didn't like it. However, I have met barmaids who returned to PI when their husbands transferred here for duty. They come to Rufadora and talk to their friends. They show off their babies and talk of how wonderful it is living in America. Moreover, not one of them has expressed a desire to remain in the Philippines. Indeed, Frank, they—"

"Wait a minute. Let me talk, Marie."

"Do not interrupt me. They all want to bring other family members back to America." Marie spoke in earnest. The haughtiness had disappeared. "I think you possess an altruistic nature, Frank, but it is misplaced in this case. I don't think you've thought through your feelings on what makes a happy marriage between barmaids and Sailors."

"Maybe not, Marie. I truly hope all the marriages are happy."

I drew a finger through a water stain on the table. Cigarette burns rimmed the edges and it wobbled on uneven legs.

"Who are you, Marie? You're not a barmaid, yet you work in a bar. Wait, let me rephrase that," I added hastily. "You're not a barmaid, yet I met you in a bar where you seem to be on close terms with the mama-san, and you served me a beer. And, I might add, somehow the bartender knew enough to use top-shelf liquor for your drink. You're a contradiction. Not to disparage the girls who work here, but you don't fit with them. You don't speak and act like the others, and your bearing suggests a life lived in the city. I would guess you're from a wealthy family, well educated, and bored. Am I right?"

"I didn't serve you; I brought you a drink out of courtesy."

"That was nice of you. Thank you."

"We've already been through this part."

"You're being evasive."

"You're being impertinent and interrogative," Marie snapped.

"Another ninety-degree turn."

"Excuse me?"

"Yes. Just as our conversation starts to warm, one of us says something that causes tension, and the thread of our conversation turns cold."

"Maybe we're not trying hard enough to make general conversation. Shall we talk about the weather? I think it will be hot tonight."

"It's always hot here. General conversation is great in a waiting room or on a bus."

"But impersonal."

"Yes. But people are only passing the time in a waiting room, not trying hard to know one another."

"Is that what we are doing?"

"I truly hope so. We seem to be aiming for some objective other than small talk."

My heart beat fast, and I was becoming emotional. My eyes tended to tear up when I became passionate. "I have an intense urge to engage with you and find out more about you. I think you want the same."

Marie's eyes softened as she smiled. "I do, Frank. I don't know what made me bring you your beer, but I wanted to be near you again." She sat back and crossed her legs, then arched her eyebrows and flipped her hair to one side. "Since you asked, I manage the bar for Helen, the mama-san and owner. She is also my aunt."

She captured me again. "I don't care what you do for a living, Marie. I'm drawn to you. I like talking with you. I can hang out with my friends and talk all night, but they can't offer a female point of view or companionship. They can't flash brilliant white teeth at me from behind beautiful lips or look at me with bright, brown eyes that make my throat tighten and my heart skip two beats with every blink. You have a firmness of character belied by a delicate beauty, and eyes expressive of two sentiments: come hither, and go away, far away. I don't know how to interpret either one. Two days ago, I launched aircraft during a battle in Vietnam; tonight, I'm battling wits with a beautiful but perplexing woman. Maybe the feeling of doom hanging over me makes me speak this way. Maybe I feel a sense of urgency to know you because I don't think I'll return from Vietnam again."

Emotions visibly churned behind Marie's eyes. She appeared anxious, like she had gone too far when speaking earlier, or she wanted me to continue. I wasn't sure which. I hoped I hadn't gone too far. It was too late now, though; I had to leave, not because I needed sleep, but because I didn't want to make another foolish ninety-degree turn.

"I'm sorry, Marie. I've said more than I should have. I usually don't speak this frankly, or this much, until I've known a woman for, oh, eight or nine years."

I couldn't take my eyes off hers. "I'd better get going. I'm exhausted and have a big day tomorrow."

She wanted to say something but remained silent. But that was okay. Her eyes told me all I hoped for, and when she lifted her hand to me, my heart melted. I took her soft, warm hand in mine and held it tight. She pressed my hand in return and smiled. Oh, how my heart melted.

"Goodnight, Marie. I've enjoyed meeting you. I hope we meet again. You're unlike any woman I have ever known." My eyes teared up as I walked away, completely in love with this beautiful woman I had known barely two hours.

Chapter Ten

Marie Taneo

My pulse raced as Frank walked away. I wanted to call him back, tell him I wanted to know him too, but I couldn't. I was too proud to be the weak one. Too independent to seem dependent. I had been wrong about one thing, though. He wasn't unlike other Sailors. He was unlike any man I had ever known. He was confident, but not aware of his confidence. He was strong, attractive, and smelled good. I took pleasure from his parting words: "Unlike any woman I've known."

I had not expected things to turn out the way they had. I was completely indifferent to the men who came to Rufadora. But Frank was different. He walked with such self-assurance. He did not leer at the girls or brag tirelessly. He did not have the slouching, ingratiating manner men assumed when asking to buy me a drink when all they wanted was to bed me. He didn't make me feel like a piece of momentary pleasure or a substitute mother trailing apron strings halfway around the world for a lonely boy.

Frank had not come to see the barmaids, and I had enjoyed his company. Any desire I had felt to be with a man had flown after Edward cheated on me. Now, for it to return when a man like Frank came into my life, I realized how lonely I had been without a man to love. What had I been thinking, though, to serve him? I caught myself wiping the table with a napkin. I would, indeed, make a good barmaid.

I hoped I wasn't about to experience another affair that would end up hurting me. I barely knew Frank, but oh, how I wanted to see him again. I loved his mellow voice; he could read me a bedtime story any time. And I liked the way he looked, just tall enough not to tower over me; I imagined resting my head against his shoulder. Were his shoulders bony knobs or broad enough to lean on? I loved the way his shirt tightened over his chest when he moved. He wasn't brawny or muscled, but fit. Very fit. Frank stirred something in me that I had not felt for so long. The way he looked at me melted my heart, and his voice warmed me in a wholly unexpected manner. I had known him only a few hours, and already I wished he would ask me to marry him.

Edward and Frank were similar in the way they leaned on the table and stirred their fingers in the water rings. I hoped Frank would be nothing like him. I did not want to ruin another pair of stilettos.

Edward. That bastard. I gave him everything and would have given more had there been anything left to give. I had placed my heart in his smooth hands with the long fingers and manicured nails. He held my heart, touched it, caressed it. Edward. Tall and dark, coal-black hair and penetrating eyes. He looked like a ghost in certain light. I could not have worshipped him more had he wore a white robe and halo. His touch seared my skin and made me tremble.

I loved it when Edward's fingers played along my spine and I shivered, and he expressed concern that he had hurt me, and I shook my head. I longed for him to keep touching me that way so I could feel the warmth and strength of his spirit through his fingertips. How could a man caress a woman with a touch so gentle yet so passionate along her entire body as to make her think of a wisp of breath flowing along her skin, raising goosebumps, and laying them down again, like a sigh of wind across blades of grass? Gentle was not the right word; Edward's caress was less a touch than a feeling. A feeling as of a dream passing along my body, so that I could not be sure I had felt anything, but knew I had felt something. Something that trickled through my skin, spread within me, enveloped me, and soothed me until I could think of nothing but that it should never stop, and when it stopped, a sadness and a hope that it would start again. I shivered. God, his touch had felt so good.

We had loved passionately, or at least I had, until that Grace turned his head. Grace, who came out of nowhere, wiggled her ass at Edward, aroused him with her breasts, and charmed him with her bedroom eyes. He had soiled my own bed with Grace. He had fallen for her without a glance at me. I found them together after returning home early from a weekend visit to the orphanage. I expected to find Edward in bed and wanted to surprise him. And so, I had. I cried out in anger and flung my shoe at him, a stiletto. I had good aim and left a long gash above his right eye. I told them both to get out, changed the locks, and sent all of Edward's belongings to the charity house. I had not seen him since. I had loved him like no other. The pain of his betrayal went so deep. However, that belonged in the past. As far as I knew, he still managed his father's construction firm miles away in Baguio.

Baguio: good. Maybe his car will plunge down a mountainside and catch fire, and he will burn to death. I stopped seeing men after Edward. They were all the same. Profess love to a woman until fresh meat became available. I came to Olongapo to be near the orphanage and to forget Edward. I had left job, family, and possessions to help Aunt Helen out as manager of Rufadora. I wanted to cleanse myself of the past and make a fresh start. I achieved all I wanted except forgetting Edward. He couldn't let go and had me watched. I hated the constant suspicion, the constant fear of confrontation. The scar I left on his face had enraged him, and he vowed retribution. I constantly looked over my shoulder. Maybe that was his retribution, his revenge. He could afford to pay thugs to make me nervous.

The door swung open and Amy looked in. "Marie, a man is looking for you in the bar. He says his name is Edward." Amy's eyes grew wide and she whispered. "He is so handsome."

I froze. That was all I needed. "Amy, do not tell him you have seen me. Tell him I have gone home. Do you understand? Will you do that for me?" Amy nodded and left, confused but happy to help me.

Chapter Eleven

Frank

Cigarette smoke assaulted my lungs as I made my way to the exit, already missing Marie's fragrance. I had reached the door when I heard my name called above the screeching racket from the jukebox. I looked above the heads bobbing on the dance floor.

"Frank! Hey, Frank. Over here."

Sam waved from the bar. I changed direction, but the door opened, forcing me to quick-step out of the way. A well-dressed man glanced at me as he entered and strode to the center of the room. He might have owned the place by his manner. He scanned the tables and the bar. Amy, passing by with a tray of empties, greeted him. They spoke for a moment before she left for the back room. The man stretched his neck and adjusted his tie, taking in the crowd. He nodded in recognition of Mama-san in her post at the end of the bar. She gave a thin, frigid smile with just the right amount of insolence. The man sneered and looked away.

"Hey, Sam. What are you doing here? Was that you on the piano?"

"Yep. But the keys are so darn sticky with who-knows-what. That's a sad way to treat a piano." He dipped his fingers in a glass of water and wiped them on a bar towel. "The mama-san said you were in the back talking to someone, so I decided to wait." Sam grinned. "I figured if it was a woman, I wouldn't have to wait long."

The bushy red whiskers around Sam's mouth lifted and fell as he spoke. I suppressed a smile. Sam cocked his head and smiled back. "What's so funny?"

"Nothing. You remind me of someone." I ran my fingers and thumb down Sam's beard.

"Don't tell me," he said. "Yosemite Sam."

"Great horny toads. Is that beard regulation, you varmint?"

"Very funny, Frank." Sam smiled at the familiar joke. "Probably not. I'll trim it up in the morning."

"I'm only joshing."

Amy returned from the back room and spoke to the well-dressed man. He clenched and unclenched his fists and pointed to the back room. Amy shook her head and backed away, but the man moved toward her.

"Still, a trim would be a good idea before you report to the squadron in the morning. You don't want the Skipper telling you to shave."

One of Mama-san's burly barbacks entered the bar unseen by the well-dressed man and stood with his back against the wall while another barback, equally burly, stepped from the back room.

The man cast a furious look at the second barback and again spoke roughly to Amy. I couldn't make out his words, but his tone carried. Amy's forehead wrinkled; I thought she would cry. The tension in the bar rose as people turned to watch the fuss. The man, with a hand inside his coat, stared at Mama-san, who stared back unperturbed. She spoke to the man behind the bar without taking her eyes off the stranger. The menacing Filipino joined Helen, standing next to her with his arms across his chest. The well-dressed man scowled again and withdrew his hand. He turned on his heel, appeared surprised by the man at the door, and left the bar, slamming the door behind him. Amy, shaken, returned to the back room.

I turned my attention to Sam, who had been speaking while I watched the action with the stranger. "I'm sorry, Sam. What were you saying?"

"I agreed with you. I said I don't want to scare the nuns at the orphanage either." Sam spun around on the barstool and leaned back, his elbows on the bar. "So. How'd the Chief's meeting go?"

"Fine. I came in at the end, just in time to have a blowhard senior chief get in my face."

"About what?"

"About her." I tipped my head toward Marie as she left the back room. Amy followed close on her heels. Marie spoke to Helen, who patted her arm. Still holding the blue clutch, Marie kissed her aunt's cheek and returned to the back room.

"Excuse me, Sam. I'll be right back."

I left Sam and crossed the bar. "Pardon me, Mama-san. What's wrong with Marie? Is everything all right? Can I do anything?"

"Yes, everything is all right. An old friend of Marie's asked after her, but she does not wish to see him."

"May I see her? May I go into the back room?"

"If you wish. However, you will not find her. She has gone home for the night. She will return tomorrow."

"Oh."

"Would you like something else? Are you returning to the base tonight?"

"What? No. I mean, yes, I am returning to the base tonight. Thank you." I rejoined Sam.

"What was that all about?"

"The woman I pointed out left. Seems she didn't want to speak to the guy who slammed the door. Old friends, apparently." I signaled for a beer. The bartender set a San Miguel on the bar, a cold beer this time.

"Or old lovers."

Sam's answer annoyed me. "I doubt it. The blowhard I mentioned told me she's pure."

"Pure?"

"She doesn't go out with customers."

"Ah. Interesting. Maybe the guy came back for more than a drink. He left disappointed."

"The blowhard's a former aircrewman who stopped flying after a crash. He's a troublemaker the Master Chief is trying to have transferred."

"Who?"

"What?"

"Who's getting transferred?"

"The blowhard."

"Oh." Sam leaned back against the bar. "Sorry. I was watching the barmaids. Don't they get cold dancing in bikinis?" His eyebrows lifted. "That one's real cold." He spun around on the barstool to face me. "You like her, don't you?"

"Who? The obviously cold one?"

"No. The other girl. The one from the back room."

"Oh. Yeah. She's something else."

"What's her name?"

"Marie."

"She's good looking. Beautiful. If she doesn't go home with men, does that mean she isn't a barmaid?"

"Yep. You're quicker than I am; that's exactly what it means. She's the manager."

"I thought the mama-san was the manager."

"She owns the place. She's also Marie's aunt."

"So, despite her job, is there any hope for you? Are you going to ask her out?"

"Maybe. We spoke for a while after everyone left. I think she's interested." I spun the beer bottle in my hands as a mental image of Marie passed through my thoughts. "She's beautiful, Sam. I couldn't help staring. She's cultured too, prim and proper, with a feisty personality. Unfortunately, we disagreed a bit, and I left her sitting at the table."

"What happened?"

"I called her a barmaid."

"Ah. I take it she didn't like that."

"Not a bit. Beyond that, we argued over the relationship between barmaids and Sailors."

"Were you at any point in the conversation not arguing with each other?"

"I think we were in violent agreement most of the time, but neither wanted to lose the point."

"Give the point, Frank. Women always win. If, by some stroke of fortune, we win, we lose. Our happiness is only possible when women are happy."

"Says the man whose wife once told me her happiness depended solely on her husband's happiness." I touched Sam's shoulder. "She was a wonderful woman, Sam. I would give anything to find someone like her."

"Susanna loved you like a brother, Frank." Tears welled in his eyes at the memory. "She spoke of you often."

"I loved her too, Sam. We had a lot of fun together, didn't we? You know, I never felt more lonesome than when I saw the way she held you on the pier when we returned from overseas."

"Susanna wanted to get you married. Remember how she always fixed you up with her girlfriends? And how you always said you couldn't talk to them?"

"How could I forget? She'd say, 'Oh, Frank' and roll her eyes and ask me what I had done wrong when a blind date didn't work out. Anyway, Miss Right will come along someday. When she does, I'll thank Susanna."

I had to look away as I, too, became emotional. My love for

Susanna had begun the day we met, the same day she and Sam met. She had an overwhelming yet subtle presence. She appeared at first ordinary, unremarkable, just another pretty bartender. But the pull Susanna exerted on me, on anyone, was spiritual, not of this world. It was as though she spoke directly to the heart, like God. A man didn't hear Susanna's voice so much as he felt it, somewhere between the mind and the heart. Like the voice that tells you what a nice thing you've done, Susanna's voice made you feel good, happy, proud, at peace with the world. Susanna made you smile because she always smiled, and her smile carried the command, *be joyful*. Her life had carried that message, and her life had imprinted itself on my heart. At one point, I became jealous of the love between my two dearest friends and avoided them for weeks. Seeing them together filled me with envy and a burning passion to take Susanna away from Sam. But that could never have happened. Their love, their bond, was unbreakable, immovable. Others could love Susanna, but Susanna's love for Sam, and his for her, had been born when time was born. She could love another man, but only as a sister loves a favorite brother. When I finally understood that, I basked in the warmth of her love.

"It's okay, Frank, to love another woman," she had said after coming to see me while Sam was away on detached duty in the Azores.

"Why have you not come to see me, Frank? I don't understand. Have I done you a wrong? Have I hurt you?"

I remained silent at first, afraid to give in and appear weak.

"If I have caused you pain, I apologize. I would not hurt you for the world."

Agony showed in her face, as though I were physically harming her. My resolve was fading. Susanna made you feel as though her happiness depended on you alone.

"I love you, Frank, and I need you in my life. You bring me a comfort no other man can bring me."

"I've loved you since that first night, Susanna."

Her eyes, when she replied, held sorrow. "Oh, Frank. That love I can give only to Sam."

I clenched my jaw until it ached to hold back the tears. Susanna's soul had spoken to me, had wrapped around my heart, and lifted away my carnal love for her. She had spoken; she could not love me the way a woman can love only one man.

I had to accept that. I had to grasp that bond and let it wrap around my heart to replace the love I could not have. The unearthly, invisible web that she cast over me remained, for Susanna's spell never left a man but for the hollow void in that part of the heart that loves a woman. Time and again, I wondered if she were an angel sent to live among man to show him the true meaning of love.

"I loved her too, Sam."

"I know you did, Frank."

"I see some of her in Marie."

"I hope Marie brings you the love you wanted from Susanna, Frank."

"You knew?"

"Yes."

"Susanna told you?"

"No."

"How did you know?"

"The way you acted around her."

"Was I that obvious? Did I act foolish, like a boy in love?"

"No. Not like that, but the way a man acts when he hopes a woman will love him. You pined for her. After a while, though, something changed. I noticed it when I returned from the Azores. You spent your free time with us again. But your tenderness toward each other was remarkable. Like that of a divorced couple who hold out hope for reconciliation."

"That came after she told me she could love only you. She came to me while you were away and told me she needed me, but as a brother. Susanna knew I was in love with her."

"Yes. I thought she must have."

"I wanted her to cheat on you, Sam. I would have taken her away from you." I couldn't meet Sam's eyes. "I'm sorry, Sam."

"There's nothing to be sorry for, Frank. We both loved a woman whose love was not of this world. You can't be sorry for that."

"Do you think she knew how special her love was?"

"Yes. She told me once that men seemed to need her, and it made her uncomfortable. She sometimes felt like a messenger come to bring comfort to those who were sad."

"But you weren't sad, were you, Sam?"

"No, Frank. It was different with me. Our love was meant to show others the meaning of love, the indescribable love, the love that binds a man and woman for eternity. Few people find that love, Frank. The selfish never find it."

I envied Sam the memory of that love.

"No, Frank. I'll never love again. No woman could replace Susanna's and the love we shared. Companionship is all that's left for me, and I don't want a companion whose love I can't return."

He wiped his eyes at the memories. It was hard watching him as he remembered and suffered. I often wondered if this were only grief but banished the thought; I'd seen people grieve for a while, then set it aside, place the memories on the bookshelf, take a deep breath, and go on living for the future. In a way, I felt sorry for Sam. Susanna had been his future, his sunrise, his good morning kiss, but her death had pulled the past, like a blanket, over his head.

Then I felt her; Susanna's presence was strong. I could smell the orange blossoms she loved to wear in her hair. "Maybe that's why she fixed me up with her friends."

Sam laughed. "I wouldn't be surprised."

Susanna's attempts to fix me up with her girlfriends invariably failed and left her perplexed and exasperated. Only one had lasted longer than six months, ending when my ship sailed for the western Pacific. I could never seem to find the kind of love Sam and Susanna had shared. Their love was special, a mutual giving and receiving, a respect for each other's feelings, and a concern for the other's well-being. They loved without expectation of a return of their love. Theirs was the rarest kind of love.

I had almost experienced that kind of love. Before I knew Susanna, I had known a woman who brought me to the brink of everlasting love. I knew the moment it happened. I had gone to her tiny, one-room cottage, my third visit there. The mood was expectation of something intense. We both knew something wonderful was awaiting us. When she led me to the bed, all sound hushed but that from the waterfall plunging into the pool at the far end of the yard. The air smelled of tropical fruit and flowers, and the breeze from the sea blew softly through the window and ruffled the curtains like palm fronds. Senses heightened and details sharpened and when my skin touched hers, it was as though silk were brushed across my body in one long sheet like a soft, warm breath. When we joined in that rapture borne from Heaven, I melted into her the way air fills the atmosphere, and when the sun burst like a supernova deep inside me, I felt as though my soul had achieved awareness. Her lips, her embrace, the pillow of heaven that surrounded us told me the love was there, that I need only give her the love that only a woman can bear.

"Women always left after growing impatient with my reserve, one girlfriend called it my unnerving dispassion, or we drifted apart. Solitude never bothered me though. If women don't like my company because I don't talk much, that's their problem. I'm not going to change for someone else when I'm happy in my own skin." I pursed my lips and rubbed a hand over my stubble. "I might change for Marie, though."

"Susanna would have liked that. She would have taken credit for your change of heart."

"Wouldn't she, though? I was afraid to face her after a breakup. She worked so hard to find dates for me, I felt bad for her when nothing happened."

"She couldn't figure out what she was doing wrong. She thought she knew what kind of woman you liked."

"That was the problem. I wanted a woman like Susanna, but she was the only one, and she was yours."

"Susanna wasn't mine, Frank. I didn't own her."

"I'm sorry, Sam. I didn't mean it that way. I only meant that you and Susanna had each other."

"We had each other, yes, but even that doesn't describe what we had. We didn't choose each other, Frank. We found each other. It's hard to explain."

The Sam of a few minutes before changed. He leaned forward, staring into the distance, his thoughts far away. He clasped his hands, and he trembled.

"There could only be one Susanna, Frank. My life began when I found her." He paused to collect his thoughts, pored over memories, touched her again. "An inexplicable feeling overwhelmed me when I met Susanna. That first time when I saw her from half a block away. As I drew nearer, a feeling of warmth and familiarity enveloped me like a second skin. My heart skipped. It skipped, Frank, and I felt a burn in my gut. It was intense, like in a dream when you love a woman and the joy you feel is so incredibly intense that your heart feels like it's going to burst."

Sam was in the moment, almost as if he were back in Spain and seeing Susanna for the first time.

"When you dream, there are no outside forces competing for

your attention, Frank, nothing to dull the effect of the emotions. When you're sad in a dream, it's the most intense sadness possible. When you're happy, it's the most intense happiness possible. Dream emotions are pure, unadulterated, undiluted. They are the form, the definition, the substance, the being, the universal truth of the emotions we experience less deeply when we are awake. The love you feel for a woman while you're dreaming is the purest, most complete, most fulfilling love there is. Do you know why that is, Frank?"

"No, Sam."

"Because in your dream, Frank, you give the woman your undivided attention. She is the sole object of your dream. The same thing occurs when you're infatuated with a woman. She is the sole object of your life. You give her your complete attention. You give up self for the one you love. That's the key to love, Frank."

I understood then the bond between Sam and Susanna. The infatuation that gave way to passion that should have given way to companionship. But Susanna died before they could move on. Sam's grief would never leave him. He was stuck in a love that had never moved past passion, that restless phase of the process that defines human love. He would never move past passion and into companionship because Susanna had died during the ultimate expression of passion: the birth of their son.

"When I met Susanna that day, I knew we were destined to be together. There was no doubt in my mind. The thought that we were not never occurred. It was a universal truth, an absolute, an a priori fact. Water seeks its own level, fire burns, gravity is, we were destined to marry. It just was."

Sam's faced glowed with the rapture of memory, and I knew Susanna was with him.

"When our eyes met, the deepest, most intense dreamlike feeling of joy and happiness, fulfillment, and inevitability came over me. It nearly brought me to tears. My knees were shaking and my face drawn, and my gut burned, Frank. My gut burned. When we reached for the same apple in the vendor's cart, our hands touched, we looked at each other, and I saw it in her eyes, Frank, it was in her eyes. She knew it too. She knew it too."

Sam shook his head. The plaintive wail that burst from his lips echoed the grief of a broken heart.

"Oh, God, I miss you, Susanna."

I laid my hand on Sam's shoulder. I understood his grief but couldn't feel what he felt. I had not suffered the loss Sam had suffered. I wanted to feel the love Sam and Susanna had shared, the love that connected them still, the love that had bound them from birth. Someday, perhaps, I would find a love that special, my own wished-for love.

Mama-san was used to crying drunks, but Sam wasn't drunk. She approached us and asked if Sam were okay.

"Yes, ma'am. He'll be all right. We're leaving for the base now."

I asked Sam if he needed anything.

"No, Frank. I'm okay. Let's go."

Later, I lay in bed, hands behind my head, my shadow cast onto the wall next to me by the glow of the bedside lamp. The shadow did not reveal my smile as I lay thinking about my encounter with Marie. Our fingers had touched too. I had touched Marie for only a moment, but it sent a thrill through my body. I had nearly dropped the bottle of beer. The beauty in the curve of Marie's neck, the glow in her face when she smiled, the way her eyes flashed in anger had made my heart race. Was this how it had been with Sam and Susanna? Perhaps. However, I hadn't felt born in love with Marie. That part of the magic had not occurred.

Love affected people in many ways; maybe the recipe differed for each person or couple. The first blush of love always appeared magical as, in Sam's words, the couple gave each other their undivided attention. Infatuation had the same impact as love but died away, whereas love, real love, heartfelt love, blossomed, nurtured by the desire for companionship and the desire to please the other. Sam and Susanna had lived to please one another, not expecting anything in return but knowing the other would reciprocate the love and the gesture to please.

What would love with Marie be like? She had a quick temper, but so did I. She was passionate while I was easy going. Easily perturbed but slow to react, I had, nevertheless, managed to bloody many a nose in my naval career and had paid a hefty penalty in punishment.

My thoughts flew too far ahead. I wondered where Marie had grown up, where she had gone to school. Her life of privilege was evident. She had too much of the finishing school in her, along with a touch of debutante arrogance. What was she doing in a place like Olongapo? She would have fit better in Manila or

Baguio. She carried none of the roughness of a woman who spent her youth working in bars, none of the provincial innocence of the small villages that made up most of the Philippines. Women like Marie had no notion of innocence and desperation; they lived lives of luxury and convenience and expected things delivered in neat bundles with pretty ribbons on them. Women like Marie used men like gym towels: nice soft cloths for wiping away sweat after a rousing bout of shopping for shoes. Not that Marie was superficial. Far from it.

None of that mattered, though. I needed a woman like Marie after Vietnam. The cold chill returned. Vietnam. I didn't want to go back. Not even to collect my belongings. I switched off the lamp and settled back into the soft, comfortable bed. I closed my eyes and fell fast asleep.

Chapter Twelve

Frank

I wasn't going back to Vietnam! Neither was Sam. Chip and the Command Master Chief said we had been there long enough. Others who needed the time in-country would replace us. I hadn't felt such relief in months. The news drained the tension from me like I was shedding a layer of skin.

Sam and I walked through the hangar bay like changed men, calling out greetings and shaking hands with shipmates we hadn't seen in months. We walked to the bus stop but missed the bus by minutes and decided to walk to the chapel. Chip would follow later after a late-breaking meeting.

Chaplain Roland was working in the flowerbed when we arrived. I called out to him. "Hey, Chaps, are you pulling weeds or planting them?"

The Chaplain wiped his forehead. "Why, hello, Frank. Hello, Sam. You know what they say: when weeding, the best way to make sure you are removing a weed and not a valuable plant is to tug on it gently. If it comes out of the ground easily, it's a valuable plant." He surveyed the chapel grounds with his hands on his hips. "It's a challenge to keep the jungle at bay. Last week I found a python hiding in the shrubbery. Yesterday, a monitor lizard decided to sun itself next to the rectory. I draw the line at cobras for neighbors, though."

He looked from Sam to me. "Welcome back, boys. I'm happy to see you both safe and sound." He wiped his hands before shaking ours. "I lit a candle and said a prayer for all of you when I heard about the firefight. I'm so sorry for the casualties."

"Thank you for the prayers, Chaplain. It could have been much worse."

"Yes, it usually is. Let's pray this war ends sooner than later.

I've presided over far too many memorial services and sent too many bodies home to loved ones."

"I couldn't agree more, Chaplain." We were silent for a moment before I changed the subject. "Do we have a truck for the supplies?"

"Why, yes we do. We'll leave now if you're ready. By the way, is Master Chief Franklin coming with us?"

"He said he'd meet us at the orphanage later."

"Good. He's always such a pleasure to have around, and the kids love him. They call him Goody-Goody, you know."

I wondered why the kids at the orphanage would call Chip Goody-Goody? Coincidence? That would be a stretch.

We loaded up and were underway with Sam at the wheel. My spirits lifted as we left the city behind and drove into the open country and away from the ubiquitous diesel fumes that hung over Olongapo like a shroud. On either side of the road, tall, graceful coconut palms lined National Highway like swaying sentinels. Carabao cooled themselves in mud-wallows along the roadside, and sari-sari stores offering cold drinks and snacks to travelers dotted the landscape. I leaned back in the seat as the truck, laden with paint and building material, lumbered along. The orphanage lay near Barrio Baretto, a small village midway between Olongapo and Subic City, favored by many guys from the base for its laid-back atmosphere.

Sam slowed the truck as we passed the hand-painted sign for the Zambales Orphanage. He strained to overcome the lack of power steering as he turned the truck onto a gravel road that nearly formed a U-turn. At the end of the long, rutted lane sat the low, unpainted cement-block buildings of the orphanage. The chapel's steeple, topped with the cross, rode along the top of a green hedge separating the lane from the pasture. Goats and chickens scattered as we drove into the dusty, gravel parking lot. Sam brought the truck to a shuddering stop next to the dining hall. A sow pig, lying in her litter against the wall and feeding her young, peered with complacence at the truck from beneath her immense wrinkled forehead.

Sam leaned over the steering wheel to look around the grounds. "Boy, not much has changed. The place looks the same as the last time we were here."

I shaded my eyes from the bright noontime sun. "Doesn't it, though? That building will look better once they slap a coat of paint over those bare walls." I slid over when the Chaplain opened the passenger door. "Are we painting the exterior today, Chaplain?"

"Not today. Sister Arnalita would like to finish the inside of the new building first." The door of the long, narrow building at the near end of the parking lot opened, and a nun walked out, followed by several other nuns and a large group of children. "Here are the Sisters and children."

Chaplain Roland stepped from the truck and looked around. "You'll find the chapel much improved. A former resident blessed the orphanage with a generous endowment that Sister Arnalita put to good use."

The Sisters and what looked like all the children in their care, about thirty kids from toddlers to teenagers, surrounded us. Sister Arnalita, a striking middle-aged woman with a round, friendly, open face, stepped from the group.

"Greetings, Father Roland, and welcome."

"Hello, Sister Arnalita." They shook hands as the chaplain made introductions. "You remember Frank Bailey and Sam McBride. They assisted here several times during their last deployment."

"Of course, I do, Father." Sister Arnalita, squinting against the sun until I moved to shade her, greeted us.

"Hello, Frank. Hello, Sam. Welcome back to Zambales Orphanage. We are so pleased to see you again. Father Roland told us you would come today." She put her arms around the shoulders of a young boy and girl and gestured to the others. "We have new faces since your last visit. Children, say hello…"

"Sammy, Sammy, you come back, you come back."

A small child rushed from the crowd and ran into Sam's arms. She pressed her face against his neck and sobbed.

"Little Lucy! Hello, darling. So, you missed me? I missed you too, sweetheart. I missed you too." Sam kissed her cheek.

"Oh, Sammy. I am so happy you came. Did you like the letters I sent you, Sammy?" She added in a whisper, "Sister Mary Ann helped me write them. She is my best friend."

"I loved your letters, Little Lucy. Tell Sister Mary Ann I said thank you for helping you write them."

Laughter rippled through the crowd as Little Lucy called out at the top of her lungs. "Sister Mary Ann. Sammy says to say thank you for writing—I mean helping me write—my letters."

"Oh, that is sweet, Lucy. You are quite welcome." Sister Mary Ann left the crowd and took Sam's hand. "Welcome back, Sam. It is good to see you. I read your letters to Lucy many times. They made her happy."

"Thank you, Sister Mary Ann. You've been so kind."

Sister Arnalita, patting Little Lucy's knee, smiled. "She speaks of you constantly, Sam. We did not tell her that you would be here today; we did not want to get her hopes up only to disappoint if you could not come."

"That's okay. So much has happened. You know, we would have adopted Little Lucy, and she would be in Spain with Susanna if … well, she'd be in Spain."

"I understand, Sam. God bless dear Susanna."

I hoped the Sister wouldn't ask about Sam's son. Sam was already on the verge of breaking down; the orphanage held a lot of memories of Susanna, who had often helped with the children before returning to Spain to give birth. I hadn't wanted Sam to come, but that would never have done; he had spoken with excitement about seeing Little Lucy again.

Little Lucy's eyes widened as she fingered the silver chain around Sam's neck. "Sammy, can I hold the chain?"

"Yes, but be careful with it." He slipped the necklace off, removed a golden wedding band, and placed it around her neck.

"Ohhhh," she murmured. "Pretty. What is this?" She held up the medallion, turning it so the ruby flashed in the sunlight.

"That belonged to Susanna's grandmother of many generations ago. It's belonged to her family for a long, long time."

"How long is a long, long time, Sammy?"

"Before you were born, sweetheart."

"What was the other thing you had?"

Sam fingered Susanna's wedding ring in his pocket. "Oh, only a ring."

"Is Susanna coming back, Sammy?"

"No, Little Lucy."

"Is she in Heaven?"

"Yes, she is. God needed another angel."

"When I go to heaven, will I see her there, Sammy?"

"Yes, sweetheart. You'll see her there."

Sister Arnalita cleared her throat. She turned to address the crowd of adults and giggling children.

"Goodness, children, come now, behave and listen. Behave, I

say, behave. Sisters, if you please." She stood with her hands on her hips and a half-hearted look of vexation while the Sisters rounded up the children. "Thank you. Now, children, say hello to Frank and Sam. And you will never forget dear Father Roland."

A chorus of young voices called out greetings. I climbed into the truck bed while the chaplain asked Sister Arnalita where she wanted the building materials.

"You may place the materials next to the new medical building. The lumber we will use next weekend when Chaplain Roland and his group of volunteers repair the roof, so, if you like, you may begin painting the treatment rooms. Shall we?"

"Okay, Sister."

He turned to me and said, "All right, Frank, hand down the material, and we'll pass it along."

"You got it, Chaplain. Here we go."

We stopped for a late lunch after unloading and distributing the material. Little Lucy clung to Sam's side. The chaplain, Sister Arnalita, and I sat together at the head of the long dining table and chatted about the orphanage, future repairs, and our plans for our next tours of duty. Sister Arnalita said she would pray for us to receive orders keeping us in the Philippines so we would always be close to the orphanage. We had moved on to discussing plans for more renovations to the orphanage when a car drove up. A car door opened and closed, and footsteps crunched on the gravel. The door opened, and Marie entered the dining hall.

Book Three

U-Tapao, Thailand

1991

Chapter Thirteen

Tom

The sun seared my skin as I walked down the C-130 cargo ramp. The terminal shimmered like an abstract watercolor in the heat waves emanating from the asphalt. I set my bags down and took in the familiar scenery.

U-Tapao had been a U.S. Air Force base during the Vietnam War, and later a processing station for refugees. Sentry towers once manned by armed guards now kept ghostly watch over the perimeter. Buddha Mountain, low and squat, and looking more like a bullfrog than a Buddha, dominated the landscape to the northeast.

A van honked and pulled up next to me. The rear door slid open, and Bob Dixon called out.

"Tom. Hop in. You're just in time to ride to the hotel with us."

"Thanks. Toss my bag in the back, would you?" I wedged myself between suitcases, flight bags, and George Avelar.

"Here you go, buddy. Drink up." George handed me a beer from the cooler behind the seat. "Hot enough for you?"

He looked on as I swallowed half the can of beer. "Sorry, man," he said. "No Klosters. PBR is all we have. Tastes like formaldehyde, doesn't it?"

"Yeah." I wiped my chin with the back of my hand. "But it's cold. Where'd you get it?"

"The embassy liaison, Dan something, gave us a case when we landed and another case before he left for Bangkok a little while ago. There's a few left. Have another."

George took another beer from the cooler, a Styrofoam model shedding white, crumbling pellets that clung to beer cans and melting ice.

"I like that guy. He sets priorities," he said, handing me the beer. "By the way, first flight is at six tomorrow morning. We're on the launch crew; the other poor bastards get to handle recoveries."

Poor bastards all right. The nominal work schedule was twelve hours on and twelve off. The aircraft launch crew had evenings free to spend in town. The recovery crew had to swap shifts with someone if they wanted a night out. Not likely to happen in Thailand.

The drive to Pattaya was uneventful, though the driver took the long route to point out potential side trips for sightseeing. The van, part of a package deal that included transportation, box lunches, hotel, and tours of local attractions, deposited our luggage and us at the Tropicana Hotel on Beach Road at the north end of town.

I checked in and gave the clerk, a good-looking Thai girl with the smoothest skin I had ever seen, my personal information. George passed around beers while he waited his turn. He crowded me at the counter, leaning against me and making kissing sounds.

"Hurry up, Nelson. I don't have all night. There are women in town waiting for my lips."

"Wait until they find out where your lips have been." I handed him the pen and smiled as he moved aside.

"Very funny, mister comic relief." George leaned over to sign the guest book, his left arm curved in a painfully awkward position.

I winced. "Doesn't that hurt?"

"Doesn't what hurt?"

"Screwing your arm around like that."

"No. We geniuses get used to our little peculiarities."

"Little?"

"No woman has ever complained about my peculiarity being little. Yours, on the other hand."

"How would you know?"

"Haha. I'm not going there, buddy."

George, of Cuban descent, was tall, dark, and gap-toothed the way women found attractive. When he smiled, the gap set off the white of his teeth. Many an unsuspecting woman had fallen victim to George's gap as much as they had his charm.

George picked up his beer and room key and reached for several complimentary bottles of water. He stuck them between his arm and ribs but dropped two when he reached for his bags.

"Tom, man, stop looking at my butt and help me pick these up.

Stick them in my arm. Not there, my arm. Thanks. Darn," he said, as another fell to the ground. "Hey, grab that, will you?"

"I'm not grabbing that."

"The bottle, wise guy."

"Why not just leave them at the counter? There's water in your room."

"No way. They might run out."

"You're funny, George."

"They're free."

"Come. I'll walk you to your room, dear."

"All right, but no kiss at the door."

Inside the room, I put the bottles in the small refrigerator, already crammed with pricey hotel swag, and turned to leave. George was already shedding clothes.

"Hey. Are you going to see Lek?" His voice was muffled as he pulled the tight undershirt off.

I rolled my eyes. "Eventually."

"Give her a kiss for me." George wrapped a towel around his neck and pushed me out of the room. "We're grabbing a bite to eat before heading into town."

"Who? You and Lek?"

"Smart ass."

"Where will you be?"

"I don't know. Go. I'm in a hurry. Just head toward the lighthouse. Maybe Caligula Club. Maybe the Pussycat. Check both. Go." He closed the door and turned the lock.

"Okey doke," I said, picking up my bags.

The door opened again. "Check Ben's too."

After settling into my room, I stripped to my jeans and dashed off a postcard of the hotel's pool area to Aida. She would tape it to her mirror alongside others I had mailed her. The quirky habit started with a postcard I mailed from Hong Kong. The hotel's rooftop pool fascinated her as the ultimate symbol of luxury. Now she made me send her swimming pool postcards from each of my trips.

I unpacked and showered. Refreshed and dressed like a tourist in shorts, loose shirt, flip-flops, and shades, I walked to the lobby. A new desk clerk had taken over, a tall, beautiful Thai woman who wore her black hair in braids tied around her head. She smiled and greeted me.

"Hello, sir. May I help you?"

A sense of familiarity rushed through me as I handed her my room key; had we met? "May I mail a postcard from the hotel?"

"Yes, of course. I will ensure it goes to the Post Office."

I had to concentrate not to stare. "How much for postage?"

"Where is it going?"

"The Philippines."

"Oh. You are with the American Sailors who arrived today?"

"Yes."

"I lived in America. My father was the cultural ambassador at the embassy in Washington."

"That explains your good English."

"It's helpful when dealing with tourists. Nearly everyone speaks or understands some English."

"You speak better English than some Americans I know."

She leaned toward me and spoke in a confidential voice. "You would be astonished by how many native Thai speakers mangle our language."

"I never looked at it that way. Say, What's your name?"

"Sasi."

"Saucy. I like that. Is it short for something?"

"Sasithorn. It means beloved moon, and it's pronounced Sahzee not Saucy; do I look like that kind of girl?"

Her smile dazzled me. She ran her finger down the guest register and placed the room key in my mailbox. "Your name is Tom?" Surprise filled her voice.

"Yes. How'd you know?" *Duh. She's the desk clerk. She's supposed to know.*

"I'm the desk clerk. I'm supposed to know." She leaned forward and whispered, "It's written by your room number. Your room number is on the key too." She smiled.

"Ah. Of course. I thought you had fallen madly in love with me and memorized my personal information so you could write love letters to me."

"Silly, man. I thought you had fallen madly in love with me and were waiting for me to finish work."

Her manner had begun lighthearted, but the intensity of her gaze and the lift of her eyebrows when she tilted her head caused me to wonder.

"Alas, dear lady. My dance card is full, and no amount of longing could tear me from my commitments. I am genuinely distressed."

She pursed her lips and frowned. "Ah, well," she said. Then, nonchalantly, as she ran her finger down the list of countries and postage requirements, she asked, "Are you friends with the one named George?"

"George? He with the black curly hair, attractive gap between front teeth, and gold necklaces around bronze neck?"

Her eyes sparkled. "Could you be a little more descriptive?"

"Funny lady. He's my roommate."

"Is he? He asked me to go out with him. Is he a good guy?"

"He's a great guy, and a great dancer too. You'll have fun with him."

"Good. I don't often go out with hotel guests, but your group has some charmers." She gave me a wink that made my heart leap.

Her lovely smile melted me, and I blushed. I didn't know what to say.

"You Americans blush more than any people I know. You're so funny that way. It is endearing, though." Sasi ran her fingers across my hand. "Are you sure we cannot tango tonight?"

"My heart breaks, Sasi, truly, but I'm engaged tonight."

Her eyes drew me in with their disappointment. "My heart breaks too, Tom. Truly." She gave the slightest pause, then said, "May I call you Thomas?"

Something in Sasi's voice, in her manner, moved me. I nearly became emotional. "You must always call me Thomas, Sasi."

I handed her the postage and postcard and walked away. Something about her tugged at me. The déjà vu had unsettled me, leaving a thrilling undercurrent of joy. The emotional lift limned our brief encounter, giving it the vividness of a dream. I wasn't the brightest intellect when it came to discerning female emotions, but Sasi was forward enough that I was sure she wasn't playing a game. Susanna hadn't played games either. Maybe that was it; her manner reminded me of Susanna. She was direct where Aida was the opposite.

Aida. Oh boy. I fluttered my lips.

I replayed our encounter as I crossed Beach Road and walked along the promenade. The crowds of locals and tourists, the traffic, the whistles of traffic police, and the bicycle bells gave the city a vibrant hum. The sun beat down without mercy, but a breeze blew in from the sea, refreshing the area between the water and business side of the street. Palm trees shielded me from the burning rays of the sun. I slowed down to take in the scenery.

What else about Sasi reminds me of Susanna?

The shoreline curved in a long arc to the southwest. Multi-colored cabanas dotted the beach while swimmers dotted the water, their heads bobbing up and down on the swell. The scent of coconut oil floated on the breeze. Further out, the blue sky met the darker blue of the sea in a distinct line across the horizon. Jet skis and powerboats crisscrossed the calm water, some towing parasails that cast shadows like moving targets across the sea. The beautiful day reminded me of Sandy Beach in Hawaii, lacking only a sky crowded with all manner of colorful kites floating on the trades. Loud cheering and laughter from a tiki bar on the beach drew my curiosity, and I walked over to see what was going on.

The thatch-roofed, open-walled bar held a kick-boxing ring. Two young Thai men sparred with fists and flying kicks. Neither looked serious about inflicting pain on the other. I had turned to leave when I noticed the bartender smiling at me. She raised her eyebrows as I took a seat at the bar.

"May I have a Tiger beer, please?"

"Okay. You want glass?" Her speech was rapid and clipped.

"No, thanks."

She leaned over and reached into the cooler. Her loose, white blouse fell open, revealing firm, round breasts. A twinge of arousal passed through me. I blushed and looked away when she grinned. She placed the bottle of beer on the bar and flipped the cap off with a twist of her wrist. Her dark, deep-set eyes turned down at the outside, giving her a sultry look.

"You American Sailor?"

"Yes. How did you know?"

"Only American Sailor turn bashful when looking."

I turned the bottle in my hands, my face still blushing. "Yeah, sorry about that. You're pretty, though."

"Look." She pointed toward the sea. Two U.S. Navy destroyers floated at anchor two miles offshore. "You from ship?"

"No. U-Tapao."

Her eyebrows rose as fast as her demeanor leaped from business to pleasure. Shipboard Sailors weren't around long enough to take care of girlfriends. Shore-based Sailors, on the other hand, were known to settle on one girl during their long stays in Pattaya. "You got girlfriend? How long you here?" Her excited, sharp-pitched voice grated in my ears.

"Shhh. Let me hear you speak softly."

"What?"

"Speak soft, like this."

Puzzled, she looked around the bar. "What you say?"

"Much better." I smiled and whispered back. "What is your name?"

"My name Amporn."

"I'm Tom."

"Okay, Tom." She pronounced it Dom. "Why we whisper now, Tom?" Amporn leaned closer, her eyes narrowing in anticipation of some revelation. "You got secret for me?"

"No. No secrets for you. I just wanted to hear you speak softly. You have a lovely voice."

Her brow furrowed and she looked sideways at me. "What you say?"

"I said you are pretty, and you have a pretty voice. Do you understand?"

"I got pretty voice? Okay."

"And you are pretty."

"Okay," she said, staring at me and waiting for my next move.

Her stare disconcerted me. I didn't know what to do next. I knew what she wanted, and it wasn't my order for another beer. I had an incredible urge to ask her out but couldn't form the words. I wanted her to say something. Her fixed gaze held a mix of contemplation and scrutiny, like a woman wondering if you're going to ask her to dance or stand there undressing her all night. I could almost read her mind. Neither of us spoke. I made several false starts but couldn't muster the courage to speak. The silence lengthened, well past the time when she should have left to tend other customers. I burned with impatience to speak, but something held me back. Aida? Susanna? Her steady gaze burned into my eyes, and I shifted on the bar stool.

We were engaged in a timeless dance, performed countless times in bars, across tables, while passing in the street. It had a name: Lust to me, Fortune to her. Where the dance would take us, I didn't know, but I was committed. One would have to lead the other. One had to break the spell.

Her lips parted. Saliva stretched between them. I wanted to push my tongue into her mouth.

"You got girlfriend in Pattaya?"

I blinked. She was leading. She spun me across the bar. My pulse raced. Bolero beat in my chest. I longed to hold this beautiful, eager, slender, willing woman, rub her body, press my belly to hers, wrap my lips around her tongue. Her beauty, my lust, her passion tugged at me. Longing stretched between us, an almost tangible band of sexual tension. My heart melted, and my eyes threatened to spill over with tears of need and joy for the tango we danced.

I wavered as first Aida, then Susanna, flashed through my mind. They appeared as wardens, frowning, forbidding, punishing, waving motherly fingers in my face. No one had hold of my heart, though, not at this moment. Not character, that judgmental jury that warned me actions had consequences. It had guilted my burning conscience with many a sleepless night. Not love, that focused a man's heart and eyes on the heart and eyes of the one he loved. Character might falter, but forgiveness never forgets. Man-up or unman, resist or give, breathe or die. Yes, die a little more with each flake of honor, each flake of trust, each flake of commitment chipped from the marble statue of Virtue.

No woman but this enchantress, this dark angel, this treasure of tempting seduction could imprison my weak heart at this moment. I was falling, falling for her, onto her, into her, under her spell. I tugged at the medallion as the dreaded weight of the sainted Susannas burdened my shoulders. The heat of their presence and the glow of their purity were uncomfortable against my neck. When I spoke, the words spilled from my lips a thousand times faster than the reproaches of Aida and Susanna could fill my head.

"No. I don't have a girlfriend in Thailand. I don't have a girlfriend anywhere."

Chapter Fourteen

Tom

Adrenaline pumped my system into a throbbing, vibrating engine burning on twenty-four cylinders. I rubbed my leg to make it stop tapping the foot rail. My mind churned with anxiety and uncertainty. Shooting up caffeine wouldn't have given me a bigger buzz. I rested my elbow on the bar and chewed my thumbnail as I stared through Amporn.

Why do you torture me, Susanna?
It is not I, Tomás.
It must be. I feel you watching me.
No, Tomás. I am not here. I'm dead. You know that.
Yes. I killed you. I left you in the cold and the rain.
No, Tomás. I died of pneumonia in the hospital after the car accident.
I couldn't find my way back, Susanna. When I found you, the rain was pouring in torrents as you waited for me on the steps of the Chapel. You were wet. So cold and wet.
Yes, and angry too, but my anger passed, Tomás.
I only came to the hospital once. You were alone while your friends had company; my heart broke for you.
I was so happy when you came. Remember how I jumped from the bed and leaped into your arms?
Yes, Susanna. I remember. I remember the smell of orange blossoms as your hair swept across my face. I feel you now, in my arms, and the softness of your lips. I taste the salt of your tears.
You are lonely, Tomás.
Yes, Susanna.
You must not be lonely, Tomás.
No, Susanna, but I miss you. I lived a life with you in my

dreams. I died when you died.
I lived a life with you in my dreams too, Tomás, but you must go on living. You will have a life with someone else, but you must first forget me.
I'm afraid.
Of what are you afraid, Tomás?
I'm afraid of losing you again, Susanna.
Oh, Tomás. I will always walk beside you. I will always be with you. Someday, we will be together again.
Truly, Susanna?
Truly, Tomás.
I love you, Susanna.
I love you, Tomás.

I drank from the bottle of beer. The golden liquid ran cold through my throat. The sun was near zenith. It was still hot. Hell hot. I constantly wiped sweat from my eyes. My thumb was bleeding where I had bitten away the nail.

Amporn stared at me, her red lips parted, tongue touching her upper lip as she wiped the deep-polished teak of the bar with a towel. She set the towel down and leaned on her forearms. Her fine, black hair fell over her shoulders and brushed my fingers. She smelled of vanilla.

She spoke in a softer voice as she traced her fingers along my arm. "You want another beer?"

I should not see this woman, but this was my last chance for a fling before I married Aida. Everybody did it. Why shouldn't I? It didn't mean I wasn't in love with Aida. When I returned to PI, it would be the two of us. Wouldn't it? I might never return to Thailand. I didn't want to have regrets later in life.

Regrets. Everyone had regrets. That's what made them mean and bitter in old age. Regrets over a life not lived full. Regrets over a wasted life. Or did they regret the things they had done, things they were ashamed of having done? Would I regret cheating on Aida, or not sleeping with Amporn? Which was worse, infidelity before or after marriage? Were they equally evil? What did the Bible say? Was infidelity, or was it fornication, a deadly sin? Yes, but only after a promise of marriage. Great. I was screwed. I was going to hell. It was hot in hell. It was hot in Thailand. It was hot everywhere. It hadn't been hot in Spain. It hadn't been hot with Susanna.

I had never cheated on Susanna. The thought of infidelity never crossed my mind. How would she have reacted if I had? Susanna was direct and purposeful and possessed a clearly defined sense of right and wrong. Her faith had instilled in her a strict sense of morality, a code she lived by and expected others to respect. Susanna disliked when others crossed the line. She never hesitated to lash out at cheaters, whether vendors cheating customers, or men and women cheating on each other. Susanna wasn't afraid to be feared or disliked.

I wavered, weighing the guilt I would feel against the hurt Aida would feel. Righteous hurt against unrighteousness. Was it wrong to cheat if you weren't married? Yes. Without having said the words, we had committed to one another in faithfulness, trust, confidence, support. Without having our union blessed in the Church, we had implicitly promised to love, honor, and obey one another. A brief, sexual encounter was a momentary pleasure when considered against the backdrop of a lifetime spent with the woman you claimed to love and promised to marry. An afternoon's delight with Amporn could cost me a lifetime of love and companionship. I had lost it once. I knew the pain. I knew how to compartmentalize it so life could go on with a partially numbed heart. I could bear it. No. I couldn't. Susanna was proof of that.

"Maybe. What time do you—?"

"Hello, Thomas."

Her voice pierced my brain like a gunshot, and I jumped in my seat.

"Sasi. What a surprise." There was no reason to feel guilty, but I couldn't help it.

"I didn't expect to see you again today, Thomas."

I stood as she approached. My heart was pumped. I forced calm into my voice. "I always exceed expectations. Or should it be, I didn't meet your expectations? That requires deep thought."

We laughed together, and Sasi, radiant and exuding pleasure and warmth, bumped her shoulder into mine. "Either way, my day turned brighter when I saw you."

"Here. Let me." I took the groceries from her arms. "Where to, dear lady? Is it far to your castle?"

"Kind sir! What will people think if you enter my abode? I am yet unmarried and you..." She paused, her eyes questioning me. "Are you indeed free after all, Thomas?"

"George expects me at Whiskey A Go Go later."

"Ooh. That's a rather wild club."

"George wanted to go to Caligula Club."

"Oh, that's a rather raunchy club." She pointed north toward the Tropicana. "I live that way. Shall we?"

Amporn frowned as she called after us. "Hey."

"Yes?"

"You don't pay your beer!"

I paid the tab and tipped her.

"I'm sorry, but I have to go."

"Okay. I wait you."

"Oh. Okay."

Amporn, my treasure of tempting seduction, faded into the background as if she had never existed. I wasn't purposely cruel, but I was relieved Sasi had come along. She had saved me. Saviors, though, came with a price.

Sasi put her arm through mine, and we walked toward the Tropicana, my heart thrumming with excitement.

"Thomas, I didn't interrupt a passionate love affair just now, did I?"

Her lyrical voice, slightly accented, filled me with a tingling sensation. I could have listened to her all day.

"Not at all. I am, however, passionate about beer. I was contemplating an affair with a second one when you called my name."

"We can fix that. Would you like to stop for a drink?"

"I will do anything that pleases you, dear lady. I'm free for a few hours." A warning in my brain short circuited, and the words were out before I could think. "I don't have to be back until tomorrow morning. The van doesn't leave for U-Tapao until five." My intentions were innocent, but I had suffered one of those lapses wherein an emotional desire overcomes the brain's check on impulsive actions.

If she inferred meaning to my statement, she didn't say. We passed the Tropicana and walked another mile on side streets before turning onto Saranchol Alley and walking toward the Gulf. I was glad we hadn't taken a cab. Sasi made me forget the heat, Amporn, Lek, everything and everyone but Aida and Susanna. Both nagged at the back of my head, wagging reproachful fingers in my face. But each time Sasi spoke or laughed, or bumped her hip against mine, I warmed inside as the tension that knotted my insides melted away. I felt almost free.

"Almost there. We'll put the groceries away, then go to a small club I frequent away from tourist areas. The view of the ocean is heavenly. I think you will love it."

She turned us onto a long, circular driveway leading to a tall building with large balconies overlooking lush gardens and a large pool. It resembled a resort but lacked hotel signage and the constant coming and going of tour buses and swimsuit-clad guests.

"Nice place," I said. "It looks like a hotel."

"This is my castle. I live in the penthouse. There." She pointed toward the center of the highest floor. "Directly above the swimming pool terrace, but waaaaaaay up at the top."

I stared at Sasi's neck, my vision flowing along perfect lines from the dip above her breasts to the hollow behind her ear. A Renaissance master might have sculpted its smooth and flawless perfection. The more time I spent with Sasi, the more enamored I became of her grace and manner, and my infatuation deepened with every pulse of my heartbeat.

A uniformed doorman nodded and smiled to Sasi, but gave me the once-over as we passed. Revolving doors led to an expansive lobby buzzing with activity and the heady fragrance of incense. Another doorman took the groceries from me and gave them to yet another employee who disappeared who-knew-where with them. Plush, high-end sofas and chairs furnished sitting areas where visitors and residents mixed. A long, brass-railed bar, busy with the lunch crowd, dominated the far end of the room. Dark, polished bookcases, and panels inset with frosted, etched glass hinted at the luxury contained within the walls of Sasi's home. At the front desk, the attendant smiled and bowed non-stop while Sasi signed the register, then bowed again before handing her the key. The elevator boy gave the same obeisance when Sasi entered the elevator. I had the impression the staff considered Sasi royalty.

The elevator opened onto a small, carpeted lobby decorated with vases of fresh-cut flowers and walls hung with oil paintings of old Siam. Sasi took my arm as she opened the apartment door and led me into a bright, well-appointed room decorated in creamy white leather furniture and sheer curtains tied back with ribbons.

"Here we are, Thomas. What do you think?"

The large, open floor plan led from the sunken living room to the raised dining room topped by a large, round skylight. Three bedrooms bounded one side of the apartment with the kitchen on another. A grand piano filled the area between the kitchen and living room. Beyond, a curved wall of sliding glass doors opened onto an equally curved balcony that displayed the Gulf of Thailand as if it belonged to Sasi alone.

I took in the surroundings and the view, speechless at the contrast between Sasi at the hotel and Sasi at home. Not that she had changed, but at the change in my impression of her as a hotel employee of modest means. Everything around me increased my curiosity for Sasi. Surprises poured from her.

"How beautiful, Sasi. And the piano. Do you play?"

"I've played since I could reach the keys. Do you play?"

"Oh, yes. My mother taught me, and I played throughout my school years."

"We must duet while you are here. In Thailand, I mean. Or today, if you like. What is your favorite music?"

"Classical, but I love jazz too. And you?"

"Classical. I practiced every day as a child. My mother taught piano from our home."

"Your apartment is lovely. I've never seen such a beautiful view." I scanned the view to the south. "There's the Pattaya lighthouse at the end of Walking Street."

"It is lovely, is it not? I felt such joy when my parents offered to let me live here. I could live here forever."

"You own this?"

"No. My parents own it, but I pay the utilities, and other bills. I could not afford this on a hotel manager's salary."

"You manage the Tropicana?"

"Yes."

"You amaze me, Sasi."

"Come. Let us speak of other things. The folding doors behind you open to the bar. You will find beer in the refrigerator. If you'd like, you may make me a gimlet while I put away the groceries. There is also sangria, wine, water, and soft drinks. Take whichever you prefer."

"You'll have to tell me how to make a gimlet." I spoke from behind the bar as I studied the contents of the refrigerator. "I may have tasted one, but I've never made one." I removed a pitcher of sangria and poured a glassful. "I'll have sangria."

"One-part sweetened lime juice, four parts gin. Add a slice of lime. All the ingredients are right there. Oh, no rocks. Help yourself."

She pressed a button on a light switch, and the wall opened at the end of the counter, revealing a dumbwaiter. She removed the bag of groceries and pushed the button again, closing the door.

"Well, that's convenient. What other surprises do you have in store for me?"

"No more, I assure you. The dumbwaiter is such a luxury, and the staff receive an extra-large tip since they see to my groceries for me." She placed her hands on her hips and smiled.

"So, what would you like to eat?" She picked up the phone to make a call. "I'm sending to the restaurant for lunch."

"Whatever you're having."

"Okay. We shall have club sandwiches and chips."

She placed the order and joined me. I handed her the gimlet. "Mmm. Perfect. I thought you said you never made a gimlet? You will be my bartender."

I smiled at the compliment. "Cocktails are like beautiful women: one-part beauty, four-parts temper. Add a slice of sweetness."

"Interesting theory. Rocks or no?"

"Rocks. Every relationship is rocky."

"Do you speak from experience?"

"Have you ever been in a smooth relationship?"

"Completely smooth? No. But no one is perfect, and forgiveness is the key to happiness, is it not?"

"Only if one can forgive himself."

"Uh-oh, that sounds deep when we should be lighthearted. Let's save that for another conversation, shall we?"

"By all means." I carried my sangria to the glass doors. "I love this balcony, or should I call it a terrace? This would be a great place for a barbecue. Do you like to cook outside?"

"No, although there is a grill in the utility room. My father loved to cook outside. He became enamored of it while we lived in Washington. However, I love the aroma of grilled hamburgers and hot dogs." Sasi joined me. "Do you like to grill outside?"

"Yes, although I'm a better eater of grilled foods than I am a cook. George and I often cook outdoors back in Hawaii. Well, George cooks. I eat."

"You're so funny, Thomas. Come. Let's sit outside. This is the club I said I would take you to: Club Sasi. There is always a nice breeze, and the building shields us from the heat of all but the late afternoon sun. No tourists either. You may relax here."

Like old friends who reunite after years apart, Sasi put me at ease. I slid the door open for her and she led me to a round, ceramic tiled café table with two seats. Sasi kicked off her sandals and sat back, resting her feet on the balcony. I did the same. We passed the time making small talk. When lunch arrived, we ate from a platter of salad, sandwiches, and chips. Afterwards, I helped Sasi clear the table and bring out fresh glasses and sangria. I settled back in a chaise lounge and yawned.

"Excuse me. Lunch made me drowsy."

"Me too. I could fall asleep right here." She had settled into an adjacent chaise lounge. Her arms were behind her head. She looked over her shoulder to me. "I like to drink sangria on the balcony in the evening. I learned to love sangria, balconies, and sunrises when I lived in Barcelona."

"You lived in Barcelona?"

"Yes. I worked for a hotel there after I finished university. I stayed for two years. I miss it so very much. I have not been back since, but I will return someday."

"My girlfriend was raised there." The words were out before I could stop them.

"Your girlfriend?"

"Yes. Susanna."

I didn't continue, and Sasi didn't press, but returned to Spain. "Barcelona is a lover's city. So many places to fall in love and be in love. I miss the plazas and dancing in discotheques until early morning and having breakfast as the sun rose. Did you and Susanna dance until the early morning hours?"

"Yes. Often. We used to take the bus or drive there from Rota. When we didn't stay with her family, we stayed in a hotel near Las Rambla. Our favorite plaza was the Plaça Reial."

"Oh! I know the Plaça Reial. In the Gothic Quarter. I spent many wonderful hours there. I worked a short walk away at the Mandarin Oriental."

"I loved Barcelona."

"You speak with melancholy. Is something wrong?"

I looked out over the sea as I sipped sangria. Seagulls rose on the wind and flew past, the same way they had done when I sat with Susanna in the rooftop bar of the hotel. Below, cruise ships sailed into port as they had there too. Sasi might have been Susanna drinking sangria with me. They had the same midnight black hair, the same direct manner, but Sasi was tall where

Susanna had been petite, tinier than petite. *Not now. Not now.*

"No. Barcelona is my favorite city. I miss it."

"Yes. It is so romantic and beautiful."

Silence lingered and grew heavy. I worried what Sasi might ask about Susanna. That could be the only explanation for her silence.

"Is ... I don't want to intrude, Thomas, but is Susanna still your girlfriend? Is she in Spain?"

"No. She isn't my girlfriend anymore. I left her in Spain when I transferred to Hawaii."

"Oh. I see. Well, you will ...." She hesitated again. "You will love again. It is our nature to be in love. Or want to be loved."

The conversation had veered onto ground that couldn't hold me. I'd sink beneath the pain of discussing Susanna with a woman who resembled her in so many ways. If I didn't leave soon, I would crumble in front of Sasi.

"Sasi. I'd—"

"Thomas. I have a confession to make. I left work early so I could follow you. I'm sorry if I was wrong to do so."

"But the groceries. How did—where did—didn't you go shopping?"

"Yes. I bought the groceries this morning on the way to the hotel. I planned to go home for lunch, but I had so much fun with you. I had to see you again." She put her hand on my arm. "It has been a long time since I've enjoyed a man's company so much. A very long time."

The longing in her eyes touched me. They held a deeper softness than they had a moment before. I looked for the right words to express my feelings without making a commitment. I couldn't just say hello at the front desk and nothing else. Not now. She expected more and, to tell the truth, I wanted more. I didn't know how much more I wanted, or how much she wanted to give, but she'd be disappointed if all I did was wave as I left the hotel. I told myself I wouldn't do more than have dinner with her once or twice. That's all. But she needed more.

"I'm glad you followed me, Sasi. I've had a great time, and I'd like to spend more time with you." Again, my mouth spoke before my brain had time to shut it. "You remind me of Susanna in so many ways."

"I am both happy and flattered. Although, I must tread carefully so you don't leave me behind, as I am sure Susanna must have felt sad when you left."

"When do you work again?"

Did I hope to avoid her, or hope to see her? I had mixed feelings for Sasi. The pain of seeing Susanna in her was hard to bear.

"I am generally at the hotel from five in the morning until five in the afternoon."

"Why don't we have dinner tomorrow night? I should be back from Utapao in the late afternoon. What do you say?"

"I say yes! I would like that very much. But it seems so far off, I don't know if I can stand the wait."

"Neither do I, my lady, but we must be patient. I think we'll have so much fun."

"I'm sure of it, Thomas."

Something she had said earlier prompted me to ask, "Sasi, what did you mean a little while ago when you said *or want to be loved?*"

Her next words pierced my heart. "You did say, Thomas, that the van doesn't leave the hotel until five tomorrow morning, yes?"

I had been wrong a moment before. I knew exactly how much more I wanted.

Chapter Fifteen

Tom

The following week passed in a blur that left me breathless. I rose early each morning to meet Sasi at the front desk for coffee. In the evenings, she showed me her favorite restaurants where we sipped sangria and watched the sunset from dockside tables. We strolled along the beach and back, then down and back again, countless times, chatting about nothing, walking in the silence of each other's thoughts, and satisfying curiosity about things we felt important. I walked her home in moonlight, reveling in her company. She never spoke of Susanna, and Aida seemed so far away to me.

Sasi's voice, her fragrance, the sparkle in her eyes when she laughed at my wit reawakened feelings I had suppressed since Susanna's death. Infatuation for Sasi turned quickly into passion. Sasi stirred in me a reservoir of love that had lain dormant while I waited for the woman who would heal my heart. When I thought of Aida at all, it was with a twinge of regret. My feelings toward her had not changed, but my commitment to her was less certain. Sasi gave me something that Aida did not: a hope and passion for the future that thrilled my heart and gave me reason to forget the past. I saw Susanna when I looked at Sasi. I loved Aida, but I wanted Susanna, and Sasi was giving her back to me. Soon, I would have no reason to remember the past.

One night, after a long day at the airfield, I returned to the hotel as George and the others were heading into town. George looked every bit the dance king with the top three buttons of his shirt unfastened and gold necklaces around his neck.

"Hey, Tom," George said. "You're going the wrong way, man; town's that way. Come with us."

Bob, minus the gold necklaces but nearly bare-chested with most of his shirt buttons unfastened, joined us. "Yeah, Tom. We're going to Ben's to look at necklaces, then to the German Restaurant for dinner. We're going bar hopping later."

Alex Severs, who exuded Southern charm, rolled his eyes. "You mean George is looking at gold necklaces. Like he doesn't have enough already."

"I'd love to go, guys, but I made other plans."

Bob smirked. "You mean you're going out with the hotel manager, right?"

I ignored him, reading the smirk as either "you lucky bastard" or "don't let Aida find out." It was none of Bob's business, anyway.

George minded my business too, but without the smirk. "Have you seen Lek yet?"

He sounded just like Phil. "Not yet, Dad, but I will."

George laughed. "Okay. But you gotta do it eventually, and you don't know what later will bring." He turned to go and said, "By the way, Sasi looked pretty busy a few minutes ago. If you end up alone, we'll be at Ben's, then either Whiskey A Go Go or Caligula Club." He walked away shaking his head. "I still don't know why she prefers you over me. Poor girl."

They left me at the curb and headed for town, arguing over which clubs to visit and which side of the street to walk on. They'd spend an hour at Ben's while George looked at gold chains, then hit the Whiskey A Go Go. Alex and Bob disliked the Caligula Club and wouldn't go there with George. At least not until they'd had a few beers first.

Sasi had met me at the desk every night for the past week, but she wasn't there when I looked for her. I walked to my room intending to call her. I didn't want to ask the desk clerk for her; I didn't want to be a bother. Besides, George had said she looked busy. The message light blinked on the room phone. It was Sasi. She had unexpected hotel business and couldn't see me. I lay back on the bed, disappointed.

The glare of the setting sun rippling across the blue water of the Gulf made my eyes water when I left the Tropicana. The heat had lessened with the onset of night, and the walk uptown was pleasant, with daytime's busy odors giving way to nighttime's entrancing fragrances. Street vendors set up their cast iron fry pans for the sausage pies, pasties, pad Thai, and fried grasshoppers tourists loved. I bought a sausage from a familiar vendor and ate it from my hand while making my way along Walking Street. I was a few doors from the Whiskey A Go Go when Lek walked out of the club, arm-in-arm with an older man. Turning into a doorway, I watched them over my shoulder. They stopped at the corner and kissed. When she turned to leave, the man pulled her to him and kissed her again. A long kiss. The kind that says *hurry back, babe; I'm not done with you.* A twinge of jealousy passed through my mind. She would deny it, but I knew she saw other men when I wasn't in town. Why shouldn't she? Each man she knew was special, her guy, the one she wanted to marry, insurance. The rich American, Australian, German. The nationality of the day.

It occurred to me that I wouldn't have a hard time saying goodbye after all. In fact, I didn't need to say anything. I came to Thailand about twice a year. Lek couldn't say we had an understanding or commitment. I'd deal with it if we met, but I wouldn't go out of my way to see her. I had no reason to tell her about Aida and me. Without realizing it, I had set myself up as her hero, her savior, the typical man looking out for the weaker sex. Seeing her with the other guy had deflated my ego. But it didn't matter now.

I waited for Lek to move on before continuing to Ben's. I had intended to check the club for the guys, but Lek wouldn't have left with the man if she had known they were there. I kept an eye out for her as I arrived at Ben's and peeked in the window. The guys were inside. I was about to enter when she called out in her throaty, husky voice.

"Tommy! Tommy!" She waved to me from the doorway of a shop up the street.

Forcing a smile, I waved back. "Hello, Lek."

She weaved her way through the crowded sidewalk and ran to me, grinding her breasts against my chest as she kissed me.

"Oh, Tom, Tom. I thought I never see you again. Why you don't let me know you are coming back? You don't write to tell me you are coming here. Oh, Tom, I am so happy you came back. How long will you be here? I just see you now when I'm going shopping. I can't believe it is you." She stopped speaking when she ran out of breath.

I leaned away from her. "It's good to see you again."

"Why you don't write me, Tom. Why? I am so worried that you don't love me anymore. I am so happy you come back to me."

She took my hands and pulled at me. "Can we go someplace, Tom? We go to my house, yes? Come."

I pulled away. "Wait a sec, Lek. I need to see my friends. Wait here." Halfway inside, I reached back and took Lek by the arm. "What am I thinking? You know them. Come on."

"Hey, guys. I finally found you. Look who I brought with me!"

George had always liked Lek and treated her with an open, easy familiarity, the way a guy treats his best friend's girlfriend. He picked her up and swung her around, drawing a giggling laugh from her and a horrified stare from the salesman behind the counter.

"Lek, you beautiful little woman, how are you? Hey, you got any t-shirts for me, honey?"

During a previous detachment, Lek had bought him several t-shirts embroidered with "Gorg." The mistake mortified the poor girl, although George had laughed it off and wore the shirts, anyway.

Lek blushed a deep red. "No-no, no shirts, George. I not buying shirts for you again."

Bob greeted Lek and asked if she were hungry. She jumped at the offer. "Oh, Tom, I am so hungry. We go, yes? Can we go? We go to Ali Baba's for Indian food? I like Indian food."

"I don't see why not. If you guys are ready, let's go. Are you coming, Alex?"

Alex had a suave coolness that I admired. Not only that, his accent sounded like music and only accentuated his appeal.

"Hey, Lek. Yeah. Ya'll hang on a sec, guys. Let me pay for this and I'll be with you. You think Bennie will like it, Bob?" Bennie was Alex's PI girlfriend, a sweet, charming Filipina who lacked the drama of his on-again, off-again girlfriend in Hawaii.

"Alex, Bennie will love anything you bring her. I've never seen a woman so easy to please."

Alex said, "Okay. Let's walk. We have plenty of time. Where are we going anyway, Ali who's?"

Everyone spoke at once, each trying to sway the others toward a particular restaurant.

"Ali Baba's. An Indian place near the hotel."

"No. Bob wanted to go to the German Restaurant."

"Who mentioned Ali Baba's anyway?"

"What about Pizza Hut?"

"Pizza Hut? Seriously? Who goes to Pizza Hut in Thailand?"

"All you talked about at work today was KFC. 'Oh, man, I'm dying for some KFC.'"

"Well, it's better than Pizza Hut."

"I'll give you a pizza."

Alex took the necklace out of its red cloth pouch and held it up. "Hey, Lek, let me see how this necklace looks on you."

Lek's eyes brightened and she turned, lifting her ponytail so Alex could fasten the necklace around her neck.

"I say Ali Baba, Alex. I say we go to Ali Baba for Indian food."

"There." He fastened the clasp. "Turn around now and let me see how it looks on you."

Lek turned, letting the ponytail fall down her back. She swung her head, tilting it to one side and stood with one hand on her hip, the other hanging loose, coy, coquettish.

"Jesus, Lek," Alex said. "You look like a model. Don't she look like a model, guys?"

The gold necklace stood out against her dark blue blouse. The tight, white jeans and the thrust of her hips made me swallow hard. *God, even the pink zories work to her advantage.* Not seeing her in so long had dimmed my mental image of her. I had to force myself to look away.

"Tom. Tom!"

Bob's voice called through the noise of a passing jet.

"Yeah. What?"

"Where do you want to eat?"

"What? Oh, the German Restaurant is okay, I guess."

"Oh, no, Tom, we not go to German Restaurant."

Alex shook his head. "Lek's right. We always go there, and I'm not in the mood for brats and sauerkraut. Let's go somewhere else." He opened a walking map of Pattaya and looked over the list of restaurants. "Hey, we should go to the Siam Elephant Restaurant. It's by the police station and closer than the German Restaurant. They serve the best Thai food in Pattaya according to Alex's 5 Star Restaurant Guide."

Bob cursed. "I don't care where we go, but let's go already. We're in frigging Thailand, for Christ's sake. Anything but McDonald's and KFC."

"And Pizza Hut," I said.

"And Pizza Hut," Alex said. "Lek wants to go to Ali Baba's."

"Lek. Do you mind if we go to the Siam Elephant?"

"I go wherever Tom want to go."

"It doesn't matter where we go. I'm so hungry, I could eat an elephant."

Lek stared at me, her face lined with concern. "You eat elephant? No one eat elephant."

The guys cracked up. Lek, confused by their reaction, joined in the laughter.

"Okay, Alex. I will take off the necklace now. I like it too, if it makes you like it on me. Does it look pretty?"

"Oh yeah, it does. You keep it Lek. I'll buy another one for my girlfriend."

Lek protested.

"No, I mean it. It looks so nice on you. You deserve to keep it. It's my gift to you. Besides, every time I see the necklace on Bennie, I'll think of you."

Lek's face glowed. She fingered the necklace all through dinner, sliding it around her neck, tugging it gently, trying it outside her blouse, then trying it inside. She acted like a little kid with a longed-for gift. She laughed, hugged their arms, and nuzzled the guys she could reach.

I was glad I hadn't been the one to buy the necklace. She was playing for the guys, enjoying her moment as the center of attention. The necklace was the barfine, and she gave the guys what they had bought, the only thing she had to give. Herself. Her body. Her sensuous movements and velvet laugh. I imagined her desperation, her crying inside. I imagined Lek yearning for one of the men to take her away. American Sailors had everything they desired, and she wanted in. She didn't feel they owed her anything, but they could give her what she wanted.

When she wasn't performing for Alex and George, she performed for me, feeding me from her plate, and clasping my free hand when I fed myself. I regretted the attention. She kept up a steady chatter about little things, domestic things concerning her apartment and roommate, her family in Chanthamuri. I joined in the light atmosphere, but my heart wasn't in it. I touched Lek when I was supposed to and smiled when she spoke to me. Something had changed. Something in our relationship had switched off when I saw her with the other man. Was it a loss of power over Lek? Was I upset that I couldn't control her when we parted? Maybe she didn't pine for me when I was gone, after all. I didn't love her, but I loved being with her. I loved being the sole object of her attention. The other guy probably did too. Lek was no fool. She knew what she had to do to achieve her objective, and she wouldn't place her bet or attention on one man. My heart turned cold and hardened against Lek. I lost my appetite and picked at my food. I was sick to my stomach.

After dinner, we made our way up Walking Street, arguing over where to go. George insisted on beginning the night at Caligula Club, but Alex and Bob remained steadfast against going anywhere but Whiskey A Go Go, where they hoped to pick up dates for the night. Lek wanted me to go to her place. I had no desire to be alone with her.

"I'm going back to the hotel, Lek. I have a headache. It's been a long day."

She took my hands and pleaded with me. "Oh, Tom. Please come home with me. I massage you and make you feel better."

"No, Lek. I need to get some sleep. I have an early day tomorrow, and I don't want to be fatigued. I'll see you tomorrow night."

Her face fell, but it held hope. The truth would hurt when it dawned on her. But she had been hurt before. She had told me of the hurts.

"Okay. I see you, then. Will you come to see me at my work?"

"Sure." I let go of her hand, once soft and warm. "I'm off, guys. I'll see you in the morning."

George understood. "Are you sure you don't want to have a drink before you head back?"

"No, that's all right."

"Okay. See you in the morning," he said as he joined Alex and headed for Whiskey A Go Go.

Lek kept trying to hold my hand, and I kept pulling away. "I really need to lie down for a while, Lek. I don't feel well and just want to sleep. I've been up since three this morning. I'll see you tomorrow. I promise."

"Okay, Tom. I will wait until tomorrow. You promise you will come to my work and see me?"

"Yes, I promise."

"Okay. Good bye, Tom."

She grabbed me and kissed me, but I pulled away and our hands slipped apart. She would probably go back to the man she had left earlier. It was apparent she preferred me to the other guy, but she couldn't afford to let preference get in the way of opportunity. I doubted the thought had entered her mind, but she probably sensed my waning interest and wanted to cut her losses. What would she do if I didn't show at the Whiskey A Go Go?

Chapter Sixteen

Tom

Sasi. I dreamed about her. I shook the water out of my hair and stepped from the shower. Except for vague bits, I rarely recalled my dreams. Not that dreams had context. Did any dream make sense? Did dreams do anything more than increase the hurt? In the dream, Sasi was swimming in a channel running through a city, tall buildings lining either side. I watched from a dock as she receded in the distance. It was night, and I feared I was going to lose her. Just as I made up my mind to swim after her, a giant wave formed and towered hundreds of feet over me, not breaking but always on the verge of breaking. Terror filled me, and I wanted to run away, but I was rooted to the shore. When the wave began to break, Sasi disappeared and I woke, covered in sweat and lying in damp sheets.

I wrapped a towel around my waist and brushed my teeth. What if Sasi were not at the front desk? No. She said she'd be there. She wasn't the type to disappoint. I grabbed my backpack, stuffed in a bottle of suntan lotion and a book, and grabbed my camera. I scanned the room and left for the lobby.

I followed the aroma of fresh-brewed coffee to the breakfast bar. The attendant filled a travel mug for me. Hot and delicious. The staff had laid out a continental breakfast of fruit, croissants, bagels, and doughnuts. I stuffed a pink frosted doughnut in my mouth and three more into a sack and walked across the lobby to the front desk. The clerk, her back to me, was sorting mail into room slots. She turned at my approach. It was Sasi looking beautiful, happy, and fresh. I hadn't recognized her with her hair in a ponytail. She laughed when she saw me, and my face reddened. I put the remainder of the doughnut in the sack.

"Oh, Thomas. Good morning. You are so funny. I'm sorry, I

could not help but laugh." She covered her mouth with her hand, laughing still as I handed her my room key. "Do we yet have a date for this evening?"

"Of course. I thought of nothing else all night."

"Does that mean you dreamed of me?"

"Of course. I dreamed I skipped work today, and we ran off to Barcelona, where we married and had ten kids. I stayed home while you ran our hotel empire. We had become grandparents when I woke."

Her ponytail shook when she laughed. Ponytails made my knees weak. They expressed fun, youth, freedom. Hers revealed a neck that cried out for nuzzling.

"You are so much fun, Thomas. I love the way you make me laugh."

"I'm glad. I'll be sure to stuff my mouth with pink doughnuts every morning."

"Doughnuts are fun, are they not? If you cannot laugh while eating doughnuts, why, you probably don't laugh at all."

"Well then, the world should eat more doughnuts, don't you think?" I looked around for the rest of the team. "Has anyone else shown up? They should be here by now."

"I have not seen George, but some of the others are having breakfast." She sorted the last of the mail, then picked up a heavy stack of international newspapers.

"Here, let me get those." I rushed to help her. "Where do they go?"

"You may distribute them among the sofas and chairs in the lobby, if you like. Here," she said, taking the top few papers. "You carry, and I will distribute. They are complimentary to guests."

I followed Sasi through the lobby. "We make a great team, Sasi. I work cheap too. Feed me, and I'll do anything you ask."

"Hey. Leave my girl alone, Nelson." George walked up carrying doughnuts, and stuffing several bottles of water in his backpack.

"Your girl, Mr. Avelar? When did you dream that this unlikely event took place?" Sasi was shining. Her eyes bore into George's. He laughed and looked away. Not many people could intimidate George, but Sasi was his match.

"Hah. Just kidding," he said. "You two sounded like lovebirds. 'Oh, Thomas. Oh, Sasi. Kiss, kiss, kiss.' I didn't know you were that close. You work fast, Nelson."

"And what is that supposed to mean, Mr. Avelar?"

George was in over his head with no way out.

"Just kidding again. Geez."

George picked up one of the papers from the coffee table. "Hey, I need something to read at U-Tapao. How much for a newspaper?"

Without missing a beat, Sasi said, "Twelve dollars."

I spit up my coffee and laughed. Sasi had her back to George, but I could see her smile.

"Holy crap," George said. "I don't need it that bad."

Sasi turned to George and said, "Just kidding. Geez."

George reddened. "Good one. How much are they really?"

"You may have it gratis, George. Compliments of Hotel Tropicana. Please come back and visit." She smiled sweetly and returned to the front desk.

Chief Goff walked in from the restaurant. "Miss, are the box lunches ready? We're leaving soon."

"They are ready, Chief Goff. I will send for them now." A few minutes later, the box lunches rolled in on a cart. The Chief directed the bellboy to the waiting van.

"Nelson. Avelar. Get your butts in gear."

"Bye, Sasi," I said. "I'll see you tonight."

"Goodbye, Thomas. Have a wonderful day. I can't wait until this evening." She smiled at George. "Goodbye, George. You have a wonderful day too." She waved to us, then greeted the rest of the crew as they dropped off room keys.

The van idled curbside while the driver sipped coffee and thumbed through the Bangkok Post.

I ran for the front seat, calling shotgun and opening the door two steps ahead of George. George tossed his bag into the backseat and flicked my earlobe.

"Hey dickhead, I called shotgun yesterday."

I reached around, grabbed George's shirt, and caught his nipple between my fingers. "Too bad, dipstick, I got here first."

"Owww. All right, all right, you can ride shotgun. Let go!" George twisted free but flicked my earlobe again before diving for the rear seat.

Chief Goff opened the front door. "Scram, Nelson. I'm riding up front. Clean up the coffee you spilled on the console. Matthews, stow the box lunches. Bennett, give him a hand. There should be two pack-ups: one for aircrew and one for maintenance.

The rest of you knuckleheads help the driver stow the gear. Avelar! The beer is for after work."

The guys scrambled to do as they were told.

"Matthews," he called. "Make sure they packed the coffee grounds."

I didn't move. "Aw, Chief, I need to ride up front so I can take photos on the way."

"Sorry, Sailor. Rank hath its privileges." He waggled his thumb over his shoulder. "In the back."

I grabbed my backpack, gave the console a cursory brush with a napkin, and moved to the rear. George mimicked my plea to the Chief, but I ignored him as the rest of the guys took their seats. The van set off, turned onto Beach Road, and headed for the airbase.

Once out of town, the miles sped by. The driver stopped so we could take photos of Buddha Mountain, but the Chief rushed us. The driver promised to stop on the way back. Before long, the van passed through the main gate of the airbase, drove through the workers' housing where clothes flapped on clotheslines, past the hangars, and stopped in front of the air terminal. We poured from the van and unloaded the gear. Chief Goff carried the box of maintenance records into the terminal and set up shop. We set up the holy coffee maker but couldn't find the coffee grounds. The chief was pissed.

"Matthews! Where the heck is the coffee?"

"I don't know, Chief. I looked everywhere."

"You should have looked before we left the hotel. Christ." Chief Goff made a cursory look through some of the box lunches. "All right, Matthews. Get your butt moving and find us some coffee. Check with the tower. If they don't have any, ask them where we can buy some."

"Aye aye, Chief," he said and ran off to the tower.

I asked the Chief if I could walk around and take photos.

"Yes, but don't go too far. I don't want to have to look for you if we need a metalsmith."

"Thanks, Chief."

George, sitting on a luggage conveyor and counting the dollar bills in his wallet, probably anticipating a night at Caligula Club, jumped up. "Hey, can I go with you?"

"Yeah, sure."

"Chief?"

"Go ahead. But don't get lost. And stay away from the women."

George tucked in his shirt and grabbed his cap. He called over his shoulder. "I can't help being a babe magnet, Chief. Women can't leave me alone."

"Tell that to the hotel manager."

Bob laughed so hard he had tears in his eyes. "Bam! Prince Charming goes down."

"Funny. Haha. Good one, Chief." George walked away. "You coming, Nelson?"

We left the terminal and walked toward the hangars a short distance beyond the terminal. American, Australian, and New Zealand P-3 Orions and British Nimrods lined the tarmac. I took photos of the aircraft and the mechanics making repairs and preflight checks. We waved back to familiar faces who promised to meet us in town for drinks. The aircrew vans drove by on their way to the terminal. One of the enlisted guys leaned from a window and called out.

"Hey, man. You guys got any coffee?"

George raised his arm high and gave the thumbs up.

"We don't have any coffee, George."

"He doesn't know that."

"You're evil, George."

We reached the hangars and showed our ID's to the sentry, who waved us through the gate.

"I saw a C-47 in here as we drove past," I said. "I thought I'd get a few shots." I adjusted the settings on my camera and took photos as we walked around the rusting warbird. "What a thrill it would be to fly in one."

George didn't say anything. I looked up, thinking he hadn't heard me, but the wrinkled forehead signaled he had something on his mind.

"What's wrong, George?"

He looked off into the distance like he was choosing his words. Finally, he turned to me with an intense stare that softened into one of concern as he spoke. "It's none of my business, Tom, but what are you going to do about Aida?"

I'd expected George to ask me sooner or later. "I don't know."

"I only ask because you're spending an awful lot of time with Sasi. I'd understand if this were just another detachment fling, but you've been seeing Aida for two years. That's a relationship."

"A year and a half."

"That's still a relationship."

"Yeah, well."

"It's pretty clear you have a thing for Sasi."

A C-130 Hercules taxied by, and we walked to the edge of the tarmac, covering our ears until the engine noise abated.

George said, "Everyone knows Sasi has a thing for you."

I stared at the C-130 as it rolled down the runway accelerating for takeoff.

He went on. "As I said, it's none of my business. I'm just concerned is all."

I snapped a photo of a wingless C-47 airframe parked outside the hangar. The wings lay in a pile with other rusting aircraft parts. We walked on. Buddha Mountain rose from the plain a few miles from the base. I must have taken a hundred photos of the landmark over the years. I looked at it then without seeing it.

"You know, George, you caught me off guard yesterday when you asked if I had spoken to Lek yet. I've spent so much time with Sasi that I didn't see her until yesterday as she left Whiskey A Go Go."

"Did you tell her?"

"She wouldn't have been with me had I told her. Besides, she left the club with another guy."

"Oh. That sucks."

"You should have seen them kissing."

"Ouch. Sorry, man."

"There's no reason to be sorry. She has to look out for herself."

"Yeah. I know how it is."

We reached the next hangar, and I took more photographs. Two Thai sentries nodded as we passed their vehicle. I motioned for an okay to take their photo, and they assented, smiling for the camera like tourists. I thanked them, and we walked on.

"Where's your camera?"

George shrugged. "I didn't bring it. Didn't feel like lugging it around."

"Well, let me know if you want a photo of something."

"Okay."

I said, "She was just having fun with you, you know."

"Who?"

"Sasi. She was only giving you a hard time. She really likes you."

"Oh, yeah. Cool. I'm not worried about it. I can almost take a joke." He grinned. "She intimidated me, though. I didn't know what to say."

"Imagine you rendered speechless by a woman. I spit up my coffee when she told you how much the newspaper cost."

"She has a forceful personality too, unlike Aida and Lek. No wonder you like her."

"What do you mean?"

"Most of the women you go out with have strong personalities."

"Really? I never noticed."

"They exude confidence and optimism."

"Don't I?"

"Optimism, yes, confidence, not so much. You can be indecisive. When it comes to women, that's your weakness."

We walked on, both lost in thought.

My indecisiveness sprung from a desire to please, to let others make decisions. Rather than risk hurting people by my choices or commands, I let others tell me what they wanted. I had treated Susanna and Sasi differently, though. They made me want to make decisions and lead. George had caught on to something. He was wrong about Aida, though. Aida had a strong, decisive personality, but she needed me and that made her appear weak to George. I had never noticed it, but George was right: strong women did attract me. I had never cared for weak, needy women, but hadn't consciously avoided them or sought strong women. Lek, who wasn't strong, and Aida, who was, needed me. Sasi and Susanna didn't.

"So, what are you going to do? Are you going to tell Lek about Aida? What about you and Aida? Or Sasi, for that matter?"

"I'm going to tell Lek I can't see her anymore. I had decided not to see her at all when I spotted her kissing that guy, but she saw me outside Ben's."

I caught George's glance and continued. "It caught me off guard. I mean, I know Lek is looking for a husband, and she can't just sit around and wait for it to happen, but it bothered me. To tell the truth, it turned me off to her. I didn't feel the same toward her after that. It doesn't matter though. I came to Thailand to tell her I was marrying Aida."

"Are you sure you're going to marry Aida?"

"What?"

"Are you sure you're going to marry Aida?"

"Yeah, I guess. Why?"

"You don't act like a guy who just asked a woman to marry him. You did ask her, didn't you? Phil told me you had. Shouldn't you be walking on air with your head in the clouds or something?"

George didn't have much room to talk. George, the ladies' man, the squadron's Casanova. George, the man who never went out with the same woman twice. His false promises of love would reach to the moon.

"Why does it matter what I do here if I mean to marry Aida, George? What about people who have one last fling before they marry? Who tells them they're doing wrong? Why do I have to be chaste as a saint just because I asked a woman to marry me? Who made everyone my judge and jury? What's special about me that people think I'm a heel because I want to have some fun before I get married? Why don't people worry about themselves and leave me the hell alone?"

"Whoa there, fella. One rebuttal at a time."

"I'm sorry, George. I'm just tired of people using my relationship with Aida to practice self-righteousness. I don't mean you. You're not always harping at me. At least when you do, you mean well."

"I only spoke up because this isn't like you, Tom. You're not the kind of guy who treats women like trash."

"I'm not treating anyone like trash," I said flatly.

"What do you call cheating on Aida? What about the way you're treating Lek?"

"I'm not cheating on Aida, George. I haven't slept with a woman, any woman, including Lek and Sasi, since we returned to PI. I made a commitment to Aida, that's the truth."

"What about Sasi? How deep is your relationship?"

"Sasi? I don't know." I turned defiant. I had grown tired of dissembling. "Yeah, I am going to continue seeing her. I don't care what people think. I like her more each time I see her."

"So, what about Aida? Do you really want to marry her?" He stopped in front of me and clasped my shoulders. "Do you love her, Tom?"

George's concern was genuine. He was a playboy, but that didn't mean he was ignorant of others' feelings. His promises to women were the obvious, false promises all men make, and women too when they're the givers, or takers. They aren't meant to hurt, only to persuade for the moment. Any hurt is the fault of the naive, hopeless romantic, not the romancer.

"Growing up, I wanted the kind of love my parents had. I wanted the woman that, when we met, we'd know instantly we were destined to be together. That's what happened to my parents, George. All my life, people told me my parents were born in love with each other."

"But that was your parents, Tom. You can't expect the same thing to happen to you. You know, it almost sounds like you're in love with your mother."

"That's bullshit, George."

"Wait. Let me finish. I don't mean in love with her, but in love with the idea of her. You're looking for the mother you never had. Your mother and Susanna were both Spanish, shared the same name, and worked as bartenders in Rota. Do you know what your mother looked like?"

I had never considered what George was telling me. Was I looking for my mother? That wouldn't explain Aida, though. Was my attraction to Sasi based on her resemblance to Susanna? Were my Susanna and my mother the same woman? But what had attracted me to Aida if I were looking for my mother?

I shook my head. I couldn't think straight. "Yes, Susanna and my mother resemble each other, but that's not why I fell in love with Susanna. When we met, I knew it was meant to be. It's happening again with Sasi."

"Did you stop to think maybe it's happening because you want it to? That your ambivalence over marrying Aida is making you act in ways you wouldn't otherwise act? You told me Sasi reminds you of Susanna. Are you looking for Susanna in Sasi the way you looked for your mom in Susanna? You are, Tom, and you don't see it."

"That isn't true. Even if it were, how does it explain Aida?"

"Even if it isn't true, you can't expect every love to be the same. As for Aida, maybe your head is telling you to look for your mother while your heart is leading you the right way."

I didn't say anything. George had poked me hard in the chest, and it hurt. What he said made sense.

"Seriously, Tom, I mean it. You need to lighten up, stop looking for a certain woman, love, marriage, whatever, and just let it happen. You can't force it. I doubt if your mom and dad were looking for each other. It just happened when they weren't expecting it."

"No, George. When I met Susanna, I knew instantly we would marry. She knew it too. After she died, I gave up. I thought it would never happen again. I stopped looking for love and began to look for pleasure instead. I didn't care how I treated women because I wasn't looking for anything. Aida attracted me because she needed me. She wanted what I could give her, a ticket to the States. I knew that, but I didn't mind because I knew Aida also wanted me for me. She could have had any guy at Rufadora, but she chose me."

George went on, oblivious to my reasoning. "Your problem is that you're looking for your parents' kind of love. That's the wrong approach. You're looking for marriage when you should be looking for a companion, someone to have fun with. Not sexually, that will come later. It's kind of like foreplay without expectation of sex."

I looked at George in surprise.

"Sorry, sorry, poor choice of words. That only leads to frustration. What I mean is, you gotta enjoy being with a woman for who she is, without expectation of anything beyond companionship. Tell me I'm wrong, Tom, and I'll shut up."

"You're not wrong. We're in violent agreement."

"We are?"

"I had stopped looking for love and wanted only a companion. That's when Aida came along. Aida is the first woman I went out with for anything other than pleasure. So, I guess Aida is an interim love. I guess she filled the gap between Susanna and Sasi."

"No, Tom. Aida is your heart love. You're just not ready to see it. You need to ask yourself if you really want to marry her. That's what you want, right?"

I looked away over the airfield, toward the rock-solid permanence of Buddha Mountain shimmering in the sun's cruel heat. "I don't know what I want, George."

Chapter Seventeen

Tom

Exhausted after a heavy day of maintenance, we dropped our dirty coveralls in a bin and trudged to the van. A local woman would collect the work clothes and wash them. For a few dollars more, she would wash and press personal clothing, a bargain considering how much the hotel charged. Supporting the local economy extended to more than buying barmaids drinks and picking up gaudy trinkets for girlfriends in PI.

The ride to the hotel was unusually quiet, with none of the banter over plans for the night. Most of the guys reclined in their seats, lost in thought or dozing. George snored once or twice, but stopped when Alex elbowed him in the ribs. The driver, normally a wildly gesticulating and verbose tour guide who spoke wickedly tortured English, fell under the spell of the somnolent atmosphere and held his tongue.

I sat in the back of the van, resting my cheek against the seatback. Sasi would have gone home by now, disappointed I hoped. Maybe she left me a note. I looked out the window. In the countryside, far away from the city, the sky blazed from horizon to horizon with twinkling pinpoints of light. Stars sprinkled across the heavens lit the night with the brilliance of a hundred thousand sparkling diamonds. I wanted to run my fingers through the Milky Way as it spanned the infinite curve of the universe like a feathery swath of white splashed upon a canvas of black.

I leaned my head against the window. It was too dark to see anything but stars. My tranquil, almost melancholy mood turned my vision inward. I closed my eyes and soon slipped into that shallow region just below alertness. My mind filled with thoughts of Aida and Lek. A turmoil of images and voices, colors and scents, a mix of faces and memories, emotions happy and sad, sensations at turns cold and trembling, warm and soothing. Aida, her long, black hair brushing across my belly sending wild, delicious shivers through me; lovely Lek, pleading for a return of the same love she gave, but which she would never receive. I had loved them both and wanted both and neither. Then Mama-san, whose sharp eyes pierced my heart and frowned in sorrow for Aida and disappointment in me for my duplicity; George berating me for trying to emulate my parents' love.

I dreamed of school and the painful, paralyzing shyness that shut me off from more than casual female acquaintance, and the years in foreign ports spent seeking easy female companionship, whatever the cost in money and drink, whatever the cost in promises and false hope. I smiled, I sweated, I laughed in my dream-filled sleep. My heart broke over and over again. I dreamed of my fear of falling in love again and my destructive behavior in seeking carnal and empty, rather than spiritual, healing love. I dreamed of my one true love, Susanna, a ghost in my dream. She had been so real once.

Alex woke me as the van pulled up to the hotel lobby, and I grabbed my backpack. I hit my head as I exited the van and cursed under my breath. I rubbed my head: no blood. Sasi was gone, and her absence left me empty. I asked the good-looking desk clerk with the smooth skin if there were any letters for me. She shook her head and gave me my room key. *Should I ask for her? Maybe she's in the office. No. She'd have known we were back. Should I go to her? Am I presuming too much?*

The key was in the lock when the night manager ran to me from the lobby.

"Sir! Sir!" She waved a piece of paper in her hand. "Sir. I have a note for you. Please accept my apology for not handing it to you at the desk."

It was a note from Sasi. "That's okay. Thank you." Excited, and forgetting the pain in my head, I read:

Thomas,
I am sorry our date is spoiled. I looked forward so much to our evening together. I ran from my office to meet every group, hoping to see you, but I am sure you were detained at U-Tapao. If you are able, please come see me. I will wait for you, though I fall asleep on the sofa. If you do not come, I will see you in the morning.
Yours truly,
Sasithorn

I brought the note to my nose and inhaled. Jasmine. I closed the door and tossed the backpack onto the chair, then stripped to my shorts. I lay in bed staring at the ceiling. Lek could wait. I had to see Sasi. I had to know. I rose after a few minutes to shower. The strong flow of hot water felt good and drew the weariness away. A lingering regret about Lek remained, but I put it out of my mind. I wouldn't string her along until I left Thailand, but she could wait one more night. Maybe the light would go on, and she'd realize something had changed. One more day and I would tell her about Aida.

Aida. I fluttered my lips.

Memories of my earlier romance with Lek had threatened to return me to Lek's arms. Meeting Sasi, though, had flung wide open a new door to a relationship that could lead me back to the capability for love I had lost. Was Aida a rebound from that loss? No. As I told George, Aida was a natural progression, a part of the healing for a heart maimed by the sudden loss of one half of my soul. Aida was the recovery of love. Lek was a blacking out of memory for the time it took to reach orgasm. Sasi was the half of my soul coming back to me. Sasi was the healing of my heart.

I brushed my teeth and washed my hair, humming while I showered. Refreshed, dressed, and ready to go, I grabbed my wallet and room key and headed for the lobby.

Bob called to me from the pool area. Mark and Don were with him. "Hurry up, Tom. We haven't got all night."

"Sorry, guys. I changed my plans. I'm not going with you."

"What the hell, Tom," said Bob. "We could have been halfway to town."

"Sorry, man. Plans change." I looked around for George. "Where's George?"

"Studly's schmoozing with the desk clerk," Don said. "Dude's hopelessly in love. At least until he sees another babe."

Mark said, "Where are you going, Tom?"

"Club Sasi. A little place by the beach."

"What? You no like hang wid us, braddah?"

Mark's Chinese-Hawaiian pidgin cracked me up. "No, braddah. I like hang wid you, but I like mo bettah hang wid da local wahini."

I found George leaning over the front desk, deep in conversation with the good-looking desk clerk.

"You're not coming with us, Tom?"

"No. I'm heading the other way. You guys have a good time. I'll see you in the morning."

"What about Lek? She's going to be disappointed."

"Tell her—no. Don't tell her anything. Tell her I'll see her tomorrow night."

George raised an eyebrow. "I hope you know what you're doing."

"I do, George. I'll tell her everything tomorrow."

We split up at the crosswalk. As usual, George argued with the others over where to go, with Caligula Club topping his list.

I crossed Beach Road and walked to Sasi's place. The international feel of the crowded sidewalk, the lights, the aromas, the sounds of a city teeming with dreams and desperation imparted an excitement that made me feel lucky to be alive and overseas. I would be an old man someday and look back on these times and wish I could relive them. Better to make happy memories now than live with regrets later.

Chapter Eighteen

Tom

Sasi's condo loomed tall before me. The sound of breakers crashing on the cliff face below and the fragrant sea breeze mingling with coconut oil by the swimming pool brought a déjà vu moment to mind. Similarities between the Hilton Hawaiian Village in Waikiki and Sasi's place abounded. The only thing missing was Don Ho.

I wasn't surprised to see Sasi waving to me when I glanced up at her balcony. I returned her wave and walked faster. When I looked again, she had gone. I pushed through the revolving door and strode through the lobby toward the elevator. The door opened just as I reached for the button, and Sasi ran into my arms.

"Thomas. How wonderful of you to come. I was worried you mightn't."

She kissed my cheek as she took my hand and led me to the elevator. The front desk clerk, a look of anguish on his face, caught up to us just as the elevator doors opened. He spoke to Sasi in Thai. She replied, then walked to the front desk, and signed the guest register to the clerk's visible relief.

"Oh, Thomas. You are a criminal. You failed to sign in. I may have to call for the police."

"Oh, no! Will you handcuff me so I don't run away?"

"Of course, but the handcuffs are in my nightstand."

"Oh?"

She took my elbow. "Come with me, you scofflaw. I am making a citizen's arrest."

"Is that a thing in Thailand?"

"You know, I will have to ask the police when they arrive."

"What did you write in the book? That I promised to always sign in?"

"I wrote that I take responsibility for your actions, though you ravish me and make off with my sangria."

The elevator attendant's normally placid face turned into a smile when Sasi stepped in. When the door opened to Sasi's foyer, he bowed and spoke to her.

"What did he say?"

"He said it was a pleasure for him to see me laughing, that I most often look serious, and it makes the staff afraid to speak to me. I had not realized that was so. I must endeavor to smile more often when staff is in my presence."

She stood close to me, and I was afraid she would hear my heartbeat. Had she pressed her palm to my chest, she would have felt its rapid beat.

"You make me smile, Thomas. Perhaps you should see me every evening." Gone was her smile, replaced by moist, parted lips that seemed to beg the press of mine.

"Then we would both smile, Sasi."

Neither of us spoke for a moment, and I thought if she were any other woman, I would kiss her. I knew she wouldn't turn away. I knew, too, I would stay with her if I kissed her, and there would be no turning back.

The long moment slipped past, and Sasi opened the door and led the way to the kitchen. Sasi had known I would come: she picked up a tray with two glasses and a pitcher of sangria and nodded toward the balcony.

"If you will open the door, Thomas, I will serve the drinks in Club Sasi."

The sangria was cold and soothing, the night breeze warm and relaxing. I was glad I had come. Sasi wore shorts and a light blouse tied in front. We made light talk for a while, Sasi asking questions about the life of a Sailor while I learned more of Sasi's remarkable life as the child of a globetrotting diplomat. My fatigue drained away as we talked, and I slid ever deeper into the rattan chair.

The oven timer buzzed, and Sasi walked to the kitchen where she was warming a late snack. She returned with a tray of sweet pork spring rolls and a dish of fried rice. We ate from small plates, using fingers for the spring rolls and forks for the rice.

"You're a wonderful cook, Sasi."

"You're sweet to say so, Thomas. The spring rolls are made from my mother's recipe and the fried rice is my own creation."

"I can't put my finger on what makes it different."

"We use jasmine rice and shrimp paste in Thailand. I add coconut water when cooking the rice, though. Perhaps that makes the difference."

Sasi watched me eat, smiling as I scooped the last of the rice onto the fork with my finger.

"I must remember to keep fried rice warm for your visits."

"Fried rice is one of my favorite comfort foods." I sipped from a glass of water and dabbed my lips with a cloth. "The first meal I ate in Pattaya during my first visit several years ago was fried rice served in a hollowed-out pineapple, along with salad and red snapper. I selected the fish myself from the display tank. Everything was so delicious. I must take you to that restaurant if it's still open."

A pleasant drowsiness overcame me just then, and I couldn't stifle a yawn.

"You must be dreadfully tired after such a long day."

"Your note invigorated me. I wondered if I should come. I was afraid it would seem presumptuous and untimely. Still, I thought about our date all day, although I grew less hopeful about seeing you as the work wore on."

"I would have slept on the sofa all night waiting for you."

"It must be a comfortable sofa. Does it double as a bed? If I pull up the cushions, will we find a squeaky, lumpy mattress or a satin divan fit for a seraglio?"

"Neither, but we could lay the sofa and chair cushions on the floor. They would make a suitable bed, yes?"

"Hmm. What if we slipped between the cracks? Would we not disturb the people below us?"

The mischievous smile gave her away. "That would depend on how much noise we made."

"I can't picture you in an awkward position."

"You haven't seen me on my yoga mat."

"Oh? Limber, are you?"

"Visualize a human pretzel and you will have some idea."

I liked the image, not because it was suggestive, but because it fit my impression of this warm woman whose charm melted my heart. Whether it was the sangria, the late meal, or the fatigue, I wanted her to know how I felt.

"There is grace in all your movements, Sasi. You are purposeful, direct, funny, thoughtful, and considerate." Her smile was almost demure, and she clasped her hands in her lap.

"You are charming, seductive without effort, beautiful beyond measure, and your smile reaches deep inside me so that I want to cry with joy when I see you." I paused. "Now, I've said too much and upset you."

"No, Thomas. I'm not upset."

"I like when you call me Thomas."

"Do you?"

"Yes."

"Did Susanna call you Thomas?"

"Yes, Sasi."

Sasi's voice was soft and tender. "Tell me about her."

"No, Sasi."

"It's okay. I understand."

"No, Sasi. You don't. You can't understand."

"No?"

"No. Someday, I will tell you about Susanna. I'm not ready."

"What if someday I am no longer here?"

Her eyes held mine in a steady gaze.

She spoke again. "What if someday you are no longer here?"

"What do you mean?"

She rose from the chair and leaned on the balcony railing. Moonlight reflected in her black hair the way it had done in Susanna's. Where Susanna's face was parchment white, Sasi's face was tan. Their lips had the same fullness, the same dip in Cupid's Bow, the same moist pull of desire.

"I don't believe in chance, Thomas. I believe we were brought together for a purpose."

"For what purpose?"

"I don't know."

"What makes you feel this way?"

She turned toward me, her hands behind her on the rail. "When I first read your name in the register, my heart seemed to beat faster."

"Perhaps it was coincidence."

"Yes. Perhaps. It happened a second time when I read your name again. When you gave me your letter, it happened a third time but with a stronger feeling."

"Maybe that's when you fell madly in love with me. Maybe angels were saying, 'Fall in love, Sasi.'"

Behind the smile, I was serious. I wanted to hear the words, "I love you, Thomas," but I was afraid to hear them too. The pull she exerted on my heart was tangible, not just a whisper of desire, not just a wish. Susanna's pull had affected me the same way. I was afraid of what was happening with Sasi, and afraid of what she might tell me. It wasn't wrong, it was just too late. Wasn't it?

She turned to face the sea and I went to her, standing so close that our shoulders bumped. I breathed in the scent of Sasi's perfume. The closeness of her body sent a thrill through me, raising the hairs on the back of my neck. The thrill passed, but the feeling remained, a warmth that seemed to buzz silently about me as the love potion cast by a fairy godmother sparkles around the virtuous lover.

I had to go before it was too late. Sasi's spell was strong, and I, being weak, could not break it. I had not come to Thailand to add guilt on top of guilt, but I could not step away from Sasi. Every bond between a man and a woman begins with a crucial moment. Our moment was at hand. Was lightning striking a third time?

"I did not want another relationship with a man, Thomas. My last one ended badly and left me with much anger and hurt. But for some reason I do not understand, I wanted to know more about you. I had to see you before you saw anyone else, before you saw another woman. I had to stop you before fate intervened and left us no more than hotel manager and guest."

Sasi walked to the end of the balcony. She stood with arms crossed and her back against the wall. The full moon shone on her face. Her eyes were wet. I didn't speak.

"I waited until you were gone, then picked up the bag of groceries and walked after you. I worried I had lost you until I saw you at the bar. Courage failed me, though, and I walked back to the hotel. I thought I should wait for your return, but I knew that would be too late. I had to go to you."

I walked to her and she turned to me.

"I am afraid of loneliness, Thomas, but loneliness flees when you are near. It flees now."

Tenderness for Sasi came over me, accompanied by sorrow and regret for myself. How could I have let things come this far? How could I have left myself so vulnerable? How could I have done this to her? Why hadn't I walked away when I had the chance? If I had not stopped at the kickboxing bar, if I had continued to Walking Street, if, if, if. So many ifs. So many possible paths. So many possible pasts. How many futures had I embarked upon through my choices? Life would be easier without the twists and turns, false roads, and dead ends. My entire adult life had been a continual search for the true path to the love my parents had shared. Instead, I had scrambled blindly through maze after maze, each stacked one atop the other and mashed down until every turn ended in disappointment, every twist ended in another crushed dream, every exit an entrance to another chasing of my own tail.

The warm breeze carried the muffled sound of waves crashing against the cliffs below. I wished I were back at sea among five thousand Sailors like me, where food, sleep, and not getting blown into the sea by jet blast were all that mattered. Life was simpler aboard ship.

"I don't know what to say, Sasi." I sought for words to express the feeling behind the pulsing in my temples. "I'm glad you came after me. I felt a strong attraction for you as I walked away. I questioned the feeling for a number of reasons and—I shouldn't say this—felt a similarity with the day I met Susanna."

I gripped Sasi's arms and held her. She gazed intently, expectantly at me. Tears rolled to the tips of her eyelashes where they hung, stretched, then dropped away. I didn't want her to cry.

"I have wandered lost in love since Susanna died. We were going to have a life together." I didn't want to cry. "We were born in love, Sasi, and we spent our lives waiting for each other. When we met, we knew, we knew we had found the one we were born to love. Born to marry, to grow old with, to die next to in old age. When I held Susanna, the world ceased to exist, and we were alone, completely alone, as though the only two people created. When she looked in my eyes, I could have lived without air. I took all my nourishment from her gaze, and the sight of her was the bread and water, the fruit and vegetable, the meat, the wine, the dessert, the sustenance to my soul. I needed nothing, I wanted nothing, I had nothing because Susanna was everything. Her touch thrilled me the way lovemaking does when you find yourself between passion and ecstasy, and you feel the breath of God waft through your soul and you understand, you realize, you know at last that she is the precious gift whose name is imprinted on your heart."

Sasi was crying, but her eyes held mine. My grip tightened, and I realized I was hurting her.

"Thomas. Thomas. I am so sorry."

"We were cheated, Sasi. Cheated. We didn't have a chance to

marry. We didn't have a chance to grow old together. We didn't even have the chance to die together because I wasn't with her when she died."

Passion gripped me. I ripped the necklace from my neck and held it up. The moon's light reflected from the medallion, the ruby, Susanna's wedding ring. Tears blurred my vision, and my voice caught in my throat.

"This. This. This is my mother's medallion. She died giving birth to me. Her death broke my father's heart. This is Susanna's wedding ring. She died when our love was still in its infancy. I knew her for a fraction of the time we should have had together. It isn't fair, but then life isn't fair, is it?"

I let go of Sasi's arms. She rubbed them where my hands had been.

"I'm afraid to love you, Sasi. I'm afraid to love you and lose you. It seems the women the men in my family love are doomed to die young. If I don't go now, you will die too, and I don't want to love you if that is our future."

"Thomas. Thomas."

I left Sasi then. Her cries tore at my heart, but my own heart beat loud as passion surged and ebbed, surged and ebbed. I couldn't bear to love her with the passion and ecstasy I had had with Susanna and then lose her. I couldn't take the pain. Not again. I couldn't take the pain of Sasi, Susanna, my father, and my mother upon my shoulders. I wasn't a God who moved pieces around on a chess board with whatever whim he felt. I was a man whose heart broke the same way in grief and love.

Chapter Nineteen

Tom

The crucial moment lay before us, quivering with anticipation, awaiting resolution. I was anxious. I had to see Sasi again, but kept putting it off. We spoke in the morning before I left for the airfield, exchanging little more than pleasantries, and again in the evening when I returned. I think she waited for my return, hoping for some break in the dam between us. She always seemed on the verge of breaching the dam but stopped short, as if having second thoughts. The same happened to me and wrenched my heart each time I clammed up instead of baring my soul to her.

I had to do something, but what? What held me back from taking her in my arms and whispering how much I loved her? I couldn't leave Thailand without putting to the test my feelings for her. To leave without seeing her meant living the rest of my life wondering what might have been. For the first time since Susanna died, I was sure of my feelings for another woman, and I needed to tell Sasi. The question of Aida, however, remained unresolved as well. How could I tell Sasi of my love without also telling her of Aida?

But Aida was the problem. I was afraid of hurting her and afraid of finding out how much I loved her. I was also afraid I loved Sasi because she reminded me of Susanna. Fear was king over me. I feared commitment, and I feared loss.

Another night on the town was in full swing. I joined George and the others and headed for Whiskey A Go Go. We crossed Beach Road and continued as it turned into Walking Street at the south end of Pattaya. Here we left behind the pleasant ocean view and fresh air of the broad, palm-lined seaside promenade and entered the nightclub district. The change of smells was immediate as the fragrant sea breeze gave way to an aromatic mingling of cooking spices, fresh fish, cheap perfume, diesel fumes, and raw sewage.

A few minutes more brought us to Whiskey A Go Go. The heavy drumbeat of the live band assaulted our eardrums well before we reached the entrance, but the full force of the music didn't hit us until we entered. Like a tsunami, the sound filled the void outside the door, temporarily vaporizing the fine hairs of the inner ear and rendering us momentarily deaf. The screaming guitars and pounding drumbeat sent a thrill through my spine. The electric atmosphere stirred some primeval human emotion and forced a surge of adrenaline into the bloodstream. Successive bursts of energy found outlet in loud, excited voices, bodies bobbing on the dance floor, and smiles stretched so taut that the face ached. A thick pall of cigarette smoke obscured the band from view.

We found an empty table, thick with spilled beer and cigarette butts, and nabbed a chair from another table so everyone had a seat. I turned at the touch of a bikini-clad barmaid tapping my shoulder. She wanted my drink order.

"What?"

"I say what you want to drink?" The flickering lights caricatured the girl's face and movements into stop-motion animation.

"Tiger beer, please."

"What you say?"

I repeated my order, straining my vocal cords to be heard.

"Okay."

Another one yelled in my ear that Lek was in the back, and she would let her know I was there. I didn't tell her not to bother.

We eyed the dance floor and occasionally caught ourselves bobbing to the music. Normal speech was impossible. We could only look at each other and smile and raise our eyebrows. A few tables away sat a group of aircrewmen enjoying a rare night on the town.

The barmaid returned with the drinks and passed them around. George raised his glass in a toast. "Cheers, fellas." As he tilted his head back and guzzled the bottle, Lek walked up, wet her finger, and poked it in his ear. He jumped, and beer dribbled down his chin.

"Lek!" He wiped beer off his face. "You owe me another beer—on the house!"

Lek sat in his lap and laughed with the others. When she caught her breath, she snatched away and drank the rest of his beer.

"Oh, George, you so funny, you make me laugh too much."

She wrapped her arms around his neck and pressed her cheek to his. She kissed him, then came to me. George leaned his chair back on two legs and grinned at Lek as he dabbed at the beer on his shirt with her bar cloth.

"I'm glad I can make you laugh, but you still owe me a free beer."

He reached out and corralled a passing barmaid.

"Hey baby, you wanna dance?"

She giggled as George swept her into his arms and carried her to the dance floor.

I asked Lek if she wanted to dance.

"No, my sweetheart. We go after I finish my work?"

"Sure. Let me know when you're ready."

"Okay. I want to walk with you. I am tired of here, the Whiskey A Go Go, and want to walk alone with you. Always we are with other people, your friends, and hardly we ever get to be alone except late after I work, and then you have to work too early."

She pressed against me and tightened her arms around my waist.

"I like to be in your arms. I like to stay here always."

She nuzzled my neck. I told her the things she wanted to hear and touched her with enough caress to reassure her that she was my girl. I had put off saying goodbye because I didn't want another crying woman on my conscience. I had to tell her that night, though. I could leave at any time, and I didn't want our relationship to remain unresolved. It was the least I could do for her.

"Tommy, you drink your beer. I go finish my work."

"What work are you doing tonight?"

"Serving in party room. They will finish soon, and then I can leave. Only two hours and I come back."

The tedium was already unbearable; two hours would seem like an eternity. I ordered another beer and settled in for the long run. Dancing might have killed time, but I didn't feel like dancing. Neither did Mark and Don.

"Hey, why aren't you guys on the dance floor? Where did Alex and Bob go?"

"They're dancing," George said as he returned from the dance floor. His face glistened with sweat and pleasure. Nightlife was his element.

"Together?" I raised an eyebrow. "I always wondered about those two."

"They're close, but not that close. Look at Alex. He's such a stud dancing with two women. He reminds me of me."

George sat on the edge of his chair, his back straight and eyes on the dance floor, still breathing hard. He downed his beer between breaths and tapped his feet to the music. "Man, I am pumped. This place is jumping. Who's up for a foamy later? Let's go to Sabailand. That's the best place for a massage."

No one else wanted to go.

"Man, you guys are wimps. We don't get to Thailand often, fellas. You gotta make the most of it while you're here. C'mon, let's go. Who's with me?"

Don yawned, looking tired and bored despite the deafening music. A passing barmaid winked at him and rubbed her hand across his face as she walked to another table. He put his hand on hers until she slipped away.

"No way, dude. I can barely keep my eyes open. It didn't hit me until I sat down. I'm going to stay here and drink for a while. Maybe Mark will go with you."

"Nah, I'm okay. I'm going to stay for a while and then get a bite to eat. Anybody want to share some fried grasshoppers?"

Fried grasshoppers tasted okay after a few beers, but not when they came up the next day.

"C'mon. You know you like them. They taste like chicken. Just grab the head, and give it a twist. The head comes off and brings the guts with it. You eat the shell. Tastes so good!"

"Grasshoppers and balut have the same appeal as fried rat, which is what I think I had for dinner last night," said George. "It was supposed to be hamburger."

"You're on your own, George," I said. "I'm going out with Lek later. Maybe Alex and Bob will go with you, but I doubt it. They look like they're having too much fun."

"When are you telling Lek what's up with you and Aida?"

"Tonight. I can't put it off any longer."

"Poor kid. It's gonna hurt, you know."

"I know."

"I mean, it's going to hurt her. You have someone to nurse your poor little heart later, but she doesn't."

"You wouldn't say that if you had seen the way she was kissing that guy last week."

"Well, good luck anyway." He patted my shoulder. "I'm off. Maybe the aircrew guys will go to Sabailand with me. See you tomorrow morning. Wake me up in time to get a shower. Unless Lek cuts off your happiness. Later."

"Smartass."

Don stuck it out for two more beers before leaving with Mark. Alex and Bob returned to the table between dances but were away most of the time. After a while, I gave the table to a group of Aussies and moved to the bar. I had another beer and made small talk with barmaids as they waited to pick up orders.

Lek finally joined me, chatting with other barmaids while I finished my beer. I observed her as she spoke, noticed her manner, how she leaned against me and smiled at the girls, how they seemed to concentrate on her words, her gestures. It was a few minutes before I realized that she drew confidence and stature from me. The other girls were jealous of her relationship with the American Sailor, while she showed pride in the attachment, almost like she owned a pet the other girls wanted to take home. It had never occurred to me that I could have that kind of effect on a woman, and I found I liked the feeling of power. However, after a few minutes of self-satisfaction, awareness thumped me between the eyes, and I understood the reality of what had occurred between the girls. I wasn't the cause of it, but what I represented: opportunity and freedom.

The sobering thought reminded me that Lek would never find with me what she sought so earnestly. I would leave in a few days and never see her again. There would be tears and hand-holding, tight hugs, and tender kisses as we parted for the last time. With pleading eyes, she would beg me not to forget her, to write her often. I would echo her words and make the promises she wanted to hear.

I knew that, for a while after I left Thailand, she would cling to the diminishing hope that I would live up to my promises. The hope would fade, and she would gradually stop expecting anything from me. She would ignore the looks of pity from her friends, who would say they knew all along that I hadn't cared for her, that I only wanted her in bed, that they had not liked me.

I downed the beer then took Lek's hand and said goodbye to the others and left the club. "Where would you like to walk, Lek?

Along the beach?"

"Yes. I like walking there. Here, I put my arms around you and hold you like this. Now you cannot escape me. I hold you forever, Tommy." Her arms circled my waist, and she rested her head against my shoulder. "Oh, you always got bony shoulders."

We strolled along window-shopping. She admired a gaudy bracelet so I bought it for her. Every few feet, it seemed, Lek had to stop and look through sale items. Her face glowed as she slipped the bracelet on her arm. "I like this one so much. I will keep it always as a reminder of you, Tommy."

She wasn't making it easy for me.

Walking Street, narrow and hemmed in on both sides by buildings and shops, ended after a half mile and turned into the wider Beach Road bordered by clubs, restaurants, and hotels on the one hand, and by the Gulf of Thailand on the other, its turquoise water now dark in the night but reflecting the white of the full moon. Running lights from sailboats and freighters riding at anchor rippled on the moonlit water.

We sat for a while on the seawall, dangling our legs over one side then turning around and digging our bare feet into the warm sand on the other. We leaned against each other, silent, not speaking of my imminent departure. I was likely on my last visit to Thailand for several years unless I found a way to stay in the squadron when my current tour ended.

I would never see Lek again. Whatever I had felt for her had fled once I saw her with the other man. Besides, I told myself, she had no right to expect anything beyond my infrequent trips to Thailand. I had never told her I loved her, had never told her I would marry her and take her back to America. She had assumed it because I came back to her with each trip to Thailand. She had assumed it because hope like that consumed her life. How many other men had dashed her dreams and broken her heart?

Lek's grasp on my arm tightened. Her shoulders shook.

"Lek, are you crying? What's wrong, sweetheart? Hey, don't cry, honey. What's the matter? Oh, sweetheart, what's the matter?"

I lifted her chin. Anguish contorted her face and tears rolled down her cheeks. My heart panged.

"Oh, Tommy, please don't leave me. Don't leave me, my sweetheart. I love you, Tommy. Please don't leave me."

Chapter Twenty

Tom

Her voice shook, echoing the sorrow and fear in her heart. Sorrow at my leaving, fear for her future.

"Oh, Tommy, I know I never see you again when you leave, and it make me so sad. I want you not to go, to stay here with me. Tommy, all the time you are here I stay only with you, I see no one else, I promise you. Even at my work, when other guys want me to go with them, I do not go with them. Even if my family in my village need money, I do not go with other guys. I stay and wait for you, Tommy. Please don't leave me, Tommy."

My anguish was palpable, but I could only listen to her pitiful cries and hold her in my arms. I ignored her shaded lies about not seeing other men and turning down their money. She was desperate and would do or say anything as she clutched at the diminishing dream slipping from her grasp.

I consoled her and stared at the ground, unsure what to say or how to act. I was going to do to Lek what I had witnessed other Sailors do to their girls. They, and I, had raised the hopes for marriage of a young girl, then dashed those hopes when the fun ended, when the time came to leave the amusement park, get on the airplane, and fly away, leaving the girl heartbroken and her hopes destroyed.

"But Lek, you knew I would leave, that we could only be friends. I didn't mean to hurt you. I thought you understood."

"I know, Tommy, I know. It's okay. You never say you will marry me. I just hope you do. Someday I find a nice man like you who will take me to America." She wiped her eyes, sniffling. She blew her nose on a tissue from her purse. "We go now, Tommy? I want to walk some more and go home."

"Of course, Lek."

I put my arm around her and she moved against me, clutching my arm, grasping for a thread of reassurance. We walked along the beachfront, talking little. I knew she hurt, that she felt empty inside, but I was powerless to do anything for her.

"Come to the hotel, Lek. We'll rest there for a bit, then get something to eat."

"Okay, Tommy."

We left the promenade and walked to the hotel. The good-looking front desk clerk eyed us as we passed. At the door to my room, Lek stood on tiptoes to kiss me as I fumbled for the key.

"Oh, Tommy."

She gave me a thin smile as I inserted the key and opened the door.

She walked in ahead of me and stopped. I dreaded what I knew was coming. She began unbuttoning my shirt. She pressed her hands to my bare chest, then moved them down to unfasten my jeans. I put my hands on hers and pushed them away, but she raised my hands and pressed them to her breasts. My pulse beat harder. The blood rushed in my head.

What am I doing?

I dropped my hands and stood still. She kissed my neck and ran her tongue around my ear. I put my hands on her hips and began to caress her. I pressed my lips to her forehead.

No. I can't. This is wrong.

She felt for me and held me.

No.

"I can't do this, Lek. I'm sorry, I can't. I can't make love to you, or see you anymore." I had not wanted to tell her this way.

"Please, Tommy."

"No, Lek."

I wanted to leave Thailand without telling her of Aida.

"No, Lek. I can't. I should have told you earlier. I'm marrying my girlfriend in the Philippines."

Lek pushed away. In that fleeting moment, she turned from lover to stranger. She stared, pale. The emotional bond between us faded as though someone had thrown a switch. Her face turned red. I knew she didn't care that I had broken off the relationship. There were other men. She cared that I had embarrassed her. She cared that she would have to face humiliation and the taunts of her friends.

She did not cry or tear up. Her body straightened as she drew her shoulders back. She confronted me with a look of defiance and determination. She wanted to shame me and then leave, proud that I had not defeated her.

"I always tell my family about you, how nice you are, how handsome you are. All the girls in my village they are jealous because I have you, and they see your picture that you give to me, and they think I am so lucky. They ask me when I am getting married to the American Sailor and going to Hawaii. All the girls in Whiskey A Go Go think you are a nice guy, and I am lucky too. They say I am going to be happy with you. But you break my heart, Tom. I love you, but you do not love me. I'm sorry I know you. I hope your girlfriend find out about me so you don't hurt her too."

She had lost a bet but retained an ace. She would leave me and run to the other man, or another man, or another. She would make love to him with renewed zeal and passion out of spite for my dumping her. Out of a need for reassurance that it hadn't been her fault. The silence drummed in my ears after she stopped talking. It wouldn't ease her pain, but I thought I should say it.

"I'm sorry, Lek."

Her eyes welled with tears, and my resolve weakened. I wanted to tell her how sorry I was. I wanted to hold her and tell her that I wanted only her. But I couldn't not. It wasn't true. I would say those things only to make her feel better. Now I only wished she would leave so I could begin to forget. I wanted to lie down until the numbness subsided, and the ache went away. But the ache would never vanish completely. It would return each time I remembered Lek and how it began when I met her and how it ended.

I stood rooted to the floor, unwilling to move a finger, unwilling to shift my body in any way lest she take it as a signal that I had changed my mind. I wanted her to go. She wiped her eyes with the back of her wrist, teardrops falling onto the nightstand beside her. She picked up her handbag and left the room, leaving the door open.

When she had gone, when the click of her heels on the hard cement became a permanent echo etched in my memory, I closed the door and leaned against it. All the excitement of the night, all the adrenaline that had kept me pumped and on edge subsided the way a sugar high subsides, and I crashed. My knees wobbled, and I trembled. I sat on the bed and ran my fingers through the tears on the nightstand. It was over. The past did not matter anymore. Only the future mattered, my future with Aida. Or my future with Sasi. I cursed under my breath. It wasn't over.

Chapter Twenty-One

Tom

Gershwin's *Rhapsody in Blue* filled the foyer. I listened for a moment before knocking. The music stopped, then began again after a few seconds. I knocked again, harder. The door opened, and Sasi peeked around the edge of the door and smiled.

"Thomas. Come in. How wonderful of you to come."

She didn't appear surprised. I glanced toward the kitchen but saw no pitcher of sangria and glasses on the counter. Wishful thinking.

I hesitated to enter, unsure of my welcome. "Hello, Sasi. I'm sorry to bother you. I'm not disturbing you, am I?"

"Don't be silly, Thomas. You are neither bothering nor disturbing me. Please come in."

She left the door to me and walked to the piano. She sat on the bench and brushed her fingers across the keys.

"What brings you here, Thomas? I did not expect to see you outside the hotel. Is everything okay?"

I had told myself on the way over that I would get to the point, speak my mind, and then leave or stay, whatever she wanted. I wouldn't press for an answer or obligate her in any way. That night concerned the truth: my feelings for Sasi, my brief life with Susanna, my engagement to Aida. The outcome depended on Sasi.

"I told you about Susanna the other night after I had said I was not ready to. Shall I tell you the rest? Do you still want to know about Susanna and me, and how my relationship with her affects us?"

"Oh, Thomas. Of course, I do. You—we—were in such a passion that night. I understood how deeply you loved her. I wanted to know everything but didn't want to intrude. Please. Tell me everything."

"Would you mind if we sat outside?"

"Not at all. I will bring refreshments. You would like sangria, yes?"

I smiled. "It's the only thing to drink at Club Sasi."

I stood on the balcony looking out over the city and the sea. The sinking sun would teeter on the rim of the horizon soon, before leaving the moon behind to cast a romantic glow across the land. Already, lights blinked on around the horizon, and the roar of daytime activity began to give way to the muffled, relaxing hum of nightlife.

Sasi set the tray on the table between the deck chairs and handed me a glass of sangria. She sat in the opposite chair and turned in the seat, one leg beneath her. She sipped her sangria and waited for me to begin.

"I never knew my parents, Sasi. My mother, her name was Susanna also, died a few hours after giving birth to me." I related the story of my birth, life as an adopted child, my romance with Susanna. Sasi listened without interrupting. When I had told her of Susanna, her eyes glistened when she spoke.

"Oh, Thomas. That is beautiful. Do you think it was coincidence, or do you think you were fated to meet Susanna?"

"I believe fate destined us to be together. When we met, I knew Susanna and I had been born in love and needed only to find each other."

"I believe it, Thomas. I believe some loves are fated, that people can be brought together and feel they have known one another all their lives."

"Her eyes made it plain from the beginning. I knew she loved me. Such joy filled me that I couldn't speak. Our hearts bonded, and I leaned across the bar and kissed her. Every new day brought deeper joy, and I wondered how I had lived before meeting Susanna. Life had changed from ordinary to a daily walk of inspiration, extraordinary happiness, and bliss. When we had to spend time apart, I was lost, cold, sad, withdrawn. We spent little time apart except the few occasions I had to travel."

My eyes blurred with tears, and I wiped them away with the back of my hand. Sasi knelt and put her arm around my shoulder. "I never dreamed she would die."

"Oh, Thomas."

"I wanted nothing to do with women after she died. I felt cheated out of a life of happiness with Susanna, and I lost interest in a life of happiness with anyone. I wanted to love again, but I wanted to fall in love exactly the way my parents had, and Susanna and I had. It was an impossible dream."

Sasi's eyes brimmed with sympathy. They spoke to me from a deep well of love. I wanted her to tell me lightning struck more than twice in the same place. Her eyes spoke for her. I thought of the night we stood on the balcony looking out over the sea and the warmth that had buzzed around me.

"My grief over Susanna's death went so deep that I resisted the will to let a woman love me. But when I met you, Sasi, the wall began to crumble, and my heart began to heal. The last time we met here, I told you what I feel for you is different than what I felt for her. I said I didn't know why, but I do. Susanna didn't have to heal a broken heart."

Sasi touched my cheeks with a tenderness that reminded me of Susanna's gentleness. She kissed my forehead, then pressed her head to mine.

"Together we will heal your heart, Thomas."

My heart pounded as I embraced her. Her words sang in my head and gave me hope, but I had to tell her everything.

"Before we go on, Sasi, there is more you should know. I didn't want to tell you this, but I couldn't hide it from you. Our relationship should not begin with half-truths. You deserve to know everything so our hearts hold no secrets."

She remained silent, watching me closely. I kept her hands in mine so if they turned cold, I would know that the other half of my heart would remain buried with Susanna.

"Before I left for Thailand, I asked my girlfriend in the Philippines to marry me."

Her expression didn't change. Her eyes held mine in a steady gaze.

"George and I discussed Aida a few days ago, and he asked me what I planned to do about our engagement. He knew I had second thoughts about marrying her. I told him I didn't know what to do. When I came here the other night, I already knew I couldn't marry Aida. I realized Aida attracted me because she needed me. After all the pain and grief over Susanna's death, after all the failed relationships, failed because I hardened my heart against loving again, I found a woman who needed me. But needing and loving are different emotions, and I can't marry Aida because she needs me when I don't love her. I feel tenderness for her, but not love. It may seem strange, but I questioned whether I should ask her to marry me and compared her to Susanna even as I proposed."

"I understand. Marrying for the wrong reason leads only to heartache. I'm glad you told me of Aida."

"There is also a girl here that I used to see when I came to Thailand. She expected more than she had reason to. I told her there was nothing between us."

She pressed a warm hand to my cheek. "I'm glad you told me about Lek and Aida. I know there will be no secrets between us now."

"You knew about Lek?"

"One of the front desk clerks told me. She said Lek left the hotel crying. They were friends, and Lek told her what happened. I'm sorry, Thomas, but I am glad it is over for you."

"Thank God. I feel a weight has lifted from my shoulders. I agonized over how to explain all this to you."

"I knew about Aida too."

"What? How?"

"First, I must tell you I didn't want to trap you, Thomas. I only wanted to know you loved me enough to tell me."

"I understand, but how did you find out about Aida?"

"I overheard some of your friends discussing her in the lobby one morning. One of them asked the others if they knew you had asked her to marry you. They turned quiet when I entered the lobby to distribute newspapers. I didn't give any sign that I had heard them, then you came into the lobby, and we spoke as we always do."

Sasi kissed my cheek to reassure me. "I'm so happy you told me everything." She picked up the empty pitcher and walked to the kitchen for more. She returned and filled our glasses. "But, Thomas, what are you going to do about Aida? How will you tell her? We cannot move forward until you resolve your affairs with her."

"I'm going to tell Aida the truth, Sasi."

Book Four

Olongapo, Philippines

1968

Chapter Twenty-Two

Marie

The astonishment on Frank's face could not have been more apparent. My own astonishment at seeing Frank having lunch with Sister Arnalita caused me to pause mid-step as though I had entered the wrong house and stumbled into a dream world. I blushed, more from embarrassment for the stumble than seeing Frank, but I recovered and composed myself as a confident woman does: I whipped my hair out of my eyes, threw my shoulders back, lifted my chin, and strode to the table. The men rose like gentlemen at my approach.

A bright flush of happiness settled over Sister Arnalita's face as she greeted me. She hugged me like the favorite she always told me I was and kissed me on both cheeks.

"Oh, oh, oh. Oh, my dear, Marie. I am so happy to see you, my child. Come. Come. Sit here, sit next to me."

Sister Arnalita tugged my hand, but Frank's presence had rattled my nerves, and I needed time to assess the situation before joining the group at the table. What in the world brought Frank to the orphanage?

"Hello, Sister Arnalita. Hello, Father Roland." I paused before greeting Frank, still enjoying his surprise at seeing me. "Hello, Frank."

My voice was hurried. I forced myself to calm down and speak normally. I took a deep breath as I paused in front of Sam. I gave him my hand and introduced myself.

"Hello. I do not believe we have met. I am Marie. How do you do?"

"Fine, thank you. I'm Sam. I'm happy to meet you."

Sam shook my hand. He seemed nice, but I sensed sadness in his eyes. His hand was soft, almost feminine, but not unmanly, and his touch was more of a caress than a grip. I warmed to him right away.

I was still a bit out of sorts, and continued speaking as I walked to the refrigerator. "I am sorry I arrived late, Sister Arnalita. I have not missed anything, have I? May I serve you anything, Frank? A bottle of water, perhaps?"

To say I was happy to see Frank would be an understatement. I felt like a little girl in love for the first time and lingered at the refrigerator until my excitement subsided. I tried to appear nonchalant when I returned to the table, but couldn't help feeling transparent.

"No, thank you. I'm fine."

I hardly knew him, but hadn't stopped thinking about Frank since he left Rufadora. Our conflicts had troubled me, but I overruled them in favor of a second chance. I didn't need another heartbreak, but there was something about Frank that made me sure he wouldn't turn out to be another Edward. That bastard.

Sister Arnalita interrupted my train of thought. "Well, Marie. So, you know Frank? No, you have not missed a thing, dear. We will be painting this afternoon and just happen to have an extra brush for you. Will you join us?"

"Of course, Sister Arnalita. That is why I came today." Sister Mary Ann slid down the bench to make room for me. "Frank and I met at Rufadora yesterday. We had some rather interesting conversations, full of twists and ninety-degree turns, did we not, Frank?"

"Yes, we did. I never thought we would meet here, though."

"You think I do not belong here, Frank?"

"That's not what I think at all. I'm just surprised at meeting you again so unexpectedly."

"I come every chance I have to help the sisters."

"She does," said Sister Arnalita. "And she is a big help. The children love her, especially when she drives them to town in her automobile. I think they love her most for the ice cream she buys them."

"It is the least I can do after all you did for me when I lived here."

I loved the surprise on Frank's face. "You lived here?"

"Yes, I came here after my parents died. I was three years old. The sisters cared for me until I was adopted."

"I had no idea, Marie. I'm sorry for the loss of your parents."

"Thank you. I have no memories of them. I was so young when they died and came here so soon after. I had little time to wonder what happened. I missed them for a while, but soon forgot them as I came to love the sisters. Everyone here treated me like a princess. I am afraid you spoiled me, Sister Arnalita."

"Yes, we did. But you have grown into a wonderful, beautiful, intelligent young woman despite our best efforts." Her eyes closed and her shoulders shook as she laughed quietly. She patted my cheek. "Marie is like a daughter to me."

Sister Arnalita shook her head. "We also owe her a debt of gratitude for the wonderful gift. It is thanks to her that we have made so many repairs."

"Oh, Sister Arnalita. It is I who owe you so much for all the love you have shown me. I am so blessed to have you."

"I worry about you, though, Marie. Why you do not marry and bring us children to play with? To play with, not to care for. There are far too many orphans in the world. When will you find a husband, Marie? When?"

"Sister Arnalita, you always want to see me married. Would you have me marry Frank just to give you children?" I caught myself and spoke quickly. "I meant marry any man, not Frank. Oh dear." I attempted to recover and made light of the slip of the tongue. "Would you like that, Sister? What do you think, Frank? Shall we marry and bring children for Sister Arnalita to dandle on her knee?" I looked at Sam, who smiled behind his hand. "Sam, you know Frank. Would he be a good husband?"

"You know, Marie, I think he would at that. He babysits a whole passel of Sailors every day."

Frank clearly enjoyed the thought. "I suppose there are worse fates in the world. If I had to marry Marie so Sister Arnalita could have children to dote on, why, I guess I wouldn't mind."

I arched my eyebrows at Frank's response. "How kind of you, Frank. Thank you."

Father Roland spoke up. "Well, to hasten that day, I'll perform the ceremony and Sam can be best man. Little Lucy will be the flower girl, and all the sisters and children will be the honored guests. When shall we begin?"

Laughter rippled around the table. Frank's wonderful laugh sent a thrill through me. Sister Arnalita leaned against me and patted my hand.

"You may laugh, but someday Marie will bring her children to see me. When that day comes, I shall retire and spend my days taking care of them. Maybe Frank's children, hey? Hey? What you think?"

Sister Arnalita's eyes crinkled and her shoulders shook as she laughed again.

"Marie, Marie, look what Sam let me wear. Isn't it pretty?" Little Lucy ran in from the playground, covered in dust and holding the medallion high.

"Ohhh, hello, dear Lucy." I hugged Little Lucy, who danced on her toes in excitement. "Now then, let me see what Sam is kind enough to let you play with." I left my reading glasses in the car and had to squint to see the medallion up close. "Why, it is beautiful, Lucy. Oh. The jewel looks alive. How odd. Do be careful not to lose it, now."

"Okay." Little Lucy ran outside again, still holding the medallion above her head.

Sister Arnalita smoothed her habit as she stood. "Come friends, we have been lazybones enough. We must begin." She clapped her hands and shooed everyone out of the dining hall, closing the door behind her. "Back to work, now. Frank, you shall paint the treatment room with Marie. I can see you want to be near her, and her eyes look at you often. Yes, yes, I see it. I know you too well, young lady. Come, Sam. Bring Little Lucy and we will clean up the dispensary."

"Sam?" The name came to me. "Are you the Sam of whom Lucy speaks so often?"

"That would be me."

"Susanna was your wife?"

"Yes."

"Ohh. I do not know how I missed the connection when we said hello. I have heard so much about Susanna. I know how much everyone loved her."

"Thank you. We had planned to adopt Little Lucy."

I placed my hand on Sam's shoulder and squeezed him tenderly. "I am so sorry, Sam. She must have been a wonderful person. Lucy would have been fortunate to call you and Susanna father and mother. I am sure I would have felt that way. I wonder that we never met when you visited the orphanage with Susanna."

"We came here often. I wish you had met her."

"I lived in Baguio for many years and could not visit as often as I would have liked. I would have loved knowing Susanna."

Little Lucy ran in and I said, "Come, Lucy, we must join the others." Sam and I took her hands and swung her between us as we walked.

Sam's loss touched me, and I resolved to cultivate a close friendship with him while I pursued a determined relationship with Frank. Sam seemed the type to cherish friendship, and I sensed a close bond between the two men.

"Oh, Sam, I nearly forgot; I must speak to Sister Arnalita. Please go ahead. Tell Frank I will be right there."

I waited as Sam and Little Lucy walked on, then looked for Sister Arnalita. She was alone in the kitchen. "Sister Arnalita, may I have a word with you?"

"Of course, Marie, what is it."

"Edward is having me followed."

"Oh dear. Does he know you are here?"

"I do not think so. I saw nothing unusual on the drive over. He knows I am working at Rufadora—he came by the bar last night—but I do not think he knows I came to the orphanage. I would not be surprised if he looks for me here, though. In fact, I know he will."

"Shall we close the gate to deny him entrance?" She pursed her lips and frowned. "No, I suppose we cannot. It would be dishonest. Well, we will just have to go on with our work. If he comes, he comes. Do you know why he is looking for you?"

"No. I have no idea. As far as I am concerned, our relationship ended when he and that woman were together in my house."

"Yes, my dear, I remember. What a sad time for you. What will you do now? Does Edward know where you live? Would you like to stay here for a few days?"

"Yes, I would like that. I do not want to worry about seeing him in town. Maybe he will get the idea, if he has not already, that I do not want to see him and will go away. Though, I cannot believe he would come all the way from Baguio to have a drink at Rufadora. Now I am even more concerned for his intentions. I hope nothing has happened to his parents. He may be a bastard—sorry Sister—but I adored his parents, and they loved me. They were as upset over the breakup as I, maybe more so since they lost not only me, but a measure of respect for their son."

"We will make up a bed for you. If you would like your own room, I will ask Sister Annabelle to move into the girls' ward."

"No, I do not want to trouble anyone. I will sleep in the girls' ward if you do not mind."

"Okay, but I must warn you that it will be noisy."

I patted Sister Arnalita's cheek. "Dear Nanay, are you forgetting I slept there for six years?"

I left Sister Arnalita and joined Frank in the treatment room. The butterflies in my stomach made me feel like a teenager getting ready for her first date.

He was painting the doorframe when I walked in. Flecks of paint dotted his face, and his hands were virtually a different color.

"There you are. Ready to paint?" He handed me a clean brush.

"Yes. I came prepared to help, although I had no idea I would be painting. I usually assist with the cleaning and preparing of meals for the children. Painting is a new exercise. Perhaps I will leave behind a masterpiece." I dipped the brush in the paint can, knocked off the excess with a flick of my wrist, and gave Frank my best innocent-eyed look. "Where do I begin?"

"The door jambs. Have you painted before? Shall I give you some pointers? It's easy."

"Judging by the paint on your face and the color of your hands, perhaps it is you who needs pointers. Are you sure you have painted before, Frank? Besides yourself?"

"There are two skills every Sailor learns early in his career, Marie: how to handle a swab, and how to paint. Oh, and a third: how to wash clothes."

"How to wash clothes. Excellent. You must be an expert by now."

"Haha. I had no idea you were a comedian."

"Oh, Frank. I am only teasing."

I gave Frank a smile and began painting the doorjamb. I caught myself several times watching Frank from the corner of my eye. I liked this side of him. No ninety-degree turns, no barroom politics to hinder plain talk, only a pleasant afternoon dotted with light, airy conversation. He had an easy manner. On the one hand, he could appear gentle, like he would fold into himself if shaken. But he also had a firmness that I was sure could stare down a tempest. I determined to stay near him as often as I could to enjoy his breezy, witty side and soft laugh.

"Frank. I want to know more about Sam and Susanna. I have heard so much about them, and Lucy shows me photos of them when I visit."

"Before I begin, you should know she always called him

Samuel, never Sam. She said they were Samuel and Susanna in a previous life." He paused to collect his thoughts. "The love they shared is hard to describe. Had you known them together, you would understand. Until I saw them together, my idea of love was what my parents had. Mom and Dad's love seemed like a constant striving for ascendancy, for authority of one over the other. Oh, they were in love, but it was the kind of love everyone else has, a normal love, so to speak."

He dipped his brush in the paint can, tapped it on the side, and continued painting as he spoke. "It was different with Sam and Susanna. It was like they shared the same love, as if, as Sam puts it, they were born in love. Their love transcended earthborn love. I wasn't the only person to see it."

"How did they meet?"

"While Sam and I were stationed in Spain. Susanna worked as a bartender at the Matador Club. The way they met makes for a funny story, almost a fairy tale, I'd say."

"How so?"

"They both reached for the same apple in a street vendor's cart."

"Annnnd?"

"He let her take the apple."

"Please tell me he paid for it."

"Yes, he did. Then she left. Sam thought he'd lost her. He was despondent. He worried he would never see her again. As it turned out, she had relocated from her home in Barcelona earlier that week." Frank pointed his paintbrush at me. "Hey, you missed a spot on the doorjamb. Do I have to show you how to paint? I will, you know."

"Frank, I will paint you blue if you don't finish telling me about Sam and Susanna."

He raised the paint brush in a mock salute and said, "Yes, ma'am."

"Well, that same night, Sam and I were to meet at the Matador Club for dinner. When I arrived, I found the two of them leaning on the bar, she on one side, he on the other, deep in conversation, talking and laughing. I walked into the dining room to see another friend and glanced back. Susanna was patting Sam's cheek."

"Ohhh, what a good story. What else happened?"

"Sam told me later that night that he was going to marry Susanna. They married two months later, but I've always believed they were married from that first night. Something clicked, and it seemed as if they had known each other all their lives. Yes, they were born in love with one another."

"That is such a sweet story, Frank. I hope someday to feel a love that intense." I daydreamed for a moment. Every girl dreams of a love like that. "How did Susanna die? She died giving birth, yes?"

"Not quite. She was a tiny woman, frail, fragile. I was always afraid the wind would pick her up and carry her away. She lost a lung to infection after a bout of pneumonia as a child. I guess her health was never the best and may have contributed to what happened after she gave birth. The autopsy was inconclusive." Frank paused. "Remember the medallion Little Lucy showed you?"

"Yes."

"There are two of them. The other is with their son's adoptive family. The medallions were in Susanna's family for generations. Susanna said they were cursed, that they damned the wearer with the thing they feared most. The thing Susanna feared most was dying young. I'm not saying I believe in curses and things like that, but it makes you wonder. All according to family legend, of course."

"Do not scoff at such beliefs, Frank. For two hundred years, science has ridiculed home remedies, acupuncture, folk medicine, and other things as old wives' tales. Now they are finding out that there is more to them than they thought."

"Why, Marie, I never would have thought anything could scare you."

"I do not take foolish chances, Frank. My own family has traditions and beliefs that would seem archaic and folklorish to outsiders. Besides, everyone seems cursed in some way. Some even seem to curse themselves. I would not recommend that Lucy play with the medallion, and certainly not wear it. It makes me nervous now that you have told me it is cursed."

"Well, as I was saying, the birth itself was normal, but shortly after, Susanna complained of pain in her diaphragm and chest. The pain became so bad that she fainted. She never regained consciousness. She died in the emergency room."

"Poor Sam. And the baby. What happened with their child?"

"Sam was beside himself with grief. Until that night, they had lived a fairy tale romance. I'm not kidding about that. To them it must have been a normal life. To everyone else he was Prince Charming to her Cinderella."

"How beautiful. But what about the child?"

"Sam couldn't look at the poor little thing without breaking down. The child looked just like Susanna, even to the way his lip curled at the corner when he smiled. Poor Sam. I felt so bad for him. Six months later, he told me he had given the boy up for adoption. There was nothing to say. I understood."

"Where is the boy now? What is his name?"

"Tom Nelson. Sam gave him up to friends, Alan and Esther, with the understanding that they not reveal his birth parents until he was old enough to understand."

"Poor Sam. His heart must hurt every day. Does he talk about Susanna and his son?"

"Rarely. He writes about her, but doesn't share what he writes with anyone but me. His writing is quite beautiful, full of love and pain. They were quite an extraordinary couple."

We continued painting in silence. Outside, children laughed and played. Now and then the sharp voices of the Sisters recalled them to their chores.

"Frank. You said they shared a love unlike any you had ever seen. Could it have been, perhaps, that first blush of love that we experience when we first meet someone? Love goes through stages as the initial overpowering attraction turns to familiarity. Continuous intimacy is an underlying effect of love, but we must reach and pass certain stages if our relationship is to last. Maybe Sam and Susanna never had a chance to reach the stage of familiarity. Perhaps Sam mourns for the loss of the first, overpowering attraction."

"I've wondered about that, Marie, even though their love seemed so natural, so unquestionable."

"Oh, Frank. I do not question their love. I only hope that someday I feel a love that intense and lasting."

"I know their love was unconditional, but I never thought there was a reason or purpose behind it. I never thought they needed each other to be complete, or that one had something the other lacked. They seemed to fit together like the pieces of a puzzle. If there were anything mystical about their love, I would say it was to show the world how to love one another."

"If Susanna had lived and Sam died, would she feel the same way that he does?"

"Without a doubt. I spent time with Susanna when Sam was away. She pined for him. She lost her appetite and wouldn't go out. She said she felt his absence when he walked into another part of their home. He was the same way."

"Maybe they broke the rules of love, Frank. I hope so. It is a beautiful story."

Frank leaned down to stir the paint can, then dipped his brush in and began to paint again. He paused for a moment, holding the brush up until paint dripped onto his fingers.

"I nearly had a heart attack when you walked in, Marie. I wouldn't have been surprised to see the Pope standing there."

"Yes, my heart jumped when I saw you." I paused, holding the brush away from me. I didn't turn to face Frank. "You left in quite a hurry last night. I was speechless when you walked away. Were you so upset with me?"

"No. I was tired and needed a good night's sleep. I'd probably still be asleep had I not promised the Chaplain I'd help out today."

"You disappoint me. I thought you would tell me you left in a hurry because you didn't trust yourself around me." I applied more paint to the doorjamb, brushing up and down with long, smooth strokes.

"Marie."

His tone gave him away. *Yes. Please, Frank. Say it.* I pretended not to hear.

He remained silent. I turned, now holding the brush the way Frank had done. "Yes, Frank?"

I caught myself and lowered the paintbrush before paint dripped onto my fingers. My heart beat so hard I felt sure Frank could hear it. A host of thoughts raced through my mind. I hoped I had not misinterpreted his signals; I couldn't bear his rejection. But my feelings for him could not be denied. I had never felt such a yearning for a man so quickly. A yearning greater than physical attraction. A yearning that had sprung to life in the moments before he left the back room so abruptly and had bloomed not thirty seconds before that. I dropped my paintbrush as Frank took me in his arms and kissed me. I did not push away.

I was breathless when our lips parted and my knees shook. *Oh God, that felt so good.*

"Yes, Frank? Did you want to say something, or do you want to kiss me again?"

He kissed me again. I felt his heartbeat. He held me by the

small of my back, his other hand on the back of my head. He enveloped me, cocooned me with his arms and hands and the length of his body. I pressed into him, my arms around his neck, pulling him into me as I fell into him. He felt so wonderful.

He whispered in my ear, "Marie. I left so abruptly because I was attracted to you, not because I had a busy day ahead of me."

"I know, Frank."

"Not because I wanted to sleep in a nice soft bed."

"I know, Frank."

"I can't explain why this happened so quickly."

"I don't mind, Frank."

"I don't usually act like this."

"You do not need to apologize, Frank."

I interrupted him before he could speak again.

"Frank?"

"Yes?"

I whispered again into his ear. "Wipe the paint from your fingers."

He laughed and squeezed me in his arms, then bent down and picked up a rag and cleaned the paint from his fingers.

He said, "Do I need to apologize for kissing you?"

"Only if you did not mean it, Frank. Only if all I am to you is 'just another barmaid looking for a rich American Sailor who will later turn out to be just another poor soul on a meager salary trying hard to make ends meet.' I think that is how you put it, yes?"

Frank smiled and scratched the back of his head. "It does sound vaguely familiar. We'll have to wait and see how it ends, though."

"Will this dream have a happy ending, Frank?"

"Do you want it to?"

"I am sure of it, Frank."

"You kissed me back, you know."

"It must have been the paint fumes."

"I'm sure of it, Marie."

We were laughing when Chip entered the office.

"Hey, what's all this? I didn't know you two made a date. Why does no one tell me these things? Uh-oh. I'm not supposed to smoke my cigar in here. Last time I did, Sister Arnalita grabbed it from my mouth and threw it on the ground. She said smoking a cigar was a nasty thing to do in front of innocent little children. I swear I saw one of those innocent little children pick it up and stick it in his pocket. Anymore brushes? Marie, you are looking all kinds of beautiful today. Have you two been doing anything I should know about?"

Frank said, "Hey, Chip. We thought you weren't going to make it. What happened?"

"Oh, a young Sailor made some trouble in town last night, and the police threw him in jail. I had to go sweet talk the police chief to let him out instead of keeping him locked up all week."

"Was he hurt?"

"Only his pride. I had the guys in his work center take him to the barracks and put a drunk watch on him."

"He was that drunk? What a shame."

"Yep. All too common over here. Seems like bases and bars are built together, doesn't it?"

"It occurs at Rufadora all too often," I said.

"It costs me a mint of money to get those boys out of jail. Oh well. So, what are we painting? Each other? How come all the paint is on you, Frank?" Chip laughed his low rumbling laugh, a laugh that built up from a low chuckle to an all-out roar. Several children ran in at the commotion and joined in the laughter. They loved Goody-Goody.

Sister Arnalita entered the room. She smiled at Chip. "No cigar, Master Chief?"

He wiped his eyes. "No ma'am, Sister. I have seen the light and given up those nasty things. Given them up in here, anyway."

"Good. I do not want anyone to smoke around Marie. I want her and Frank's babies to be healthy."

Sister Arnalita winked at me and wagged her eyebrows toward Frank. I blushed again.

Chip's mouth hung open in surprise. "Babies?"

Chapter Twenty-Three

Marie

God, his arms felt so good. My heart ached for more. I wanted Frank's arms around me again, all night if possible. Forever. I hadn't known such happiness since Edward swept me into his romantic world. It was hard to believe fewer than twenty-four hours had passed since Frank and I met. The emotional rollercoaster since then had taken me through despair, disdain, anger, bewilderment, pleasure, and now, a softening of the purple and black bruise on my soul, a budding happiness, and a heart beginning to feel again. The reflex action against falling in love had not materialized. I had changed from a woman wanting never to love again, to a woman who thought she might have found love once more. The heart that for three years lay dormant and cold had sprung to life, thawing the frozen tendrils of passion that had gnawed at my dreams since Edward broke my heart.

Nearing sunset, painting finished, brushes and rollers washed, children and adults cleaned of the paint that speckled their arms and faces, it was suppertime. The sisters served the children their evening meal at the long dinner table, running back and forth, cleaning up spills, urging good manners, praying to favored Saints for patience. Afterwards, Sister Arnalita gathered us all to rest in the shade of a great acacia tree where we enjoyed cold drinks and quiet conversation.

Heat radiated from the blacktop of the highway, and the air smelled of asphalt. Sister Arnalita and I, sitting on the bench of a picnic table, cooled our faces with fans we wove from palm fronds while the men, not acclimated from childhood to the tropical climate, suffered in the heat. The blazing sun would soon sink below the jungle treetops, leaving behind a dark canopy of night awash with twinkling stars to chase after it, a comfortable lethargy, and a blanket of satisfaction for the day's accomplishments.

No one had the energy or desire to disturb the peacefulness of the twilit evening. The only sound came from the buzzing of insects and an occasional shriek from something creeping, crawling, or climbing in the jungle. The whish of vehicles passing on the highway whispered every few minutes across the fields surrounding the orphanage I still called home. A feeling of blessed serenity floated through the comfortable atmosphere.

Chip, sitting with his back against the acacia, chewed a stub of unlit cigar. Sam, eyes closed, lay propped up on his elbow, his head in his hand, Little Lucy nodding by his side. Frank sat next to me, his face the picture of contentment. Sister Arnalita and Father Roland spoke quietly, discussing the day's work and the work still to come. No one wanted the restful evening to end.

The crunch of tires on gravel broke the quiet, and we all turned toward the sound. A car had turned onto the driveway. Sister Arnalita smoothed the front of her habit as she stood. I joined her, and we walked around the tree to get a better look. Frank joined us too. The car drove a few yards and stopped, dust swirling in the dim light. A man exited and raised the trunk lid. Trees obscured a clear view. After a moment, the trunk lid shut and the man re-entered the car. The car continued toward the orphanage, crawling along as if the occupants were uncertain of their location or reception. Whoever they were, they were well-to-do: few people in this part of the province, other than I, drove a new American sedan. A foreboding passed through my mind, and my heart sank. I felt Frank's glance as though he sensed my worry. I felt safe with him near me. Sister Arnalita pursed her lips and frowned, wrinkling her forehead, and put an arm around my waist. I was glad I had told her of Edward. She called to Little Lucy and sent her to the dining hall. The little girl kissed Sam on the cheek and left the group of adults.

The black sedan stopped behind the truck from the Navy base, blocking its exit. The engine idled several long seconds before falling silent. Darkened windows made it impossible to see who was inside. A few moments passed before two men clad in street clothes stepped out. After a moment, a third man exited the far side of the car and paused, apparently buttoning his coat: Edward. He spoke briefly to the men, then straightened his tie as he walked to the near side and approached the group. He was a handsome man of above-average height, well groomed, confident, and I hated him. My anger rose and I confronted him before he could use his charm to his favor. I took a step forward, clasping and unclasping my hands.

"Why do you come here? What do you want? Get away. I told you I never wanted to see you again."

Edward smiled. "What kind of greeting is this, Marie? Surely, Sister Arnalita taught you to be polite, even toward those for whom you feel such loathing."

His men joined him and stood a few paces behind, far enough away to avoid appearing threatening, close enough to lend a hand if needed.

"Hello, Sister Arnalita. It's been a long time. I trust you are well?" His measured voice was a half octave too sharp to be pleasant. Sister Arnalita was charitable but did not smile.

"Welcome back, Mr. Soriano. I am well, thank you. Is there a particular reason for your unexpected visit?"

"Ah, Sister, you make it as plain as Marie does that my presence here is less than welcome. I assure you I come only to pay my respects to you and express my admiration for your good work."

"You lie," I hissed, conscious of the spittle flying from my lips. I didn't care. "Why do you need these other people if all you intend is to admire the orphanage? Hey? Go. Leave now."

"Now, Marie." Sister Arnalita patted my arm. "There is no need to be upset. I will be happy to show Edward around if he would like to see the orphanage."

I pulled my shoulders back and stood straight, never taking my eyes off Edward. I hated that my heart was black with disgust for this man who had caused so much pain, but I would never acknowledge the power he once wielded over me. Had I the chance to do it over, I would have done more than scratch his face with my shoe. As an orphan, I had grown used to the taunts of other children at the school my parents enrolled me in. I had learned to fight back, and had been disciplined for going too far, for not knowing when to stop beating the other child. I learned quickly to inflict more pain than I received. It was a lesson other kids learned quickly, too.

"I said go, pig. Go back to the whore with whom you soiled my bed."

Edward's eyes acknowledged the depth of my anger and hatred, and he turned away. He smiled graciously at Sister Arnalita.

"Thank you, Sister. I would enjoy seeing the orphanage."

"It has been a long time, Edward, has it not, since your last visit?"

"Yes. It has been quite a long time since Marie showed me the place of her greatest happiness and to seek your blessing for our relationship. Years that have passed so quickly it seems impossible they ever occurred. So much happiness followed by such a turn of events left me an empty man for so long. I come not only to pay my respect, but to beg Marie's forgiveness."

"Bah. You have some other reason for coming here. You are nothing but a liar. What is it you want, you pig?"

Sister Arnalita tut-tutted. "For shame, Marie."

Edward's eyes flashed and the thin, white scar above his left eye stood out in the dark of his face.

I couldn't refrain from laughing at him when I saw the scar. I couldn't help taunting him either, although it would distress Sister Arnalita. "What happened to your perfect face? Is it flawed? Is that a scar I see? Ohh, too bad for you. I think now, you will always remember me when you look in the mirror. What a pity. I will forget you one day, but you will carry me with you for the rest of your life."

"Yes, Marie. I see you every time I look in the mirror." A thin smile crossed his lips. "Sometimes, I see a scar on your face." The smile grew.

Sister Arnalita stepped forward, motioning toward the Sailors.

"Mr. Soriano, I am so sorry to interrupt, but I have not introduced our visitors. I am ashamed for not making them known to you before, since they have come from the Navy base to help repaint the orphanage. Without their help, we should never keep the buildings looking so fresh." She introduced the men. "This is Father Roland, Chip Franklin, Sam McBride, Frank Bailey."

"Good evening, Father." Edward granted the other men a slight inclination of his head. "Gentlemen."

Father Roland replied. "Good evening, sir,"

Chip stared at Edward while chewing on the fat stub of his cigar. Sam, arms crossed, and Frank, alert and on edge, stood by while Sister Arnalita continued.

"We have had a busy day and are now relaxing and enjoying each other's company. Will you and your friends join us, Mr. Soriano?"

"I am so sorry Sister Arnalita, but I would like to speak with Marie alone, if you do not mind."

"I have no interest in anything you have to say. I wish you to go."

Edward gave a slight nod and his men spread out, increasing the distance between themselves. Edward reached for my arm, but Frank intercepted him and grabbed his wrist.

"I don't think Marie wants you to do that."

"I would ask you to remove your hand. My friends might mistake your intentions as hostile."

"Let them. Marie has asked you several times to leave. Why don't you do as she asks?"

Chip spoke around the stub end of the cigar. "Frank. Stay out of it. This is none of our business. If Sister Arnalita needs our help, she'll ask for it."

"You should do as your wise friend asks. It will spare us all needless aggravation. In fact, if Marie will give me just a few minutes and listen to what I have come to say, I will leave without further imposing on your evening."

Frank released Edward's wrist and stepped back.

Edward rubbed his wrist. "Marie?"

"No. There is nothing you have to say that I want to hear. Go away from me."

"You always were an angry shrew, Marie. I may have 'soiled your bed' with another woman, but you drove me to it with your jealousy. If I spoke to another woman, however innocent the conversation, you flew into a rage. You were convinced I was cheating from the day we met."

"I may have never met the other women, but your actions proved me right. You were evasive about your plans, what time you would return, going away without notice."

"I had private business affairs that were none of your concern. Their confidential nature required a certain level of secrecy."

"You still lie. Your father never entertained a thought about keeping secrets from your mother."

"Father has his business. I have mine."

That surprised me. I thought I knew everything about the family's concerns. "What business did you have that father was not a part of? He owned the family business. You worked for him."

"My business is my affair."

"So are your women. Go away now, you pig."

Edward stood impassively, staring at me as though he were in a daze. I had never seen his face so dark, so twisted with anger and hatred. I didn't recognize his manner and grew nervous. When Edward signaled his men, I moved toward Frank. The men drew butterfly knives from their pockets and approached me. I shrank from one as he grabbed me. The other flourished his knife at Frank and the others to hold them at bay, but Frank side-stepped the knife and cold-cocked the man with a heavy fist to the temple. The man stumbled back and fell. The other, distracted by Frank's move, doubled over when I kneed him in the groin. The knife flew from his grip. Frank dropped him with a blow to the neck. Edward lunged for the knife, jerked my foot out from under me, and slashed my cheek as we both fell. I shrieked as the blade sliced my flesh. Frank kicked the knife out of Edward's hand, then grabbed him by the hair and slammed his head into the ground.

The two thugs rushed back in, but Sam stiff-armed one while Chip grabbed the other's wrist and spun him around.

"Whoa there, fellas, where do you think you're going? I think we've seen enough excitement for one night, don't you?"

Chip was a big man, bigger than Edward's men, and stocky. Sam was smaller but solid-built. The thugs looked at Edward. He shook his head.

Frank knelt beside me while Sister Arnalita dabbed at the wound, but I pushed her hand away and screamed at Edward. "You Pig. You bastard. Go. Go away now. I hate you. I hate you."

Edward rose to his feet. He straightened his jacket and tie and brushed his pants legs off. "Well, my little Olongapo whore, your perfect face is forever marked with a scar of remembrance. Remembrance for what you did to me. You will see me when you look in the mirror." He spat blood from a split lip and wiped his face on his pocket handkerchief. As he turned, I kicked my leg out, catching Edward behind the knee. He went down, crying out as he landed with an awkward twist on his elbow.

"You bitch." His eyes narrowed and he hissed at me. "You will pay for this." He cradled his right forearm as he rose to his feet. "You will pay."

Edward and his men returned to the car. The one Frank decked wobbled on his feet. Edward glanced at us and smiled as he entered the car. He spoke to the driver and closed the door. Seconds later the engine roared to life, and the car sped away, gravel flying from the spinning tires. The car turned onto the highway and headed toward Subic City.

I couldn't stop sobbing as Sister Arnalita led me to the dispensary to clean and mend the wound. The smell of fresh paint nauseated me, but I wouldn't let myself get sick. The men waited helplessly outside. The cut was deep, but the wound was clean. I would need stitches, but Sister Arnalita did not believe there would be a scar.

"Thanks to God. I would hate to be reminded of him when I look in the mirror. I would rather die than face that for the rest of my life."

"Well, young lady, I have not forgotten the first time I gave you stitches. Those were in your foot after you stepped on a broken bottle. You were six years old. You cried so loud, but you seem to have healed well. Let us see if I still make good stitches. No more crying now, anak ko. Hold still. This will hurt, my daughter."

I winced as the plunger pushed the anesthetic into my cheek. After a moment, Sister Arnalita pinched near the wound and asked if I could feel anything.

"No."

"Okay now, good. I will stitch the wound."

"How many stitches will you give me?"

"Oh, I think maybe four stitches are needed. It is fortunate that your aversion to Edward made you move away so quickly, or the wound would have been much worse. The knife was razor sharp, which is also good. God protected you this night, Marie. You will be thankful, I am sure." She brought the needle up. "Okay now, hold still."

Years of caring for young children and treating their scrapes and cuts had kept her fingers nimble. They fairly flew as she closed the wound and tied off the suture. She admired her work as she applied a small bandage to my cheek.

"There," she said. "You look like the six-year-old girl who cut her foot on the bottle so many years ago. The same big eyes full of tears, the same manner of looking away from the needle, the same look of relief when all is done."

Sister Arnalita looked down and shook her head. She looked

up again and smiled, her head to one side. The stern face had given way to sympathy. Tears filled her soft, brown eyes.

"Oh Marie, I have missed you so much, my child. Hush. Tell no one I have said you were always my favorite. When you and Frank—no, no, do not deny it, I have eyes, I see—when you and Frank have children, I will retire from this place and live with you and take care of your children. They will be beautiful children. I will love them the same way I love you, Marie Elizabeth Taneo."

Chapter Twenty-Four

Marie

With the evening's drama behind us and the children sent off to bed, the rest of us gathered in the dining hall where the encounter with Edward was the topic of discourse. None of the men knew of my history with Edward, so I explained with little detail, just enough to satisfy their curiosity. They wanted to know more, particularly Frank, but with Edward gone now, his desire for revenge satisfied, I felt I had told them enough. I would explain more fully to Frank later, I was sure.

When the men realized I was not prepared to say more, Chip suggested we all go to a club he frequented in Subic City. The bar at Subic Bay Hotel was situated on a large pier over the Bay with plentiful tables and scenic views of the mountains. Chip recommended the bar as therapy for me. I'm sure he thought we all needed the kind of therapy a visit to a bar would provide.

"Good idea, Goody-Goody," I said. "I will enjoy some real alcohol instead of what Sister Arnalita dabbed on my cheek."

"Hey," Frank said, his voice filled with surprise. "Hey, I wondered where the kids heard of Goody-Goody. Chaplain Roland mentioned him earlier today, and it puzzled me how they could have known his nickname."

Sister Arnalita smiled at Chip and said, "The Master Chief has helped here for many years. Marie once called him Goody-Goody in front of the children. They liked it so much they continue to call him by the name. I also refer to him as Goody-Goody. I think it a fitting description of such a sweet man."

"But Marie and Amy both called him Goody-Goody at Rufadora."

"Yes. Amy lived here too. She also helps out when she can."

"Oh. Amy's adopted?"

"No. Poor thing. She grew up here, then moved to Olongapo when she outgrew the other children. We are the only family she ever knew."

"Okay, folks." Chip clapped his hands together. "Enough old history. I'm thirsty. Let's go, whoever is going."

The dining hall echoed with the sound of chair legs scraping the floor as the six of us stood.

Chip said, "We can't take a government vehicle to a bar. We'll have to go in Marie's car."

"Okay," I said. "But I do not want to drive. I am too nervous, and my cheek is sore. One of you must drive."

I looked around for my clutch, which held the car key. It was next to Frank on the table by the nurse's station. "Frank, hand me my clutch, please."

"Your what?"

I rolled my eyes but spoiled the effect when I smiled. "My purse, Frank."

"So, that's a clutch. Huh."

Sister Arnalita smoothed her habit as she spoke. "We are so happy you could come today. Please know how much I appreciate your assistance. Sam, it was so good to see you and Little Lucy together again. I hope you will come back often. Frank, thank you again for coming today. Please come anytime." She turned to the Chaplain. "Father Roland, are you accompanying the young people?" She winked at Frank. "And Chip?"

Chip guffawed. "Sister, you are such a comedian. Why, I'm younger than—well, I guess I am the oldest one here. I'd say the wisest too, but you're with us."

"Chip, you bring happiness and laughter wherever you go. God bless you. Come often."

"I will, Sister, I will. Bye now."

"Goodbye. Thank you all again." Sister Arnalita waved as the men walked to the car, then took my hands. "I will see you later, Marie? Are you sure you don't want to press charges against Edward?"

"Yes, Sister. We will not be long. I will stay with you tonight. And, no. No charges. I will call Edward's father. He will know how to deal with Edward."

"Please be careful, my dear. Stay with your friends so Edward, if he sees you again, cannot harm you. I could not bear to see you hurt."

The rattle of the truck keys as Father Roland took them from his pocket caught Sister Arnalita's attention.

"Oh, Father, I am so sorry. I am neglecting you. I am so absent-minded. Oh, oh. I beg you will forgive me. I am so, so sorry." She tut-tutted and bustled around, apologetic, patting the Father's arm as he stood amused. He caught her arm and looked fondly into her face.

"Sister Arnalita. I would wait on you all day and night if needed while you shower your love and affection on those around you. Marie must be a special woman to have you as her friend. Everyone should be so fortunate. But then, you have been this way since the war when you comforted those harmed by the Japanese. I'm amazed that someone could have so much love to share for so long."

"Oh, Father Roland. You making me to cry. That awful, awful war. After all the killing, I pledged to our Lord that I would never again fire a weapon in anger, but only spread His word with love."

Red-eyed now and sniffling, she dabbed at her eyes with a tissue, then took Father Roland's arm and walked him to the truck. "You will not go to Subic, then?"

"No. I'll take the truck back to the base. Frank, Sam, and Chip will ride back with Marie or take a jeepney."

"Okay. Goodnight, Father. We will see you next Saturday?"

"I'll be here with the whole gang, Sister Arnalita. Goodnight."

After Father Roland left, Sister Arnalita took me by the elbows. "Oh, Marie, my dear. I hope you will marry soon. A man like Frank, hey? Hey? I like him, and I see that you like him. Is it true you met only yesterday?"

She paused, but cut me off before I could reply.

"No, no, what am I saying? It is none of my business. Go, young lady. Enjoy your night out. Your bed will be ready when you return. Go now. Go."

"Goodbye, Sister Arnalita." I walked to the car. Frank held the door for me.

We left the orphanage behind as Sam made the turn onto National Highway and headed for Subic City. The short drive took us past White Rock Beach Resort, a nice, clean, family beach with decent facilities, and Marilyn's Super Head Inn, a bar notorious among Sailors and Marines for its raunchy entertainment. I knew of its reputation but remained silent. I would blush if anyone mentioned the place. The avalanche of quiet that descended on the car as we drove by faded when Chip, sitting in front with Sam, spoke up.

"It's a Sailor thing."

I said, "What is?"

"Marilyn's."

"Why do you say that?"

"I heard you thinking."

I punched his shoulder. "Oh, you men are all the same. You have but one thing on your mind all the time."

I was embarrassed as they laughed, but it was impossible to resist playing along. "Goody-Goody, I think I shall call you Naughty-Naughty instead."

Sam, following Chip's directions, turned off the highway into the parking lot of the Subic Bay Hotel.

"Well, here we are." Chip opened the door and climbed out of the car. "The hotel shares the parking lot with Rosemarie's Bar out back. It's a tiny place, only a few tables and barstools inside, but the pier is what brings folks here. The view is great. Come on. This way."

Chip led way along the shrub-lined path next to the hotel patio bar. Inside, couples danced to music from the jukebox. A young girl sitting at the bar laughed at her unseen partner, her teeth flashing brilliant white.

Moonlight washed out all but the brightest stars and glistened in the glass tables on the pier. Music from the jukebox hung over the bay, muted in seeming deference to the warm, comfortable, almost sentimental atmosphere of the night. To the north, the amber and white lights of Subic Bay Shipyard shone like daylight on the massive oil tankers in dry dock for repair and overhaul. For miles in either direction, piers, illuminated by colorful strings of lights, jutted into Subic Bay, its warm saltwater sending up sea-fragrance to mix with the smell of beer and whiskey, the overdone spritzing of cheap, cloying perfume, and the pheromones of a thousand men and women colliding like pool balls in search of a pocket of quick love.

Rosemarie, the mama-san, greeted Chip with a quick, warm smile as he ordered drinks at the bar. He came to Rosemarie's often to get away from the hustle and bustle of Olongapo, and to relax without the constant interruption of friends from the base wanting to drink with him. Gregarious by nature, he needed an occasional night to himself to unwind. He spoke a few words to Rosemarie, then paid the tab and led the others to the pier. He found a table with an unobstructed view of the bay, and the mountains across the way silhouetted against the light of the moon.

Waves lapped at the pilings. The low hum from a passing boat reminded me of rides to Corregidor Island with Edward. I exhaled a long breath. There will always be memories, I told myself. Most of our time together was good. Too bad he turned out to be such a bastard. I had not foreseen his violent nature. I sipped my drink, reflecting on the scar my anger had left on Edward and the likelihood that the cut he left me with would satisfy his thirst for revenge. I felt certain it had, especially since his parents would admonish and chastise him for his behavior. They had called me their daughter and welcomed me into their home from the day they met me. I would always have their support. I tipped my drink in a silent salute to Edward's future discomfort.

Two attractive barmaids, barely clad in short shorts and loose tank tops, approached the table, flip-flops slapping their heels. They backed off when they saw me. My clean, well-dressed appearance set me apart from the local, dressed-down sort looking for a free drink or quick score. I didn't particularly care if the men wanted to mingle with the girls, but I didn't think they would, certainly not Frank, and Chip was happily married. But Sam, unattached, was a different story. However, he confirmed my opinion of him when he showed no interest in the bargirls that came and went.

The drink warmed me as I sipped from the glass. I was careful not to move my cheek too much. It was swollen and felt fat, and ached like a bad tooth, but the alcohol would soon render it numb. I set the drink down and rested my arms on the table, listening to Sam as he spoke to Frank and Chip.

My parents had been a childless couple who searched orphanages all over Luzon for a child to adopt. Although they had known Sister Arnalita for many years, the Zambales Orphanage had been the last one they visited. I knew right away I wanted to go home with them. Of course, all the children knew that for themselves. No child ever gave up hope that she would be the next child adopted. In my case, magic struck with the young professionals from Manila, Warren and Esper Taneo. After several months visiting back and forth, the authorities approved the adoption, and I moved to Baguio with my new parents. After six years with the sisters of Our Lady of Lourdes, I had a home.

"Marie. Marie."

The alcohol was working. I gradually became aware someone was speaking my name. With my chin in my hand, I lifted my eyes to Frank's. "Hmm? Yes?"

Frank looked concerned. The thought pleased me.

"Are you okay? You seemed far away for a moment there. Does your cheek hurt?"

"Yes, it is sore and throbs a bit, but I am okay." I spoke dreamily as I rocked side to side slightly. "It must be the night air. It could be the medicine Sister Arnalita gave to me. Of course, the alcohol does not hurt." I laughed at the unintended joke. "Haha, the alcohol does not hurt. Alcohol does not feel pain." I felt good, all right.

Frank suppressed a laugh and smiled behind his hand. "Should you be drinking? I'm concerned, not telling you what to do."

"No, I know that. Thank you for your consideration. I am okay. One drink will not hurt me. I would like another, though. Two drinks will not hurt me even more."

"Are you sure?"

"Oh, yes, Frank. I am sure. It has been a long day. I want to have my drinks, go home, go to my bed, and forget all about it." I smiled and patted his cheek. "Except for the good parts."

He pressed his hand to mine. I liked the feel of his beard stubble. It tickled my palm and made me shiver, raising goosebumps along my arm. Our faces were close enough for his breath to waft over me. I inhaled and exhaled, a deep, long exhale of satisfaction, pleasure, and anticipation. I wanted the moment to last forever. I was falling in love. I liked it.

"Well, all right. One more drink, then we'll take you back to the orphanage. Maybe I'll tuck you in." He smiled and winked and signaled for the barmaid.

I remained as I was, head in hand, a slight smile on my lips, my eyes half-closed as the excitement, medication, and alcohol held me in a state of drowsy relaxation. I covered my mouth and yawned.

Chapter Twenty-Five

Marie

I scrunched my nose and puffed at the strand of hair tickling me between the eyes. It flew up, then settled back again. I resisted the urge to brush it away. Moving my hand meant effort. The tickling proved too much to bear, though, and I reached up to tie my hair back.

"Oh, I'm terribly sorry."

My elbow had jabbed a man in the abdomen. He grunted and stumbled against the table, then steadied himself with a hand on the back of Frank's chair. It was Senior Chief Kelly. I recognized him from Rufadora and the several times Shore Patrol had been called to remove him. His face was blotched from drinking. He leaned down to peer at Frank.

His voice was thick, and his foul breath washed across the table.

"Hey, it's the Flip lover. How you doing? Hello, Goody-Goody."

He brought his face close to Sam, who was quick to turn his head away. "Hey, who are you?"

I had been watching Frank with eyes half-closed. I began to worry when his jaw tightened. I knew the signs of a bar fight and didn't think he'd take the insult sitting down. He stood a head taller than the skinny senior chief and seemed to grow larger with anger.

"Senior Chief, why don't you go back where you came from and let us enjoy our drinks."

"What? It's too early to go back to base."

He noticed me on Frank's right and stared at me. A half-decent smile appeared on his face for a moment before turning into a mocking leer.

"Hey. Hey, I know you. You're the pure girl. The pure girl." He tripped as he laughed and spilled beer on his shirt. He ran his hand over it. "Ohh, that's cold."

"Hey." He called out loud enough to be heard at the next pier. "Hey, looky here, it's the pure barmaid."

People nearby stared at the commotion, probably weighing the odds of a fight between the giant and the drunk. I felt their eyes on me and moved closer to Frank. I appealed silently to him, telling him I wanted to leave before he beat the drunk to a pulp. Frank looked more annoyed than angry and clearly regretted the interruption for my sake.

"Senior Chief, I'm warning you." Frank's fists were balled, and a vein in his temple throbbed. His patience was wearing thin.

"No, no, no. You don't warn me. You're only a Chief, a little Chief." He indicated a little Chief with his thumb and index finger, then pointed at Chip. "He's the biggest Chief. I outrank you, and he outranks me. See?" He swayed on his feet. Bar patrons at the closer tables laughed while a group of Sailors a few tables away shook their heads.

"Hey. Little lady. Get me a beer, would you? Hey, what's the matter with your face? Did the little Chief hit you? 'Little Chief,' he laughed."

Chip left his seat and stepped between Frank and the senior chief.

"Why don't you head on back to the base, Paul? I think you've had enough to drink."

"You don't tell me what to do when I'm on liberty." His slurring worsened. "I don't take orders from you off-base."

"Paul, I'm going to ask you one last time to go back to the base, or I'll call Shore Patrol and have them take you back. I'm sure you don't want that now, do you?"

"I don't care what you do, big man. Screw you, anyway. You don't like me because I quit flying. You think I'm a coward." He hid his face in his hands and began to sob. "You don't understand. I'm not a coward. He was my friend. We flew together for six years. He was my friend. He was on fire. I watched him burn. I can't stop seeing him. He reached to me for help, but what could I do? I watched him burn." He picked up a beer bottle from the table and smashed it against the deck railing. "He was on fire. What could I do! What could I do? I can't stop seeing him." His shoulders heaved as he cried.

"Come on, Paul. Let's go back to base. You'll be all right."

"No! I don't want to go back to base. I said screw you."

"All right, Paul. I warned you."

Chip turned to Sam. "Be a good fellow, Sam, and flag down Shore Patrol, would you?"

"Sure thing, Master Chief." Sam grabbed his beer and headed for the street.

The senior chief wouldn't shut up. "Who's he, anyway? Her boyfriend? Hey. Where's he going?" He gripped the back of a chair to steady himself and leered at Marie. "Hey, Miss Pure. How much for a short time?"

I ignored him.

Frank reached around Chip and grabbed Paul by the throat. Paul struggled. Frank squeezed.

"Frank, you'd better let go. I'll take care of this."

"Not until he apologizes."

"Frank."

The senior chief twisted free of Frank's grip. His eyes blazed with anger. Spittle lined his lips. He hissed between clenched teeth. "I ain't apologizing to no whore."

"You ... Frank lunged and punched the man in the side of the head. His glasses flew off and into the bay. He stumbled and knocked over a table, scattering beer bottles, ashtrays, and people. He hit his head against a table and fell unconscious to the deck. People on the next pier over cheered and clapped. Bar fights were always a welcome diversion.

Chip raised his eyebrows and rubbed his chin as he considered Paul. "Well, you certainly pack a punch, Frank. That about does him for the night. I guess we can manage him now." Chip corralled a barmaid and asked her to call Sam back. "No sense having Shore Patrol arrest him. Heck, it's no fun getting arrested when you won't remember it."

Sam returned with Rosemarie, who assessed the damage.

"Is he hurt, Master Chief?"

"No, Rosemarie. No one is hurt. The Senior Chief is out cold, but he's still breathing. He'll be okay. His glasses fell into the water, though. I'd appreciate it if one of your boys would see if he can find them tomorrow."

Frank lifted the table upright and set his beer down. "I'm sorry for the trouble, ma'am."

"It's okay. No trouble. Nothing broken except Senior Chief.

Poor man. He often crying about his problem when he's getting drunk."

"Come on fellas," said Chip. "Give me a hand getting him to the car. We'll go to the orphanage and have Sister Arnalita look him over."

I was disappointed that we had to leave. I wanted another drink. I took Frank's hand and ran my fingers over his knuckles. "Never a dull moment with you, Frank."

"It has been pretty exciting, hasn't it? I'd have less trouble in Vietnam." He made no move to pull away from my touch.

"I'm sorry about all this, Marie."

"No need to apologize, Frank. The senior chief is only an annoyance, and I would have had to face Edward, eventually. Having you and the others with me prevented the meeting with Edward from turning worse. If he had meant to hurt me, this cut on my cheek would be minor compared to what he might have done. Truthfully, though, I think he lashed out as he did because he was embarrassed by you, Sam, and Master Chief. He felt his manhood was demeaned, and he could not stand the shame."

"Well then, I'm glad we met Paul here tonight."

"Why is that?"

"We don't want to take him back to base in his condition. If Sister Arnalita will let us, we'll stay at the orphanage tonight. If Edward believes we would return to the base, he might return to the orphanage to confront you again."

"I would be surprised if he tried anything criminal. Edward is vindictive, but he will not risk having the police involved. Cutting my face would give him great pleasure, but he would not chance it unless sure he would get away with it. His father would remove him from the company if he is involved in a crime. Edward will not risk that."

"That's good to know, but I think we'll play it safe." He turned to Chip, who was pressing Rosemarie to accept money to cover the damage. "What do you think, Chip?"

"I think it's a great idea. I'll call my wife from the orphanage and let her know."

At the orphanage, they wrestled Paul out of the car and onto an examination table in the dispensary. I left to find Sister Arnalita while Chip called his wife.

"Oh dear. What happened?" Sister Arnalita's nose wrinkled, and she leaned over Paul's face and sniffed. "He's drunk." She clucked her tongue and asked again what happened.

"Another fight, Sister Arnalita. This time with a person from Chip's place of work."

"My word. Sailors seem to fight a lot."

Chip returned and watched Sister Arnalita look the man over. "Frank had to restrain him when he got out of hand."

Sister Arnalita, and Sister Mary Ann, who came along to assist her, didn't appear to believe Frank had merely restrained the man.

"Well, I guess you could say he ran into Frank's fist," said Chip.

Sister Arnalita turned Paul's head side to side and examined his face. She clucked her tongue, making a sound that resembled cricket clackers.

"From the bruises, I would say he ran into Frank's fist a number of times." She sighed and shook her head when she looked at Frank. "That is two men you have knocked out in one day, Frank. You should seek employment as a prizefighter when you leave the Navy."

"Well, Sister, maybe I'll return here and work as your bodyguard. This place wasn't exactly a place of peace and serenity tonight."

"Speaking of peace and serenity," I said. "May the men stay here tonight? Paul is in no condition to return to the base, and they don't want to leave him. Are there rooms for them?"

"Of course, Marie, of course. I'll have Sister Aileen prepare the rooms." She looked around the room. "Where is Sister Aileen? Ah, there you are, Sister Aileen. We'll have guests tonight. Please see that their rooms are prepared. Marie and I will tend to the drunken Sailor."

"Yes, Sister."

"Now, Master Chief, Sister Aileen will show you men to your rooms."

"Are you sure you can take care of him by yourselves? We'll stay and help. We're not going anywhere tonight."

"I have handled many a man larger than he, Master Chief. You would be surprised at the strength of a woman with a firm hand and a firmer voice."

Chip scratched his temple and grinned. "Aye, aye, Sister. You don't have to convince me."

The men were leaving for their rooms when Paul moaned. He held a hand to his forehead and tried to sit up. The effort was too much and he fell back, still holding his aching head. His face was blotchy red, and a heroic blue-black bruise colored one side, like a prizefighter who failed to avoid a strike.

"Well, Paul isn't dead after all." Chip walked back to check on Paul as he tried to sit up. "He's coming around—a bit dazed—but he doesn't seem to be as drunk as he appeared at Rosemarie's."

Paul moaned and fell back. "What happened? Where am I?" He turned his face away from the bright light of the examination lamp. "Turn that thing off. Please."

"Oh. I am so sorry." Sister Arnalita turned the lamp off. "How thoughtless of me. How are you feeling, hey? Hey? You must have a headache. I will give you some aspirin."

"A headache is putting it mildly. My face hurts and my head's going to explode." The unfamiliar surroundings disoriented him, but he seemed reassured by the sight of Chip.

"Chip? What are you doing here? Where are we?"

"You're in the dispensary of the Zambales Orphanage, Paul," Chip told him. "The good sister, Sister Arnalita, has been looking over your injuries. We brought you here after you had an accident at Rosemarie's."

"I remember now." He turned to Frank, who had returned with Sam. "You pack a punch."

Frank said, "You feel all right? You hit your head against a table when you fell. You might have a concussion."

"Except for a massive headache, I feel all right," he said, shutting his eyes tight and clenching his shoulders to ease the pain.

I moved from behind Paul so he could see me. He paled, then turned red when he recognized me. He had upset me at Rosemarie's, but after what I had learned of his situation, I couldn't hold a grudge. My concern was genuine, and I wanted to put him at ease. Besides, it had been the alcohol talking, not him.

"I am glad you are okay. I was afraid your injury might be severe. You had a nasty fall."

"I'm okay. I think I owe you an apology."

"I understand, Senior Chief. I forgive you. I do hope you feel better soon. Sister Arnalita is a wonderful nurse."

He looked at each of us in turn. "I owe all of you an apology. I've been so, so—"

Chip cut him off. "Rude? Mean? Unfriendly? You've been a real jackass lately, Paul. I was concerned for you. You weren't the same man I've gone on liberty with for nearly twenty years. By

God, I hope my shipmate is back."

"Yeah. I feel a bit sheepish about all that. I'm truly sorry."

"Marie accepted your apology," Chip said. "That's good enough for me. Let Sister Arnalita look you over, put the fear of God back in you, and send you to bed. We'll head back to base in the morning"

Chip's face took on a look of worry as he was leaving. "You do have coffee here, don't you, Sister? We must have coffee in the morning. Please say yes."

Sister Arnalita's eyes grew wide. "I cannot tell a lie."

Concern gave Chip's face a comical appearance.

She smiled sweetly at him. "We do drink coffee."

"Sister, you old fox. I think I'm going to hug you."

"Ohh." Her eyes crinkled when she laughed. "Go to bed now, Goody-Goody. You making me to blush. You always making me to blush."

Frank grabbed Chip's arm. "Let's go, Goody-Goody. You need a nap."

"You're killin' me, Frank."

Wishing to be alone with Sister Arnalita, I took her by the elbow and led her out of Paul's hearing.

"Sister." I didn't believe Edward would return, but Frank had made me worry.

"Yes, Marie. What is it?"

"Sister, I must inform you that, although I told Frank that Edward would attempt nothing tonight, I have a sense of foreboding that he may indeed return to the orphanage to confront me."

"Yes, I knew something bothered you, my dear. I knew you would tell me when you were ready. But come, we must attend to the senior chief first, then we will speak of Edward."

I stood by while Sister Arnalita tended to Paul. "Come now. Sit up so I can clean your face." She dabbed his head gently with a cotton gauze. "Oh, oh. That cut will need stitches."

She smiled as she gathered needle and stitching.

Chapter Twenty-Six

Marie

I luxuriated in the soft linen and the cooling breeze from the ceiling fan. Sister Annabelle had moved to the girls' ward so I could have my old room to myself. Exhausted, I lay on my side, hands under the pillow, and fell into a deep sleep.

I woke as a knife slashed my face again and again. I screamed, but no sound came from my throat. I couldn't lift my arms to shield my face. Blood filled my mouth and eyes, ran down my neck, my breasts and belly, my legs. Edward's horrible laugh filled the room, taunting me, ridiculing me. I screamed as he dug his fingernails into my cheeks. Then I watched, helpless, as the razor-sharp blade, at the top of its rise, glinted in the moonlight. I shrank in terror as the knife arced toward my heart.

A noise in the dark chased the dream away, and I woke to a hand mashed against my mouth. Another gripped my hair and pulled my head back. I couldn't breathe and fought against panic. I bit the hand covering my mouth and kicked under the bedsheet. Whoever held me cried out but retained his iron grip on my face. There were two of them. Hands on my legs restrained me. A shaft of moonlight through the window showed two dark figures, silent but for heavy breathing. One held me immobile while the other attempted to tie my arms behind me. Why were they kidnapping me? Who—Edward. The bastard had returned as I had feared. *Frank. Where are you, Frank?* The hand slipped from my mouth.

"No. No. Let me go!"

Someone slapped me across my face. Again, and my eyes watered from the pain. Hair tore from my scalp as the other hand yanked my head back so hard it forced my mouth wide open and bared my throat to the knife. I screamed, but the only sound was a gurgle in the back of my throat. The knife flashed in the shaft of moonlight. *Oh, no, no, please, God, no.*

I forced a scream. "Frank!"

The knife hovered above my head. I closed my eyes.

"No." Edward. "I said restrain her."

The men lifted me to my feet. My knees gave and they yanked me upright. I cried out in pain behind the hand still pressed against my mouth.

"Enjoy the pain you feel now, dear Marie. It will be worse, much worse, in a short while."

Edward, his right arm in a sling, held a knife as he spoke, pricking the tip against his finger and drawing a spot of blood.

He's mad.

"You will wish for this pain to return. Gag her."

His voice was sinister, menacing. I struggled to break free. Edward raised his arm and I flinched. He brought the back of his hand against my head with such force I blacked out. When I came to, they had dragged me into the hallway and gagged me. One of Edward's thugs opened the door at the far end. I moaned through the gag. My face hurt, my head hurt, and I couldn't focus my eyes. Blood filled my mouth, and I couldn't breathe through my nose. I was suffocating. Panic returned. My heart raced. Blood rushed in my ears, and I began to cry. *Where are you, Frank? Help me. Please come, Frank.*

"Hey. What's going on out here? Keep it down, will you? I can't sleep."

Small sleeping quarters lined both sides of the hallway in the T-shaped building. A head appeared from a doorway just beyond me. Paul looked down the long, narrow corridor, saw what was going on and rushed from the room.

"Hey. What are you doing with that woman? What have you done to her?"

It was clear from the surprise on the men's faces that they hadn't expected to find anyone but women at the orphanage. All three appeared frantic as they looked down both ends of the passageway, obviously expecting to see the men they had fought with earlier. Paul took a step toward me, but Edward stepped between them, brandishing his pistol.

Paul backed away when Edward pointed the pistol at him.

"Whoa. Okay. Okay. Put the gun away. I don't want any trouble. I'll just go back in my room and go to sleep."

"It's too late for that. Move away from the door."

Paul's appearance relieved me. If he had heard the commotion maybe Frank and Chip had too. With the men distracted by Paul, I twisted against them and lunged, kicking Edward in the back of the knee. He didn't fall, but braced himself for Paul's lunge. The thugs let go of me and went for Paul, but I flung myself against them, giving Paul time to wrap his arms around Edward. They grappled, each trying to throw the other. Edward freed his arm and raised the gun. One of the men slashed at me with his knife, but missed. I kicked him between the legs. He howled in pain and fell. He was fortunate I was not wearing my stilettos. The other man grabbed me by the arm and threw me against the wall. I fell, too tired and hurt to move, but screamed for Frank. Paul yelled for Chip as he grabbed Edward's arm. The gun went off. They struggled with each other. The gun went off again and Paul fell, bleeding from the shoulder.

"Chip!" The senior chief yelled again. "Chip!"

"Frank!" I yelled.

The men rushed in from the corridor next door.

"No! He has a gun!" I struggled to my feet, bracing myself against the wall.

Edward turned, placed the gun in his pocket, and drew the knife from his jacket. He stepped toward me, staring like a madman, oblivious to everyone but me. White, frothy spittle lined his lips and he breathed with a labored, harsh, raspy sound. He reared back and brought the knife down as Frank, two steps behind him, lunged, stretching frantically for his arm. I had nowhere to go and shielded my face. A shot rang out. I screamed. I screamed again as the knife nicked my belly. Edward's head thudded against the floor. A button from my blouse rolled round and round and round before falling over next to his face. The body lay still, lifeless eyes staring at the button as blood spurted from a hole in the back of the neck. Sister Arnalita calmly lowered the rifle when the body stopped twitching.

"No one harms my daughter."

Chapter Twenty-Seven

Frank

The inquest into Edward's death ended after months of legal formality and a finding that Sister Arnalita was justified in using lethal force against Edward. I held Marie's hand as we left the Olongapo courthouse with Sam and Chip and walked to Triangle Park. Marie, on edge for months as the investigation unwound, gave a deep sigh.

"I am so happy. Not that Edward is dead, of course, I would not wish that for anyone, but that the whole thing is over. I have not slept well since the... since it happened. To put it all behind me is like starting a new chapter in life."

"A new chapter with a new mother," I said.

"Indeed, Frank. I still cannot believe Sister Arnalita is my mother. Looking back though, a lot of things I puzzled over for years make sense now. Her tenderness toward me, why it took so long to be adopted, the way we remained in touch. She had to let go of me, yet wanted me within reach."

"She's an amazing woman. Did you know she and your father fought with the Filipino underground in World War Two? That he was killed while attempting to rescue allied prisoners of war?"

"I had no idea until the inquest. She never spoke of the past or her guilt over killing so many Japanese soldiers. It also explains my parents' apprehension whenever I told them I was going to visit the orphanage. They must have worried I might discover the truth. God bless them, for all they did for me."

Our relationship had blossomed during the ordeal. Marie relied on me for strength and support during the months of the investigation and inquiry. For my part, I had found in Marie a companion, someone whose company I looked forward to rather than turning inward and seeking the solitude of my own thoughts.

I had discovered the truth in Marie's words about the stages of love. I had also shared my life story with Marie after years of keeping my inner life private from all but a few people. Marie occupied my thoughts throughout the day, and I found her part of my dreams at night. I was deeply, completely in love with a woman for the first time in my life.

"All of a sudden," she said, "I am so relaxed with the pressure gone. I could fall asleep right here."

"Sleep as long as you like, Marie. I'll be here when you wake."

"Ohh, thank you, Frank. But I would not have you bored while I sleep like Rip Van Winkle."

"How do you know I would be bored? I like watching you sleep. You are the quietest sleeper I know."

"You make up for it by snoring enough for four people," Sam said.

"I don't snore. I'm a heavy breather."

Marie leaned against me and said, "He can snore all he likes, Sam, as long as he is there when I wake."

A jet from the base roared through the sky, making talk impossible. When it passed, Chip rose and stretched. "You know, it's a good thing Sister Arnalita kept that rifle after the war. She said she would never be caught unprepared again."

"I can't believe the shot she made," I said. "I felt the bullet fly past my ear. Had I moved an inch to the left, I wouldn't be here now."

Marie leaned forward, looking far away. "I saw only the knife in Edward's hand, and the next moment his body on the floor. Thanks to God that Paul woke when he did." She leaned against me again and nuzzled my neck. "I am most happy that you were there that night."

Chip said, "Hey. What about Sam and me?"

"Yeah. Why does Frank get all the attention?" Sam, his head in his hand, lay stretched out on the park bench. "Chip and I are jealous. We want some loving too."

Marie leaped to her feet. She ran to Chip and kissed him on the cheek. She knelt next to Sam and kissed him too.

"Ohhh, you know I love my heroes." She clasped her hands over her heart and gave her best imitation of a woman rescued from danger. "You all were so brave and manly, and I so weak and terrified."

"I seem to remember you landing a few blows. You know

where to hurt a man."

"That's right," said Chip. "You held up your end all right. Remind me not to put myself on the wrong side of your kick. I wouldn't want to give orders in a falsetto voice. It just wouldn't get the right response from my Sailors."

"Nevertheless, it might have turned out differently had you not been there. Especially Sister Arnalita and Paul. How is he, by the way?"

"The wound has healed, but he'll be stiff for a while." Chip chuckled and said, "He'll also have to drink left-handed."

"Please tell him again, I said thank you."

"You can tell him yourself at the next Chief's meeting. We're holding it at Rufadora next Wednesday, before Frank, Sam, and I fly back to Vietnam."

"Vietnam? Frank, you did not tell me you are returning to Vietnam. Must you go? How long will you be there?"

"I didn't want to worry you, Marie. Not while all of this was going on. You've had enough to think about."

"Yes, but... Oh, Frank. When will you return?"

"After a week or two so the guys there now can come here for R&R."

"I am afraid for you, Frank. What if something happens? What if ... no, no. I do not want to think about it. Please be careful. You too, Sam, and you, Chip. I need you all. Little Lucy needs you. I do not know what I would do if anything happened to you. All of you. I love you so much."

Sam said, "We'll only be gone a short time. What could happen? We'll be okay."

Sam might have projected confidence, but my neck tightened as the feeling of doom returned. I didn't want to go back, but I went where I was needed. If I was needed in Vietnam, I'd go. Still, I felt like I was wearing a bullseye between my shoulder blades.

We left the Triangle and walked to Via's Tacos for dinner. Afterwards, Marie and I said goodnight to Sam and Chip and walked along Gordon Avenue toward Marie's bungalow in west Olongapo. At the turn for the street to Marie's house, I gave her a nudge, steering her toward the market.

"Let's walk through the market tonight. I feel like hearing people laugh."

"I would like that. I will buy a fan too. It is so hot and the air so still."

We often strolled through the market looking for bargains and picking up knick-knacks. Everyone welcomed Marie, and me too, once they sensed the relationship between us.

A saleswoman caught Marie by the wrist as we walked past a display of cheap costume jewelry and pulled her into the vendor's stall. She reached for a golden ring on a display table and placed it on Marie's finger.

Her eyes twinkled as she looked first to me, then to Marie. "Now she got ring, you marry her. Yes? You marry her."

Marie blushed and laughed.

"Well, if she would like me to ask her," I said.

"Oh, you are so funny. You are embarrassing me. Stop it now!" Her smile betrayed her. She peered at me from beneath her brows. The ponytail gave her an impish look, one that never failed to move me.

I moved now, kneeling on one knee as the saleslady shushed onlookers and opened the curtain at the back of her stall. Marie watched, amazed, as Chip, Paul, and the Chaplain appeared. She stared as Sisters Arnalita, Annabelle, Aileen, and Mary Ann gathered next to her. Sam entered, carrying a radiant Little Lucy smiling ear-to-ear, and stood next to me. Marie stared blankly, uncomprehending.

"Frank, what are you doing? Mother, why are you here? Oh, Little Lucy, you look so lovely."

"Shhh. Little Lucy." I held my hand out to the little girl who came forward and placed her hand in mine. She carried a bouquet nearly as tall as she, and wore her best dress, picked out at the Navy Exchange with Sam by her side. She beamed proudly and reached into a pocket, careful not to drop the flowers, and withdrew a blue silk pouch. She handed it to me. I kissed her cheek and opened the pouch. I turned it up, and a sparkling ring fell into my hand. I reached for Marie and took her hands.

"Marie. I knew love only as a family feeling before I met you. I didn't know loneliness until we were apart. I didn't know what it meant to be a man until you leaned on my shoulder and I put my arm around you. I don't want to live another day without you. You once told me, Marie, that love passes through stages, and that the first blush of love does not last forever. A relationship must grow and evolve or become stagnant. I didn't know that until I met you, and it explained my inability to find lasting relationships. I was looking for something that could never be. I'm glad that it was you who taught me what love is. I love you, Marie. May I spend the rest of my life with you? Will you marry me, Marie?"

Marie covered her mouth with her hands and choked back tears. "Oh, Frank. Oh, Frank. Yes. Yes, Frank, I will marry you."

The crowd cheered and clapped until the saleslady shushed them again.

"Wait, wait, there is more, there is more." She pressed her hands together as in prayer as I placed the sparkling ring on Marie's finger.

"This ring belonged to Susanna, Marie. Sam once told me that if anything ever happened to him, he wanted you to have it, so that he and Susanna would remain a part of our lives forever. But things moved so fast for us that Sam wanted you to have it now. You would have loved Susanna, Marie."

Sam stepped forward and took Marie's hands. "Susanna would have loved you, Marie. You and she are so much alike." He stopped, overcome.

Marie pressed a hand to his cheek. "Sam. No one could have said nicer words to me. I feel like I know Susanna through the words and memories of those whose lives she touched. I know she was a wonderful person, Samuel."

"Frank told you, didn't he?"

"May I call you Samuel?"

His voice choked with emotion as he spoke. "You must always call me Samuel, Marie."

Marie touched his hand gently, then turned as I touched a finger to the golden ring the saleslady had slid onto her right hand.

"This ring is my promise to you. I will love you forever, Marie. And these," I said, as Sam lifted Little Lucy onto my shoulder, "are the papers that will allow us to adopt Little Lucy as you said we should." Marie gazed at the papers, clasped her hand to her cheek, held the other out so she could gaze at the ring, then looked at her little family.

"Oh, Frank. Oh, Little Lucy. Oh, Samuel. Thank you, dear, dear, Samuel. I am so happy."

Book Five

Vietnam

1968

Chapter Twenty-Eight

Chip Franklin

I recall it like no time had passed between then and now. My skin sizzles every time I think of that damned heat. Georgia never had heat like Vietnam. The gravel of the aircraft taxiway still grinds into my knees as I kneel beside Sam. Every helicopter is a Huey gunship chopping the air with its rotor blades. The flak vest still chafes the back of my neck, and the sweat still rolls down my armpits. Some people look back with happy memories of the things they did even under the worst conditions. Not me. Not about Vietnam. That place was hell and nothing good comes out of hell. And I sent both those boys to hell.

It was Sam and Frank's last day in Vietnam. Frank was leaving for the USS Midway, while Sam would follow later in the afternoon. I would fly out the following morning. We'd sail for Subic the day after and spend the rest of the deployment in PI.

One week in Vietnam turned into three, and they were anxious weeks, especially for Frank. Boy, he was jumpy. I never saw a man dive under a Jeep so fast in my life. Every time he heard a gunshot, his shoulder blades would meet in the middle of his back and he'd run for cover. He always said he'd get it in the back. I never thought I'd get shot. It's strange how some folks think. Frank told us every day he wouldn't feel safe until he was with Marie again. Marie was something else. She was beautiful and sweet and smiled at everyone like she loved everybody. She and Frank were meant for each other; sometimes you can just tell. Frank knew what he had and counted his blessings every day.

I walked with Frank to the chopper. He fingered the ring and necklace Marie had given him like a rosary. Frank said she had clasped it around his neck and told him to be careful, that she didn't want to lose the man she loved. Well, a few more days and he'd never have to leave Marie again. I shook his hand and told him I'd see him aboard the Midway, then joined Sam at the edge of the taxiway. Frank climbed the ladder and stopped at the top for one last look around the airfield. I would always remember the relief on his face.

He was waving goodbye to Sam and me when a puff of something red appeared just above his vest. The impact of the sniper's bullet spun him into the side of the helicopter. I couldn't believe my eyes. Not as he was leaving. A dark, wet spot appeared above the edge of his flak vest. His knees gave and he crumpled, sliding down the steps to the ground where he lay motionless as his life slipped away in a growing pool of blood.

His arm stretched out like he was reaching for something. I got to him just in time to hear him whisper, "Marie."

* * * * * * * * *

Sam had raised his hand to wave back when Frank jerked and spun around. The puff from Frank's chest spread outward in slow motion. Everything slowed down. Sam's scream of disbelief seemed to reverberate across the airfield.

"Frank!"

Sam dropped his tool pouch and raced across the tarmac. I ran after him and knelt beside Frank to see if there was anything I could do. Sam unfastened Frank's flak vest and ripped his shirt open.

"Oh, man, Frank, hold on man, hold on. Hold on, buddy."

More shots came from the perimeter and we ducked against the spray of fragments of asphalt.

I yelled for a corpsman as Sam pressed a towel to the wound to stanch the blood streaming from Frank's chest.

He was frantic. "Frank, Frank, can you hear me, buddy?"

No response. He felt for a pulse.

"Christ, man, my hands are shaking. Calm down. Calm down. Where's your pulse, Frank? Frank!"

He checked again. "He's not breathing."

"Okay, Frank. I gotta get you out of here. Hang on, buddy. You'll be okay."

Sam pushed me away when I tried to help him lift Frank.

"No. No. Frank's my best friend. I got him. I got him."

The safety of the maintenance shack was a short sprint away, but Frank was dead weight, and Sam had to run hunched over to run at all. I ran ahead to open the door.

"Almost there," Sam said. "Almost there. We're gonna make it, Frank. Hang on. Hang on, buddy."

What happened next will stay with me until the day I die. The bullet smashed into Sam's back, ripping through muscle and tendon and pulverizing bone. The pain must have been excruciating as it filled his brain because the groan wrenched from behind his clenched teeth sounded inhuman, animal-like. I never heard anything like it. Sam staggered, took another step, and staggered again as another round smashed into his back. His knees buckled and he fell forward. He reached out to brace himself and his wrist snapped with a loud crack when he hit the ground. His sunglasses and helmet flew off when his head slammed into the concrete taxiway. Frank's body rolled from Sam's shoulders and over his head, mashing his face into the hot, jagged surface and scraping the flesh from his chin and cheek.

I ran over to help Sam. The blazing sun beat down on the asphalt, heating it to a point just short of boiling. Sam's face was bleeding. He tried to roll onto his back, but his legs wouldn't move. He twisted his upper body and forced himself over with his good arm, his legs flopping like the legs of a stuffed doll. He screamed with pain, then turned to look for Frank, whose still body lay just out of reach. Sam stretched to pull him closer but screamed again.

A moment later he stopped moving. I thought he was going to pass out, but then he began to speak like nothing had happened. It was like listening to a dead man.

"It's strange, Master Chief. You'd think two bullets would have a lasting impact."

Blood pooled beneath him.

"They're right, Master Chief. You don't hear the bullet that kills you."

"Don't talk, son. You're not going die. Help is coming."

"Master Chief? No, Master Chief. Not me. Frank. Frank's hurt. Help Frank."

He closed his eyes against the blazing sun.

"Where are my sunglasses? I need my sunglasses."

He coughed and spit up the blood filling his throat. A tooth fell from his mouth. His face was messed up.

"Frank. Frank. Wake up, Frank. Please be okay, buddy. Wake

up, Frank. Please don't die. Make him wake up, Master Chief. Make him wake up."

Sam was beyond any help the Corpsman, Lopez, could give him. I lifted Sam's head into my lap and brushed away the flecks of dirt and gravel on his face. The pool of blood spread beneath him, an ominous, dark red that soaked into the asphalt and stained my fatigues.

Sam's eyes followed the sound of shots beyond the perimeter as Marines pursued the sniper. Two Hueys flew a tight circle as they fired into the brush.

Lopez pursed his lips. "Pray for a miracle, Master Chief."

Anguish twisted Sam's face, and he cried out for Frank. "Where's Frank? Frank? Frank? Wipe my eyes, Master Chief. I can't see."

I had to wipe my own eyes before wiping Sam's. There was nothing I could do for him but hold him and tell him I loved him and not to die. "Hang in there, Sam. Don't leave me. Don't you die on me, Sam. Don't you dare die on me."

"Okay, Master Chief, I'll try." He coughed again. Blood bubbled from his mouth, dribbled down his chin and onto his neck.

"Master Chief. Take my necklace and the medallion…give them to Little Lucy. My boy …. My boy … Tom … has the other …. I haven't seen my boy … since he was a baby."

The medallion flashed in the sunlight as I removed the necklace.

"Not since …. I'm sorry … I'm sorry …. I couldn't … take care of him. She died, Susanna died and … they said they would take care of him …. They said they would take care of him …."

His voice drifted away as he drifted into delirium.

"Susanna?"

I think I fell in love with you this morning, dear lady.
You think you did? Are you not sure? Perhaps we should try again. Shall we meet for an apple in the morning?
I had already planned to meet you for an apple tomorrow. And the next day, and the next, and the next, and every day until…
Every day until what?
Every day until you marry me?
That is a question I am not quite prepared to answer. Let me ask you a question.
Okay. Yes. I will marry you.

What will you have, silly boy?
A glass of Rioja, lovely lady.
Crianza? Reserva?
Gran Reserva. I want to celebrate that you didn't return to wherever you came from.
Barcelona.
That's my favorite city!
Oh! You know Barcelona?
No! But I'm going there with you.
Oh. I see. And when will this highly anticipated excursion take place?
I thought Spanish women had brown eyes.
I am not Spanish.
You're not Spanish?
I am not Spanish. I am Catalan.
That explains the green eyes?
Perhaps. Though my sister has brown eyes.
Is her hair also black as a starless night?
Of course.
I feel like I'm dreaming. I don't want to wake up.
Why not?
I have thought about you all day.
All day?
Yes... By the way, what is your name?
I am Susanna. But you may call me... Susanna.
I love the way your eyes crinkle when you're being silly. Will you tell me your name?
My name is Sam.
Sam. Hmmm, I think I will call you... Samuel. May I?
You must always call me Samuel, Susanna.
Will I tell you something, Samuel?
Yes, Susanna.
I knew you when you entered the room. I turned so you would not see my smile.

He lifted his arm and whispered, "Susanna."

Sam blinked against the tears falling on his face. They dotted the dust on his cheek and dribbled to his chin where they clung for a moment trembling before dropping away. He moved his lips but made no sound. He moved his lips again. They were dry and cracked.

"It's okay, Sam," I said. "You did the right thing. She would have wanted it that way. It's okay."

"Yes. I did the right thing …. Susanna would have …." He coughed, a dying rattle in his throat. "I'm thirsty, Master Chief."

"Sure, Sam." I pulled the canteen from my belt and loosened the cap. I brought the canteen to his lips, but he wouldn't drink. I set the canteen down and brushed my fingers through my friend's bright red hair. I caressed his cheek.

"You did the right thing, Sam. You did the right thing. You did the right thing. Don't die, Sam. Please don't die."

Sam stared past me, his eyes fixed on the vanishing point of light. The flow of blood dribbling from the corner of his mouth had slowed.

"Frank is dead, Chip …. What am I going … to tell Marie?"

I'm leaving Spain, Susanna. I'll be away for a year.
I know. You told me you wouldn't be here forever.
I wish I could stay. I don't want to leave you. You've made this a home for us.
It won't be the same without you. I'll miss lying next to you, shielded from the sea spray that blows in the window. I won't be able to bury my face in your pillow and breathe you in. I'll wake up every morning at five, but I won't be able to watch you dress for work. I won't feel your lips brush across my forehead before I turn and wrap my arms around your neck and hold you until you kiss me and tell me you must go.
I'll wake up every morning at five and feel you next to me from seven thousand miles away.
I'm going to set my clock to yours so we wake up together.
You won't return to Barcelona? You'll stay here?
Yes. I'll wait for your return.
I'm glad. You make me so happy, you know, staying here while I'm away. I love our little bungalow. I wish we could stay here forever.
Forever is a long time.
Forever isn't long enough for me to love you, Susanna.
I'll love you beyond forever, Samuel.

Book Six

Olongapo, Philippines

1991

Chapter Twenty-Nine

Tom

The Victory Liner carrying Aida and me back from Bataan sped through the countryside, bouncing side-to-side on the rough road, belching black clouds of diesel smoke every time the driver shifted gears. At frequent intervals along National Highway, children in blue and white school clothes waited for jeepneys to carry them to school. Between those intervals, carabao seeking relief from the blazing heat wallowed in mud-holes lining the edge of the jungle, a jungle not long removed from the horror and bloodshed of World War II.

The Kodak moments whizzed by, unseen, as my thoughts lay elsewhere and my camera lay unused in its case. The bus lurched as it hit a pothole. I rubbed my eyes and looked around. A woman on the other side of the bus crossed herself. The bus had passed a church. I leaned back. I'd asked Aida once why people crossed themselves. She explained that, to Catholics, it was a sign of respect when passing churches, funerals, even roadside markers for victims of vehicle accidents. She had asked me if Americans crossed themselves.

"Not that I know of."

Aida had remarked, "Oh, maybe Americans always in a hurry and don't see out the window even when they looking."

Aida dozed against my shoulder, her breathing a soft purr in my ear. The even rise and fall of her chest might have indicated a dreamless sleep, or a pleasant dream. She wrinkled her nose at a fly buzzing around her head. She stirred but didn't wake when I waved the fly away. She looked innocent and vulnerable in her sleep, and beautiful too. My heart leaped at the depth of tenderness I felt for her. The visit to her village, seeing her family and friends, the drowsy bus ride all combined to relax her. Happiness had smoothed the worry from her face and replaced it with contentment. *Is she dreaming? If so, they must be happy dreams to bring such a sweet smile to her lips.*

I had always felt tenderness for Aida, but always questioned my love for her. Fear of ridicule for marrying a barmaid, a prostitute in some people's mind, plagued me too. I believed her when she said she never took a man's money. She dated men because she liked them, and if they slept together—were American women prostitutes because they slept with the men they dated? I disliked judgmental people like Kenny and others who poured scorn and opprobrium on those who saw through external appearances to the soul inside the person. A person often beat down by life but urged on by a spirit that refused to give up. When refusing to give up meant performing work that others found abhorrent and beneath contempt. I knew Aida's story. She had refused to give up. She had worked as a barmaid to support her family and to meet a Sailor who might take her to America with him. She could provide better support for her family from America. I knew Aida viewed me as her ticket to a better life, and I didn't fault her for that. People everywhere looked for someone who could help them, lift them up, give them a fresh start. Some people weren't honest about it. Aida had never hidden what she wanted from me: love and a better life.

"Honey ko. What you are thinking?"

"Oh, nothing much, Aida. I'm just thinking about life and the universe. That's all."

"Okay. Think about me too, a little, okay?" She nestled her face into my neck, her lips pressed against me.

I smiled at her words. *If she only knew.* I rubbed her shoulder and hugged her. *Maybe she does know.*

She had once told me the things she observed in me: insecurity and indecisiveness. I sensed she kept others to herself. I had told my friends that Aida had me wrapped around her little finger, and they had laughed and called me pussy-whipped, and I had laughed with them at the truth in her words. But I could not shake the fear.

I could not shake the fear that always weighed on my mind. The fear of committing myself. Aida believed others caused my indecisiveness with their remarks about barmaids. But I worried over the strength of my commitment to Aida, not Aida's work. I had always believed marriage the natural course when two people loved each other, but I hesitated at the thought of binding myself to one woman for the rest of my life. I believed marriage was forever, that marriage vows were not to be taken lightly. What if Aida wasn't the right woman, though? What if we married after all and I realized I didn't love her? What would I do then? What about other women? What if I wasn't ready to give them up? I was young and might regret marrying too soon. I didn't want to grow old wondering what I had missed. I wanted to know marrying was the right decision. If Aida were the one, I wanted to feel it in my heart. I wanted to know without reservation that she was the one. I wanted Aida to be my Susanna, my meant-to-be-from-birth love.

Those thoughts were the old ones. They had plagued my restless sleep as thoughts and dreams. I had found my Susanna, my meant-to-be-from-birth love. Aida was not her. Susanna represented the past, a glorious past; Sasi represented the future, a glorious future. Aida linked the two as a softening agent for the cold, hard heart I had thrown up as a defense against another hurt as terrible as Susanna's death. I knew that now and felt as though I had known it all along.

The conductor rose from his seat and changed the movie on the television mounted behind the driver's seat to *Missing in Action*. I had seen the movie dozens of times, but a Vietnamese actress reminded me of Sasi, and I watched for a while. I soon drifted off, waking again when the bus slowed for the exit to the bus station in Balanga. I nudged Aida awake and retrieved our bags from the rack above the seat.

"We have a couple hours to kill before our next bus, Aida. Let's get something to drink. There's a refreshment stand in the terminal."

"Okay, Tommy. Anyway, I'm thirsty. I want iced tea."

I carried the bags into the terminal.

"Hey. What are you two doing here?" I called to Phil and Lucy who were studying the departure schedule above the ticket counter.

"Hey, guys," Phil said. "We're heading back to Olongapo. I thought you were going back tomorrow."

"We decided to head back today instead of rushing around at the last minute. I hate coming back from a trip and going to work the next day. Our bus leaves in a little over two hours. Looks like we'll ride back together. Do you and Lucy want to join us for a drink?"

"Sure, why not?"

We ordered drinks at a table on the sidewalk beneath a red and white umbrella that deflected the scorching rays of the midday sun. I tipped the waiter who bowed and said, "Salamat." We sipped our drinks with gasping relief while making small talk and passing the time.

I slurped the last of my tea through the straw and signaled for another round. The waiter set the drinks down, then scurried off to wait on another table. The sun was sinking below the brim of the umbrella, and Aida was squinting.

"Tommy, move the umbrella, please. The sun is in my eyes."

"Sure, Aida. Hang on." I turned and lowered the umbrella to block the sun. "How's that?"

"Thank you, honey ko. That's better."

"God, it's hot out here," I said. "It wasn't bad on the bus with the breeze coming through the windows."

Phil nodded. "Yeah. We baked at the resort too. We practically lived in the hotel pool. Have you been there?"

"The pool?"

"No. The resort."

"Oh. Which one?"

"Mariveles."

"Mariveles? No. We've been meaning to go, but we usually go to Baguio or Manila. I like the quiet of Baguio and the excitement of Manila. Besides, Grande Island is as good as a resort for me."

"You and Aida ought to come with us next time. Maybe she'd like something different from Grande Island."

"How about it, Aida? Would you like to spend a weekend at the Mariveles Resort?"

"Okay, yes. I go there many times, but I will go with you. Let me know, and I will tell my family to expect us so we can have a picnic together with them."

"Hey, that's a great idea. Aida's dad has a couple of banca boats. He's a fisherman. Maybe he'll take us out and we can spearfish for the picnic."

"Sounds good to me. Lucy? What do you think?"

"I would love to. I'd like to meet Aida's family."

"There. Done deal." Phil finished his tea and signaled the waiter for another round. "Who else needs another tea? Tom?"

The girls declined, and the waiter brought two more and a dish of peanuts for them to snack on.

Phil paid the waiter. "How was the visit? Were Aida's parents happy to see you?" Lucy and Aida stood and began to walk away. "Hey, where are you two going?"

"To the sari-sari store. We'll be right back."

"Okay. We have plenty of time."

"Yep. They fawned over her, of course, and made me feel welcome. All four of her brothers were there and her two sisters still live at home. The house is so small I don't know how they all fit under one roof. But we had fun, and we ate all day long. Neighbors kept calling and bringing more food, people stayed on, playing mahjong all night, and the beer never stopped flowing. If you think keg parties at the Bowdoinham Ranch were something, you've never experienced a weekend-long party in a Filipino village. If we hadn't slept at Aida's grandmother's, we wouldn't have slept at all. People kept wanting to drink with me."

"Did her folks ask if you were going to marry Aida?"

I paused while the waiter cleared away empty glasses. "Aida told them. I had the feeling the weekend was a bridal shower without anyone explicitly saying so. Half the village wanted photos with me, and the other half wanted photos of Aida and me with their kids. I never held so many kids in my lap. I'm probably godfather to a hundred kids by now. I hope I don't have to buy them Christmas presents."

"Will you marry Aida, Tom?"

I shook my head. "No, Phil. What happened in Thailand showed me I couldn't question my motives in marrying Aida. I had to be sure I wanted to marry her or call it off. If I knew beyond a shadow of a doubt that I loved her, I would marry her. But I don't and I can't. I know she wants to go to the States, but I can't marry a woman for a reason like that. I wouldn't respect myself or Aida if I did. There can be no love in a relationship that lacks respect."

The last few words I spoke in a raised voice as two buses pulled in and bled off their air brakes. The sound of hundreds of people filing off the buses and gathering their belongings filled the terminal while the sound of a hundred more lining up to board echoed around Phil and me. A teeming mass of humanity, most brown, a few white, shoulders bowed under the pressures of life and love. Two languages expressing the same thoughts.

Lucy and Aida bounded up to the table, chattering away in Tagalog. Phil and I stood to meet them. Phil looked over Aida's head at me and said, "What did you say?"

"I said there can be no love in a relationship that lacks respect."

Chapter Thirty

Tom

I jumped from the jeepney and ran up the sidewalk. I could barely contain my joy: my request to re-enlist and stay in Hawaii had been approved. That meant another tour of sea duty and two more deployments. The gate squealed as I opened it. I pushed the brick aside and opened the front door and took the steps three at a time, meeting Aida on the landing. She frowned but, heck, I always sounded like an elephant when I ran up the stairs.

"Hey, Aida. I have good news. I get to stay in Hawaii for another three years."

"Who Lek?"

My scalp tingled at Lek's name. For a moment, I lost the ability to form words. I brushed my hand through my hair and down the back of my neck, a nervous habit probably intended to buy time to come up with a believable lie. Aida stared, her eyes red and puffy, and her lips pressed into a thin line. My mind whirled as I stammered and tried to make sense of the black hole I found myself in.

I made like I hadn't heard her. "What? Who is who?"

"I said, who Lek?" She spoke each word deliberately. "How she knows you in Thailand?"

My brain scrambled in a desperate search for something to say. How had Aida learned about Lek? From George? Bob? Don? It wouldn't have been Alex, I was sure of that, and certainly not Mark. Both were good friends, all the guys were, but …. No, it would not have been them. I knew them too well. It had to have been someone else, but who?

"I waiting."

Pain showed in Aida's eyes. I could see how deeply she hurt, how embarrassed, how betrayed. My presence made her feel ridiculous, as though I were laughing at her stupidity and blindness. In her mind, I was openly parading another woman in front of the world so the world could laugh at her too.

"Lek?"

"Lek."

I had done nothing with Lek a girlfriend could take fault with except buy her dinner. But I had done that with the intent of telling her about Aida. Lek had wanted to make love, but I had stopped her. However, Aida wouldn't believe a word I said no matter how hard I protested my innocence. It would have been different had she asked me who Sasi was. At least then I could have spoken the truth instead of lying my way out of trouble.

"Ohhh. Lek. She works at the club the guys and I used to go to. We went there after work to unwind. Why do you ask? Did one of the guys tell you about her?" I half expected Aida to flourish a butterfly knife while screaming, "You butterfly me? Hey? Hey?"

I tried to sound nonchalant, but my voice and burning ears gave me away. She knew something had happened in Thailand, and she wanted an explanation. She wanted me to tell her it was all a mistake, that I had angered this woman somehow, perhaps snubbed her advances, and this was her revenge. Which was exactly what had happened, but Aida wouldn't believe it, no matter how much she wanted to. Something drastic loomed on the horizon. Lies would not help, and pleading turned my stomach.

"No. She send me this."

Aida held out several sheets of a letter. Her hand was steady, but her face contorted as she held back the tears. How in the world had Lek gotten hold of the address? Who would give it to her? None of the guys would have. The only people at the hotel to see Lek had been the staff, the maids and front desk clerks. I recalled the dirty looks from the good-looking front desk clerk. She must have given Lek the address. No. That couldn't be it. I had left the squadron address in the hotel register, not Aida's. Oh no. The letter. Aida's letter. I had left it at the front desk to go out with the mail. The good-looking desk clerk must have given it to Lek.

"She said you slept with her. She said she didn't know about me, or she would not go with you. She said she slept with you last year too, and that you promised to marry her. Why you butterfly on me, hey? Hey? Why? Why you cheat on me? I haven't cheated on you since all the time we have known each other. What you got to say? What? I know you going to lie to me, like you lie to them.

Also, now I want to know, you got a girlfriend in Japan too? And Hong Kong too? Probably you do, eh? And Hawaii? Why you butterfly on me, Tommy? Why? Why I'm not good enough for you? I know how Sailors are. You think because I a barmaid I sleep with the guys all the time. That is a lie. I don't sleep with any guys but you since all the way to last year. But you do. You sleep with all the girls. What other girls in Olongapo are you sleeping with? When you stay to the barracks, do you sleep with a girl there too?"

"Aida, we're not married. What if I did sleep with another woman while away from you? I never slept with other women here. Are you telling me you never slept with other guys while I was back in Hawaii? Besides, I didn't sleep with Lek this time. I slept with her last year. She wrote that because I told her you and I are getting married and I couldn't see her again. I didn't even want to see her, but I had to tell her about us. I couldn't just walk away without saying goodbye. That's the truth, Aida."

She spoke as though she had not heard me. Her voice grew soft, the words painted with sincerity, but framed in hurt.

"No, Tom. I don't have other guys when you are in Hawaii. I'm faithful to you the whole time, but you are not faithful to me. How many Filipina do you sleep with? Are they my friends?"

"I never slept around, Aida. I've been faithful to you since we committed to each other last year."

Her eyes filled with tears. She didn't speak, but stood before me, innocent, on the high ground, out of my reach, a righteous soul spurned by a soulless lover. I had hurt her, but for something done long ago, before we became a couple. She didn't care. She believed I had cheated on her; that's all that mattered. I had made her feel worthless, a joke, provincial, unwanted, ugly.

I would always remember Aida's appearance at that moment and the truth she didn't know yet. I would hurt her soon, destroy her dream, her brightening life, and I would hate myself for it. The realization of what I was about to do hit me between the eyes. My heart seemed to grow in my chest, and a sob caught in my throat. I was filled with shame as I fought back tears. I was going back to Sasi. Wasn't I?

Through all of this, barely registering in my brain, Yoshi barked while other neighborhood animals squealed and squawked. The neighborhood sounded like a farm. The floor seemed to move, but it didn't register in my brain as my mind churned over Aida and Sasi.

Inexplicably, the passion I had once felt for Aida returned. I wanted to take her in my arms, press her to me, hug her tight, and tell her how sorry I was for the hurt and pain I had caused her. I took a step toward her, mouth open to plead with her, to tell her I loved her, only her. The low-toned, rising rumble made me stop. I tensed as the apartment began to shake. Pictures fell and crashed on the floor, their glass frames shattering in the rumbling, hellish noise of the earthquake. Aida's eyes widened and she cried out as the room shook. She braced herself against the sofa. Dishes fell from the counter. Yoshi barked non-stop as he ran back and forth between the stair landing and Aida and me. A woman's scream ripped through the window, jarring my nerves. The floor lifted and rolled like an ocean swell. Was this it?

"We have to get out of here, Aida. Come. Outside." I grabbed her arm, but she resisted and pulled away.

"Come on, Aida. Let's go. It's too dangerous to stay here, sweetheart."

"No. You go. I go by myself. Here, take the letter from your girlfriend."

She threw the letter at me, its sheets fluttering to the floor.

"And I not your honey ko."

She ran into the bedroom, returning a moment later with her purse, the swimming pool postcards, and the ring I had bought for her birthday from the Navy Exchange catalog. She slipped into her street shoes. Then, for some odd reason, she ran to the bathroom and returned, stuffing a hand towel into the pocket of her jeans. She ignored my pleas and ran down the stairs, Yoshi close on her heels. I ran after her but stopped and ran back. The rolling motion threw me side to side as I dashed into the bedroom, ran to the nightstand, and retrieved the silk pouch from the drawer. I took out the necklace and looped it around my neck, then ran after Aida. The gate squealed like a stuck pig.

I ran into the street, avoiding places where the sidewalk buckled and debris blocked my path. The earthquake stopped and I hesitated, unsure when another would hit, unsure what to do. I picked my way along, keeping clear of already-flimsy buildings teetering on the edge of collapse. Another earthquake rumbled through. An aftershock? I looked for an ash plume but didn't see one. Pinatubo hadn't blown. Aftershocks continued and the damage increased. The streets were a tangled mess of abandoned cars and jeepneys. Power lines and telephone poles ripped from their foundations lay crisscrossed in the streets. Electrical power had gone out, which would only add to the misery. Animals roamed everywhere. People crowded the streets, some bleeding, some crying and wailing, many in shock. Children screamed for their parents. I stood out of the way as a group of Sisters from the Catholic church marched along, collecting children, and herding them to safety. Sailors and Marines from the base added to the growing number of volunteers and first responders rushing to help those in need. Fire trucks pushed their way through vehicles blocking the road, clearing a lane for ambulances. Bargirls clustered in groups, clinging to one another.

The last big earthquake—there had been three and several aftershocks—had died away by the time I reached the base. I didn't have to wait for someone to send for me; all hands returned to base immediately in the event of an emergency. As I passed through the gate and approached the taxi stand, Phil called to me from the duty truck. He asked if Aida were okay.

"I hope so, Phil. I lost her in the commotion. I ran back into the apartment to get something, and when I returned, she had disappeared."

"Go back and look for her. The duty officer sent me here to muster the guys who stay off base. There are enough people at the hangar to take care of everything. They don't want more people getting in the way. Just make sure you're at work on time tomorrow. They're also evacuating all but two aircraft to Okinawa and Guam until the volcano danger subsides. I'll get word to you if you're on one of the flyaway crews."

"I have to find Aida, Phil. Ask the Chief to let me stay rather than fly away. If I can't find her today, I'll stay at the apartment tonight, if it's still standing. I'll be on time tomorrow."

"I'll do what I can. I don't think they'll lack volunteers to fly away. Good luck."

I headed back into town without a clue where Aida may have gone. Possibly to Cora's house. I'd look there first. My shirt clung to me in the humidity, the fear, the worry. God, it was hot. The sweat rolled off the tip of my nose in big warm drops.

Someone called my name as I passed Mariposa's. Mama-san. I wiped the sweat off my face and went to her.

"Tom. Where is Aida? Is she all right?"

"I don't know, Mama-san. We were in the apartment when the earthquake struck. I lost her when she ran outside. I'm just coming from the base. I had to check in."

"Where are you going now? To look for her? Would you like help? The other girls might know where to look."

"I'm going to Cora's. Aida would have gone there first."

"Come with me. You look thirsty. I will give you some water. Come."

I followed Mama-san to Rufadora's. Her concern touched my heart, and I was grateful for her friendship.

"Please come back and tell me when you have found her."

"I will, Mama-san. Thank you for the water." I reached out to take her hand, but she took me in her arms instead. She hugged me tight, not speaking for a moment. Her gesture, extended from fright or relief, bewildered me. I didn't know what to say, so I stood still, somewhat embarrassed.

"You must call me by my name, Tom. Marie. Marie Elizabeth Taneo Bailey. My husband is Frank Bailey, a retired Sailor. You have not met him, but you will soon when he returns from the States. You will be here, yes? You are not returning to Hawaii yet?"

"As far as I know, Mama … Marie, I'll be here." I pushed away. "Please. Let me go. I have to find Aida."

Chapter Thirty-One

Tom

The aftershocks rattled my nerves. Night would fall soon, and I was anxious to find Aida. I didn't want her spending the night alone and exposed if she were hurt. I retraced my steps until I came to the market, where I turned toward Cora's place. I uttered a prayer that I would find her there.

Crumbled plaster covered the floors of Cora's apartment building. Displaced concrete blocks, some whole, some shattered, littered the area. It was eerily quiet for a building usually filled with the laughter of children. They must have evacuated to one of the nearby shelters. I banged the door knocker several times. No answer. I banged it again, louder, then tried the doorknob: unlocked. I wrenched the door open and called up the dark stairwell.

"Aida? Cora? Anyone home?"

Silence. I fought a surge of panic as I climbed the stairs and walked through the rooms. Where could she be? Plaster had fallen from the walls, and shattered glass lay strewn about the rooms. I picked up a crucifix and placed it on its wall hook. In the kitchen, cupboard doors hung ajar. Cora had been eating when the quake struck: food was scattered among broken dishes. I walked through the rooms again and left, disappointed with myself for not remaining with Aida. Back on the street, I considered my next move. She hadn't gone to Rufadora's, and she wasn't at Cora's. She had friends nearby, but none as close to her as Cora; if she had gone anywhere, it would have been to Cora's. Where else might she have gone?

Home? Would she have gone back to her village? Maybe. Were the buses operating? Lamao was further from the volcano; she and Cora may have gone home thinking it would be safer, or they might have gone home to check on their families. I had to be at work early the next morning. That didn't give me much time. There would be hell to pay if I was late for work. I cursed again. No. I couldn't Where else could she have gone? I racked my brain. Think, think. Where is she? Only one thing made sense. I must go back to Bataan.

I bought a ticket at the bus station and settled into a seat. As soon as the driver arrived, we left the station and headed east for Bataan. I was nervous, and it showed in my rapid foot-tapping. The passenger next to me, agitated by the earthquakes, asked me to stop shaking my leg, couldn't I see it bothered others, the constant knocking? I apologized but couldn't help myself. I continued to tap and shake, catching myself and stopping and starting up again. *Aida, Aida, Aida. Where are you, sweetheart? Please be in Lamao. Please.*

Another earthquake struck as the bus left town and turned onto the highway. A cry rose among the passengers, but most rode it out in silent fear. A man across the aisle held his two young children tight as the bus shook, at one point pressing his forehead to theirs. Poor guy. I wondered where their mother was? When the bus stopped, I rose and took the empty seat across from the man, and had the boy sit next to me. The father nodded over the daughter's head.

"Salamat."

"You're welcome," I said. I smiled at the little girl to reassure her, and she smiled back. The little boy looked at me, calmly sucking his thumb.

We'd change buses in Balanga about an hour away. I settled back, resting my head against the window. I loved the long bus rides. Yes, it was hot, but I usually fell in and out of a light sleep while Aida dozed against my shoulder.

I missed that. The expression seemed such a small thing, but held such significance. By leaning on me, Aida showed she trusted me, depended on me, wanted to touch and feel me. I became protective of her when she dozed with my arm around her. The gesture was part instinct, sure, but more than that, it showed a tenderness on my part. Some might say it demonstrated ownership, possession, domination, but those people were probably lonely and angry, and didn't understand the giving and receiving nature of relationships. When I enclosed Aida in my arms, she snuggled against me, trying to move deeper into my arms, trying to cover more of her body with mine. She wanted to feel more of me, to feel she was a part of me, and I wanted to hold as much of her as he could.

Our lovemaking was the same way. I wanted to press as much of myself against her as I could, to feel as much of her as possible. I wanted to touch all of her at one time. As our relationship developed and deepened, sexual desire transformed from a frenzied, lust-filled sport, to one of passion, romance, emotional embrace. Making love had become more than having sex, more than a goal. It had become the ultimate demonstration of love: to melt into one another as a single being, to possess one another not from ownership or domination, but to feel two hearts beating together, to mingle body to body, soul to soul. Why had I not understood that? Why had I not realized Aida was the one woman who made me feel a part of her? She was my friend and companion, not just a lover. I knew now why I always came home to Aida. She was my home. If only I could find her and tell her.

The dispatch radio crackled to life in a burst of static and broken words. The driver listened for a moment before picking up the microphone and speaking. I didn't understand Tagalog, but the man with the kids frowned as the speaking continued. He crossed himself as the driver hung up the mike and spoke to the passengers. The man with the kids translated for me. "Radio man say bus accident nearby, and tell driver he must go and help take passengers to the bus station in Balanga."

"Which bus? Is it from Olongapo?"

The man questioned the driver, both speaking back and forth while my foot tapped an impatient drumroll against the floor. *What are they talking about?*

"Okay. Driver say a bus leaving Olongapo before this bus. He says there are many injuries. Police and ambulance go there to help. We will take okay passengers to Balanga. You know someone in Balanga?"

My nerves, already frazzled from the earthquake and the fight with Aida, nearly snapped when I heard the bus came from Olongapo. Aida would likely be on it if she had decided to go home. I hoped not, but I hoped she was too. I couldn't stand the uncertainty of not knowing where she was. I trembled as I answered the man. "No. Yes—I mean, no, not in Balanga, in Bataan, a village in Bataan, Lamao."

"You okay? Your face is white like paper."

"I don't know. I think my girlfriend may be on that bus."

"Ohh, I so sorry. I hope she is not there. Your girlfriend is Filipina?"

"Yes."

"She work in Olongapo?"

"Yes."

"Ohh. You American Sailor?"

"Yes."

"Ohh. Station dito?"

"No. Stationed in Hawaii, but deployed here with VP squadron."

"Ohh. You BP Sailor."

"Yes. My girlfriend, Aida, like the... well, we had a fight today, and I think she went to see her parents in Lamao."

"Ohh. She will be okay. You will see. I am Bernard Pancho. My son is Ray and my daughter, Mila. What is your name?"

"Tom. I'm happy to meet you, Bernard." I smiled and shook Bernard's hand. His friendly manner put me at ease. I liked the man. His open face carried a broad smile reflected in his children's faces.

"Tom." Bernard held out a paper sack. "You are hungry? You eat balut? We got plenty." Bernard looked earnestly at me, but the kids appeared to be wondering if the American would be mean enough to eat their snack.

I politely declined and pushed the sack away, telling Bernard, "No, thank you. I ate before we left the station."

"Okay. Hey, we arriving at bus crash. Look there."

The bus eased out of a curve into a broad, open plain of dry fields and pastures. The bus driver slowed at the direction of a policeman and pulled onto the shoulder. Police cars and rescue vehicles lined both sides of the road, ambulances jammed in among them. People wandered around trying to get a glimpse of the overturned bus at the bottom of the ravine. They reminded me of moths circling a light. I couldn't see the bus, but the crowd stood at the edge of the road, peering down. I had to see for myself.

I left my seat and walked forward. The driver, talking to a policeman through his window, opened the doors. I left the bus and joined the crowd, pushing my way to the front, dreading what I might find. I brushed my hand through my hair and down the back of my neck. I was trembling again and clenched my teeth as I stepped from the crowd to peer below. My heart fell. The bus lay on its roof in a shallow stream at the bottom of the ravine, leaning against a huge boulder that must have stopped its roll. Bus seats, clothes, and suitcases littered the scene. Bodies lay everywhere, some moving, some still. Passengers, bloodied and in shock, sat on the ground as rescuers attended them. A line of stretchers covered with sheets lay ready to receive the wounded, and the dead whose loved ones cried and hugged their lifeless bodies.

My heart beat loud in my ears. I didn't see Aida. A hand touched my shoulder. I whipped around. "Aida!"

It was Bernard. "Come, Tom. I take you. We go down and look for Aida." Bernard took me by the hand and led me down the hill. "We will find her. She will be okay. You will see."

At the bottom of the ravine, a few yards from the bus, I stopped and picked up a swimming pool postcard. I had mailed it from the Singapore Marriott the previous year. Why did she grab this? I put the postcard in my back pocket and walked around the front of the bus. Among the wounded passengers, a few feet from a narrow stream that flowed through the ravine, I saw her. I clenched my fists and took a deep breath, blinking through tears. Bernard squeezed my shoulder as I knelt next to Aida, her battered body lying on a pink blanket. Blood covered her face, and shards of glass glittered in her hair. Her bloodied clothes were ripped, and she had lost a shoe. I reached out a trembling hand and caressed her gray face. Her lips moved in a faint whisper.

"Tommy."

"I'm here, Aida."

"Tommy?"

Her eyes opened long enough to see it was me. She tried to rise, but the effort spent her, and she fell back crying.

"Oh, Tommy. I'm sorry I got mad to you. I'm sorry. Oh, please forgive me. Don't leave me, honey ko. Don't leave me."

"Oh, Aida. No, no, sweetheart. Oh, no Aida. I'm sorry. I'm the one who should be sorry, Aida. Not you. Oh, my dear, I'm sorry for hurting you. I'm sorry for accusing you. I'm sorry for not trusting you, Aida. Oh, sweetheart, I've treated you so badly. Please forgive me, sweetheart. You've done nothing wrong. Oh, honey. I am so sorry."

She struggled to rise. I put my arms around her, pulling her to my chest. I rocked back and forth while she cried in my arms.

Bernard's children came chattering and laughing from the bus, carrying water and towels. Bernard shushed them and took the towels and water. He moistened a towel and dabbed Aida's face. She had several scratches and a large bruise on her right cheek. Cora appeared, bloodied and bruised, but walking, and took the towel from him.

"Oh, Aida. I am so glad you are not hurt. I tried to wake you after the bus crashed, but you are knocked out. Is your head hurting now?"

"Thank you, Cora. Yes. I have a headache. I'm thirsty, though. Please, can I have a drink of water?"

"Of course. Here. Drink slowly. No, no, not too fast." Aida guzzled the bottle to Cora's horror. "Aiii. Stop, Aida, or you will get sick."

"Ohh, that's better now. I feel okay. When do we go? Do they take me to the hospital? I want to go home, back to Olongapo. I'll see my family later. Are you okay, Cora?"

"Yes. The bus crash was scary. I am awake the whole time. We tumbled down and rolled over until the bus crashed against the boulder. I thought you are dead, Aida."

I looked around for a paramedic or policeman. "Let me see if they will let you go." I returned moments later with a medical technician. "The police said you can leave if the technician okays it."

The medical technician listened to Aida's heart, shined a light in her eyes, and asked her to follow his finger. He felt her ribs and looked over her scratches and bruises. Satisfied, he said she could go. He gave her instructions to cope with head and body aches and told her to drink a lot of water. After leaving her name and address with the police, she and Cora collected their belongings and, together with me and Bernard and his kids, took seats on the bus, waiting for the drive to Balanga, where we could board a bus back to Olongapo and home.

Back in the apartment, I cleaned up what little damage there was while Aida rested. Stiff and sore from the accident, she could barely bend over. I helped her out of her clothes.

"Lie back, Aida, so I can pull your jeans off." I unfastened her jeans, but she laughed and moved away, the jeans stuck at her hips. "Hold still, Aida." I tugged at the jeans. "Aida, why are you laughing?"

"Because you are tickling me, honey ko. Hahaha. Ohhh, stop, Tommy, stop. It tickles. Hahaha." She giggled and tried to avoid my fingers as they ran along her legs, pulling her jeans down.

"Oww. Ohh, it hurts when I laugh. Oh, stop it, stop it. Hahahaha! Tommy!"

"Aida."

"Yes, Tommy."

"You were so beautiful in your green and white uniform when we met, even though it looked like a tablecloth."

"Oh, honey ko, that so mean to say. But it did look like a tablecloth. I will put it on if you like me to."

"Maybe later. Come. I'll help you in the shower."

We both looked up as another earthquake shook the room.

I took her hands and helped her up. "I wonder how long this will go on."

"I don't know, but I think Bacobaco is angry."

"Bacobaco?"

"That's the name Pilipinos give Pinatubo so long ago. They say a giant sea turtle escaped from hunters and buried itself in the top of Pinatubo. She threw rocks and boulders at the hunters until she escaped inside the mountain."

"Well, I hope nobody gets hurt when Bacobaco erupts. Come, Aida."

Neither of us could see the magma eruptions occurring on Bacobaco. We couldn't see through the jungle and across the mountains to the great volcano to the northeast. Bacobaco was biding her time. She grumbled now and then, sending earthquakes in every direction, seemingly warning Filipinos she was awake and ready to burst, and they should flee to safety. Phreatic eruptions had begun as rising magma caused water to evaporate into steam, the resulting effect an explosion of steam, ash, rock, and volcanic bombs. Bacobaco inflated as magma rose toward the surface, building a dome within her crater. When she could wait no longer, when the bowels of Earth miles below her surface had fed all the magma her bloated belly could hold, Bacobaco would erupt in a tremendous fury of molten lava and a deadly wall of hot, suffocating gas and ash.

We showered together. I washed Aida, glad when her back was to me so she couldn't see me weeping at her bruised body. I regretted being the cause of so much pain, both mental and physical, and putting her through so much anguish. She chattered away like a little girl while I soaped and washed her. I washed her hair, careful of the bits of glass she had not been able to brush out earlier. The water ran red with blood before finally clearing. I applied shampoo and worked it in with my fingers, careful not to hurt her.

"Tommy, you can wash harder. You won't hurt me. I can barely feel your fingers."

"Okay. I'm just being careful."

"I know. I like when you wash my hair. It feels like a massage to my head." Aida closed her eyes and let her head fall forward, the hot water falling on her neck. "Ohhh, this feels so good, Tommy. I will sleep good tonight."

I dried Aida off and helped her dress. She was hungry, so I seated her at the kitchen table and brought her a glass of water and a plate of rice and pork. I was making my own plate when I heard a scratching at the front door. I ran down and turned the knob as Yoshi pushed the door open with his nose and ran upstairs.

"Yoshi!" It was good to see the handsome fellow. I gave him a bowl of rice and chicken and then sat with Aida while she ate, turning over in my mind what I had to tell her.

"Aida."

She stared into the distance as she chewed her food. Life had returned to the city, people chattered as they passed on the street, and birds chirped in the trees in the courtyard. Now and then, Yoshi barked, at what, I didn't know. It was good to be home, though, no matter what happened next.

I repeated her name. "Aida."

"Yes, Tommy?" She looked at her plate when she spoke.

"Aida, I didn't realize how much you meant to me until I lost you in the earthquake. When I saw you lying on the ground, I thought I would die if you weren't okay. I thought about all the times I held you in my arms, and we made love, and you kissed me and told me you loved me, and I realized you do love me, not because I can take you to America, but because I am me, that you love me for who I am. I knew then that I didn't care what anybody else thinks, that it only matters what I think and what you think, what we think about each other."

"Tommy."

I waited, but she didn't speak.

"Yes, Aida."

"Tommy. I always wanted to go to America since I'm a little girl, but that's not why I love you. I don't care if I don't go to America. I only wanted you to love me and marry me. That's all I wanted, Tommy. I only always wanted you since we met in

Rufadora. Right when I see you the first time. You only mattered to me for loving me, Tommy."

"I remember the night we met like it was yesterday, Aida. Do you remember the night on Grande Island when I asked you to marry me?"

"No, Tommy."

"You don't remember?" Surprised, I wondered if she had hurt her head in the accident.

"Are you okay, Aida?"

"I remember, Tommy, but I won't marry you. You made me so happy when you asked me, but I cannot."

My heart fell. "But Aida, why not, sweetheart? Why not?

"Oh, Tommy. I know you are not sure you want to marry me. I know you think you love me, but I won't marry the man that doesn't know he loves me for true. I don't want you to marry me because you feel obligated or you feel sorry for me. I think you are wonderful to marry me even though you don't want to, but it isn't right, Tommy. Someday, you will regret it and then we will fight, and if we have kids, it will be hard on them too when we are getting a divorce."

Aida took my hands and clasped them to her chest. Her eyes told me she had made up her mind. They told me she loved me but understood my heart.

"No, Tommy. I would rather let you go now to be happy with someone else than marry me and we are unhappy."

Tears filled my eyes as my heart filled my chest. Every feeling I'd had for Aida since the day we met rushed into my heart. I thought it would break, but I knew it bled for Aida. Love for this beautiful, wonderful woman filled me. Love for the kindness, sensitivity, consideration, and perception of a woman sure of herself and her future.

"On the bus, before we crash, I know I cannot marry you," she said. "When I receive the letter from that woman, I understand your heart. I know other women know you before me and maybe you like them still. She, that woman, say the manager of the hotel where you stay likes you. She said you are always going to dinner and dancing and you go to her home."

"Yes, Aida, but to talk. That's all."

"It's okay, Tommy. I know you talk only. But, even yet, if you spend a lot of time with the other woman then maybe your heart isn't only true to me."

I sought for the right way to explain what I felt. What I said next had to be right.

"Do you remember what I told you about Susanna?"

"Yes."

"The hotel manager, Sasi, made me feel the way Susanna made me feel. I thought they were the same feelings, Aida, but they weren't."

Aida looked out the window while I spoke, but she turned now and looked at me, puzzled.

"I don't know what makes a man and woman fall in love, Aida. I don't know why when I met Susanna, I knew instantly that I loved her, but I did. When I met Sasi, I thought it was the same feeling, but it wasn't. I wanted it to be the same because Sasi reminded me of Susanna. They looked alike, they had the same strong personality, they had the same mischievous sense of humor. The similarities drew me to Sasi and began to soften my heart. In that way, falling in love with Sasi would give Susanna back to me."

I moved my chair closer until our knees touched, and I took Aida's hands. I leaned close to her.

"You began to soften my heart when we met, Aida, because you needed me. More than that, you loved me for myself. I knew you didn't love me only because I could take you away from here. But I was looking for Susanna, grieving for her. Grief takes a long time to go away, or at least ease enough to live with, and I had not reached the point where I could tuck it away and then pull it out when I wanted to remember. Because Susanna's death affected me so deeply, I couldn't give you the love that I needed to give you. Men and women must give love as well as receive it, but I couldn't, because I loved Susanna more than you. That made me question my love for you."

I paused, more to see how Aida reacted than anything else. She might have sensed I wanted her to say something. She looked up, first into my eyes, then off into the distance as though weighing her words. She might have wondered if she could believe me. I feared what she would say.

"I know, Tommy, and it hurt me when I tried to love you, even though you sometimes didn't want me to. I knew also you thought a lot of times about Susanna, and that made me cry, but I don't say nothing because I don't want to hurt you more."

"Oh, Aida. I'm sorry."

"It's okay. I think now maybe we are okay."

"You know, Aida. Falling for someone because they remind you of someone else is the wrong reason to love someone. I fell in love with you because I wanted your companionship, honey ko."

Tears rolled down her cheeks and I wiped them away, close to tears myself.

"When I saw your battered body lying in the ravine, I thought you were dead, and my heart broke. Oh, Aida. Sasi woke my heart. She brought it back from a cold, hard, unfeeling organ to a living, loving heart. Her similarity to Susanna made me hope she was the one, and I thought that was so, until I saw you hurt and bleeding. That's when I realized Sasi was the conduit through which all the love I had for Susanna finally found its way to you. But my heart wouldn't feel it until it broke for you. My love for you began the day we met, Aida, but I wasn't ready to call it love because I had not yet found a way for my heart to heal. Sasi did that for me. For us."

I clasped Aida's hands and kissed her fingers. "Susanna wasn't healing a broken heart. I had a whole heart to give her. I only have half a heart to give you because you already hold the other half. You hold the half of my heart that I buried with Susanna. Heal my heart completely, Aida. I want to grow old with you, and then I want to die before you because I couldn't bear to wake each day and not be able to brush my fingers through your hair and kiss you good morning."

Her eyes grew wide, and I wanted to dive into the womb of Aida's soul.

Book Seven

Olongapo, Philippines

1991

Chapter Thirty-Two

Tom

I leaned on the bar, rolling the bottle of San Miguel between my hands while Aida told the story of our shower together. The story amused Frank and Marie, but the graphic depiction embarrassed me. Aida slipped into heavily accented English in her excitement.

"Ohh, Tommy washing my hair 'cause still it has glass in it from the bus crash that I couldn't brush out with my brush, and I hope he don't getting a cut on his finger 'cause already dried blood is falling out of my hair in the shower, and now it's on the floor, and I'm not wearing shoes. Then Tommy, he's afraid to wash my hair too hard so he washes too soft so I tell him, 'Tommy, it's okay for you to wash harder or not all the blood is coming out and the glass too.' Oh. He so exasperating, but I smile 'cause he always like that anyway."

She paused, presenting an opportunity for escape. No one stirred. Aida took a deep breath and a sip of water and continued.

"And then Tommy, he so sweet, he say, 'Oh, Aida, I think I lose you in the earthquake when I can't find you,' and then he say he think he will die, himself, if he don't have a luck to find me when the bus crash, but then he find me and Bernard is with him. Tommy meet Bernard on the bus and his two children—we are all friends now, so nice, and Cora too—oh, I forget, she there with me, on the bus—then Tommy—do I tell you this already? Tommy say he think about when we making love before, and he holding me, and when he knowing he finally love me for true, and he don't care what other people thinking about us, he just wants to marry only me."

Marie waited a moment, as if expecting Aida to say more, then took her hands. "Oh, Aida. We are so happy for you. Frank and I wish you both the best."

Aida smiled demurely and looked at her lap. "Yes. Thank you."

"We will be happy to have you work here, but are you sure that is what you want?"

"Yes. I need a job and I like working here. I like to work for you and Frank until I go to Hawaii."

"Well, Tom, Aida," Frank said, raising his beer to us, "here's to your journey."

"Thanks, Frank. You and Marie have been so kind to us."

Marie jumped, startled by the rumble and the shaking of the walls. "Oh dear. Another eruption, and larger this time. They are almost continuous now, and the ash cloud has not gone away for several days. I fear the volcano will soon explode. I feel so sorry for all those poor people in the small villages. First the earthquakes and volcano, and now they are in danger from the typhoon, as well."

Frank pursed his lips. "The government enforced its mandatory evacuation order. That will save lives, but most will return to find their homes and farms destroyed and their livestock scattered or dead."

I said, "What do you think will happen here? Will Rufadora withstand the ash cover?"

"I hope so," Frank replied. "We've made a lot of structural improvements since buying the bar from Helen. If not, we'll either rebuild or relocate. We'd rather stay, though. We love the Subic Bay area."

"What made you stay after you retired? You could have lived in Hawaii, or back on the Mainland."

"Marie didn't want to leave the orphanage or Sister Arnalita. We knew she wouldn't leave the Philippines, and there's nothing tying me to home anymore, so that made living here an easy decision."

"Yes," Marie said. "Sister Arnalita gave up her position, but still works at the orphanage. She took care of our children when the Navy sent Frank back. Also, my parents are only two hours away in Baguio, but may move down later this year. So, you see that everything worked out well."

The door opened. Phil and Lucy, arm in arm, joined us at the bar.

"Hi, everyone." Lucy hugged Frank, then leaned over the bar to kiss Marie's cheek.

A flash of silver caught my eye. "Lucy, may I see your necklace?"

"Sure." She unclasped the necklace and handed it to me.

A chill ran down my back. "Where did you get this? I have one just like it." I slipped mine off and compared the two medallions. Each held a ruby. I held the medallions to the light; dual flaws in each ruby flashed red. Aida leaned over, her chin on my shoulder.

"Ohh, they are the same," she said.

"It was a gift from the man who was going to adopt me when I was a little girl."

My heart pounded. "My mother died giving birth to me. My father gave me up for adoption when he couldn't take care of me."

Lucy's voice trembled when she spoke. "Are there initials on the back of your medallion?"

"Yes. SRM, SAM, and a date, 7 March 1964. Samuel Richard McBride and Susanna Avila McBride, and the date of their marriage."

"Oh my God. Sam and Susanna wanted to adopt me."

"My parents?"

"Mom! Dad!" Lucy looked at her parents. "What does this mean?"

Frank's mouth hung open. Marie, however, smiled and said, "It means, Little Lucy, that a miracle has brought Sam and Susanna's son to us."

"Well, I'll be," Frank said. "Even the reddish hair is about the same."

"Oh. Oh. One moment." Marie stepped behind the bar and removed the photo from the wall.

"Do you know, I always felt Tom reminded me of someone. Look." She held the photo up and showed it around. "Look behind the sunglasses and beard. Do they not resemble each other?"

Aida darted around me and gazed at the photo.

"Let me see. Let me see." She looked from the photo to Tom. "Ohhhh, I think he looks a lot like him. I think maybe this is Tommy's father. Oh, Tommy. I am so happy for you."

I stared at the photo. "I always wondered who he was. But what does it mean? How does his photo come to be here? How did you all know him?"

"Sam and I met on the USS Midway and became close friends. We were in the same squadron you're in now. That isn't uncommon. Many fathers and sons served at different times in the same squadrons. We went to Vietnam when the squadron deployed to Cubi Point, and then came here on R&R. That's when I met Marie. For a few months, we—the three of us—were inseparable. Well, almost inseparable." He grinned at Marie.

"Yes. Frank was a good boy back then, and smart too."

He winked at Marie. "More careful than smart on occasion."

Marie kissed his cheek. "Yes, but our ninety-degree turns are infrequent now."

Little Lucy looked at Marie. "Mom. Dad. What are you two talking about?"

Marie smiled at Lucy. "Oh, just some old memories Sam is bringing back to us. Dear Sam."

Emotion overwhelmed me. Everything I knew of my world had turned upside down.

"How did he die?"

"Die?" Marie cut in before Frank could speak. "Oh, Tom. Your father isn't dead. He's alive. He lives in Florida."

My body went numb at the revelation in Marie's words. My brain scrambled to make sense of the sudden change in the beliefs I had carried since I was old enough to understand.

"What?" I said. "I thought he died saving his best friend's life." I paused and looked at Frank. "Wait. You were my dad's best friend?"

"Yes. I'm still your dad's best friend. He almost did die. His recovery took a long time, but he's fine now. We visit each other every year. He'll be here next week."

"Next week? I return to Hawaii next Wednesday." My head began to spin.

"He arrives in Manila early Wednesday morning."

"Will he want to see me? Will there be time?"

"I don't know, Tom," Frank said. "I'm meeting Sam at the airport. I'll tell him you're here, of course, and ask if he'd like to see you. Would you like that?"

Phil, silent up to then, said. "Boy, won't he be surprised."

"Phil," Lucy said as she punched his shoulder.

Aida clutched my hand. No one spoke.

Marie put her arm around my shoulder. "We will do anything

you ask of us, Tom. We love Sam dearly, and you too. We would love to see the two of you together. Now that I know who you are, I want to cry tears of happiness for you and Sam. For you and your father." She hugged him. "Oh, Tom. Who could have imagined this wonderful turn of events?"

"Yes, Frank. Please tell him about me. Please, please, please tell him I want to see him. There must be time."

"I'll tell him, Tom."

"What I don't understand is why my parents would tell me he died?"

"They told me they thought he had died. We thought so too. There was a lot of confusion at the time."

Frank looked faraway as he sought the words to explain. He must have returned in thought to that day in Vietnam when he and Sam were shot and the events that culminated in the discovery that Sam had not died. And here he was, so many years later, explaining it to the son of his best friend, the son neither had seen since I was an infant.

"Tom," he began. "Your dad's identity was mistaken for another man who was killed in the attack. The mistake was discovered when Sam nearly died during a blood transfusion. Somehow their dogtags were mixed up, and he was given the wrong type blood. There was so much confusion at the time. We didn't find out he was alive until six months later when he called me. I thought I was dreaming when I heard his voice."

My mind was tumbling. I could barely hear Frank through the sound of blood rushing in my ears. "But why has he never tried to reach me? Can I call him? Would he want to see me?"

"The adoption papers stipulated that your parents' identities would not be disclosed. I guess your adoptive parents thought it best not to say anything since they had agreed not to reveal his identity. They left it up to him to initiate contact with you."

"But I don't understand. Why did they not tell me before I left for bootcamp?"

"I don't know what to tell you, Tom. As for calling him, why not wait until he arrives in Manila? There's no sense in worrying him while he's travelling. A few more days won't do any harm."

"I guess you're right. There are so many things I want to ask him. So many things I want to know about my mother and him."

"I have photos of Sam and your mother. Wedding photos,

photos of them with Little Lucy. I can tell you about your mother. She was a fine woman, Tom, beautiful, tender, loving. I see her, and Sam, in you. Would you like to see the photos?"

"Yes. I would. I want you to tell me about them too. I know so little about them."

"I met Marie the first time I came to Rufadora. That was in 1968. Sam and I had a beer here that night. He sat on that barstool."

The others stood quietly as I placed Sam's photo on the bar and sat on his barstool. Tears dropped from my eyelashes as I tried to stand the frame, but it kept falling. Marie leaned over the bar and brought out several books from the shelf below.

She spoke softly as I stared at Sam's photo from beneath a furrowed brow. "Here, Tom. Let me help."

I stood still, unblinking, as Marie arranged the books. She leaned the frame against them.

"There. Is that better?"

I stared at the photo through a mix of emotions I had never felt, through the delicate veil of an obscure life I had never lived, a life that could have been, should have been. I didn't brush away the tears that dripped from my eyelashes like so many grains of an hourglass. I didn't blink away the misty film that blurred my sight. The blood rushed in my ears and shut off sound. The world around me disappeared as I gazed at Sam. My world consisted solely of myself and my father, my real father, the man whose image I now looked at, a one-dimensional image behind a bushy red beard and blue-lensed sunglasses and a cheerful smile that seemed to say, *I will live forever.*

My chest was full of another Tom I didn't know. The Tom that lived on another plane of existence with his father and mother. I wasn't aware that I wasn't thinking at all. In the time it takes to voice a hope, to make a wish, to shed a tear, I lived another life with Sam and Susanna. I breathed in a new childhood and adolescence, new joys and sorrows, motherly love and fatherly advice, and exhaled them into my dreams. Into a world that began and died in the same moment. A life that lasted one short breath, one fleeting spark. The time it takes for a mother to open her eyes, to see her newborn son, to smile, to blink, to die. The time it takes for a heart to break.

Marie's voice penetrated my dream. I blinked and looked at

her. "What? Yes. Thank you, Marie." I looked around, meeting the eyes of each of them. "I don't know what to think. This is so sudden and overwhelming. How did Sam ... how was my father wounded, Frank?"

"While saving my life. A sniper shot me in the chest as I boarded a chopper to leave Vietnam. Sam raced across the tarmac, under fire, picked me up, and carried me to safety. But not before the sniper shot him twice in the back. Sam tried to cover me with his body even as his own life was slipping away. Chip, another friend, said Sam thought I had died, and wondered what he would tell Marie, how he would tell her I had died. Those were his last words before he lost consciousness. But before Sam passed out, he gave the medallion to Chip and told him to give it to Lucy."

The jolt of an earthquake startled us and broke the spell of reminiscence. The quake was followed by a loud, thundering roar as Pinatubo erupted. This time the roar didn't stop. Pinatubo was finally venting the fury she had built up over the centuries.

"This is it," Frank yelled. "Get outside. Hurry!"

The floor rumbled beneath our feet, making it difficult to run. The building shook. Liquor bottles fell and smashed to pieces. The few servers on duty ran screaming into the street. Frank took Marie and Little Lucy by the arms and ran them outside while the rest of us followed. Torrential rain from Typhoon Diding poured from the sky. A thick morass of mud-like ash already filled the street. The rain fell so hard it splashed mud-ash waist high. Frank ran into Rufadora and returned with umbrellas, barely useful in the powerful wind gusts. The six of us huddled together as Pinatubo blew her top in a rage of red-hot magma. Her ash column towered into the atmosphere, unseen through the thick rain. Streets filled with people too terrified to remain indoors for fear buildings might collapse, and too afraid to remain outdoors as hell broke loose around them. Ash bombs fell from the sky. The stench of sulphur mixed with the smell of gas leaking from cracked pipes. Terrified children clutched at terrified parents as they huddled together against the hellish nightmare. Fragile, puny humans stood in waterlogged groups and helplessly faced nature's greatest wrath, a trifecta of natural fury as Pinatubo erupted, earthquakes tore the city apart, and Typhoon Diding shut out the sun and turned day into liquid night.

The worst of the disaster ended nine hours later. From the roar, the torrential rain slowed to a drizzle, and the ground stopped shaking and rolling. Pinatubo belched the last of her ash into the sky and slowly returned to the semi-dormant state from which she had awakened just a few months before. The dread and strained nerves of the population around her flanks disappeared as the Filipino's natural tendency for hard work took over. They wiped their brows, straightened their backs, spit in their hands, and began to rebuild their villages, towns, and lives, one shovelful of ash at a time.

Chapter Thirty-Three

Tom

I didn't sleep much. The prospect of travel had thrilled me since childhood and made it nearly impossible to sleep the night before a journey. What a journey I was embarking upon.

"Baluuut. Baluuut." The tremulous voice of the old Filipino broke in on my thoughts. I ran a finger along the window sill, drawing a long, straight line in the thin film of white-grey volcanic ash. A strong odor of sulphur drifted on the night air.

"Baluuut. Baluuut." The call faded as the old man and his mule shuffled away.

I shook Aida's shoulder. "Aida. Sweetheart. It's time to get up."

She stirred, then drew the bedsheet over her nose. Sad eyes peered from behind the sheet.

"Oh, honey ko. You leaving today."

She sat up and leaned on my shoulder, aching already for my absence. She clung to me, unwilling to release her grip until I whispered that I had to get ready. She rose and helped me pack. After we showered and dressed, she packed the lunch she had made for me the night before, my favorite: sweet and sour fish with celery, carrot, red bell pepper, and snow peas, all in red sauce. And rice, too. I would warm it in the aircraft galley.

I shut the squeaky gate behind me, smiling for the umpteenth time at my promises to bring home oil for the hinges. Aida shook her head. I walked on but stopped to wait for her. She was moving the gate back and forth, letting it squeak without pause.

"Aida, what are you doing that for?"

"Oh, honey ko. I'm glad you don't bring home oil for the gate. If you do, I'm going to miss the squeak and thinking about your promises. This way, when the gate squeaks, I will think of you."

I gathered Aida close and put my arm around her. We walked to the base through a white-gray city resembling a scene from a black and white disaster movie. Evidence of the calamity lay everywhere, coated with a thick blanket of human misery. Ash had fallen for three days after the eruption, mixing with heavy rain, and turning into a thick, muddy mixture that collapsed roofs and clogged drains. We passed beneath Mayor Gordon's *Aim High, Olongapo* banner as all around us people shoveled pathways in the ash-mud or pushed it off roofs with brooms and shovels. Bulldozers coughed and sputtered as they cleared and razed. Filipinos were resilient and resourceful, proud of their city; they would rebuild. Their beloved mayor would provide the inspiration.

It had been an emotional few days that left me deeply affected. I had found my father and mother, and the people who could tell me about them. I marveled at the circumstances that brought us together. How five people from my unknown past turned up in the present and changed my life. One of them was only a memory, remembered by four who had loved her.

We passed Rufadora without stopping. Frank and Marie had gone to pick up Sam in Manila. If all went well, I would meet my father before leaving for Hawaii. I tightened my arm around Aida's waist as we navigated bricks from a fallen wall. I had spent most of my relationship with Aida navigating bars and nightclubs looking for a mythical love while she waited patiently for me with a love that was timeless. It took an embarrassing confrontation in Thailand and Aida's near-death for me to understand that she loved me the way I had longed to be loved. I had come to realize I loved her the way I had always longed to love a woman. A love of the heart, and not of the head.

Aida was my companion now, my best friend, the half of my heart that brought happiness and meaning to my life. She had waited patiently for me to work through my fears and foolishness, for she knew me better than I knew myself. In her few years at Rufadora, she encountered every kind of man from the virgin boy too timid to approach a woman, to the cynical man whose bravado couldn't hide a weakness of flesh; the shy, lonely ones whose lack of confidence inhibited intimacy, to the cruel, rough creeps who vented their anger and filth on innocent young girls seeking a better life. I was none of those but, like any man, I could be some of each. I needed Aida's tender but firm character to ground me in the reality of a living love and not some magical love that existed only in fairy tales and family legend. I touched her often, as though to make sure she was still there, to make sure she wouldn't leave. I didn't want to leave her, not for the short time before we reunited in Hawaii.

Aida's vise-like grip on my hand telegraphed the fear that had increased in intensity over the past few days. She was unnaturally quiet. I remained silent too, from fear of spoiling our last moments together by saying something forgettable. We would say goodbye at the hangar gate, the eight-foot tall chain-link fence the last thing to come between us. Where had six months gone?

"I'll send for you, Aida, once I do the paperwork and get the approvals. I'll fly you to Hawaii, and we'll be married in the base chapel, okay?"

"Okay, Tommy. You will write to me, Tommy, won't you? Please write to me. I'm afraid that when you leave and go back to America, you will forget about me. You won't love me anymore. Please write to me, Tommy. Please, honey ko."

"I will, Aida. I will. I'll write every week until you leave PI. I'll send you enough money to pay the rent and other bills. Remember to send me your paperwork as soon as you can. I can't send for you until I have all of your documents."

"Okay. I will go to my parents and stay for a while. Cora will tell me when you send a letter for me. She will receive my mail when I am in my village."

"I can't wait to come back next year and see Marie and Frank, and Lucy too, if she hasn't married Phil by then. We'll have so much fun with them. I can hardly believe what has happened in the last week. I found my father and mother. I found you too, for true."

I was nervous for what seemed like the wrong reasons. Nervous to get the goodbyes said and the tears wiped away. To get on the aircraft so I could calm down and breathe easy. The last few days had exhausted me, and my mind was full of thoughts, memories, and emotions that my brain needed time to absorb, classify, and file away. I wasn't anxious to leave Aida, but ready to embark on the next stage in my life.

I pulled her close. "Little Lucy nearly became my sister! I'm so happy we met all of them. Isn't it strange, though, Aida, how everything worked out, how small the world is? To think that here, in the Philippines, nine thousand miles from home, I found my parents. It's amazing."

"Oh, honey ko. I am so happy for you. I happiest, though, that you found me. I happiest that we are together, and happiest that soon we will be a husband and wife. You make me so happy, Tommy. I love you, honey ko."

"I love you, too, Aida."

We kissed long and passionately. I folded Aida into my arms and felt her heartbeat. Her black hair brushed my cheek and tickled my forehead. I ran my hands along her sides and over her hips. When I opened my eyes, I found her looking at me.

"I wanted to be sure it was you," she said and closed her eyes. She opened them again at the sound of rapid footsteps as Phil ran to meet us. Lucy followed behind him.

"Goodbye, Aida," Phil said. "I'll see you when you come to Hawaii. Stay close to Lucy. Let her know if you need anything. Come on, Tom. We gotta go. Give me your bag." Phil waved as he raced to the aircraft with my bag.

I held Aida's hands. "Well, Aida. I guess Sam won't get here in time. I'm sorry I won't get to see him."

"Oh, Tommy. I sorry for you because I know how much you want to see him. My heart breaking for you. I will tell him how sad you are."

"Thank you, Aida."

Phil called to me again. "I have to go, Aida. This is goodbye for now. Take care of yourself. Let me know if you need anything. If you have any problems at all, go see Frank and Marie."

"I will, Tommy. I will." Her lips trembled as I caressed her cheek.

"Tommy," she cried.

"Yes, Aida?"

"What do you see?"

"I see you loving me despite my faults, Aida. I see myself grateful for your love."

"I love you, honey ko."

"I love you, Aida."

Now, as we parted, as I walked toward the aircraft that would carry me away from the woman I loved, I found myself thinking of Lek and Sasi and the other women I had known. Susanna, the woman whose death had broken my heart just as I began to understand the love a woman can bring out of a man. I remembered the happy times with each of them, the lovemaking and the strolls, the laughs and tears. Someday, I would look back with fondness on those times. I had made happy memories in the Philippines and Thailand, Spain and Hong Kong, and many other places, and I would find there was always room for sentiment among the many years of happiness I would find with Aida.

I picked up my pace. I didn't want to keep the other guys waiting. We were spending the night in Guam, and everyone wanted to get there in time for a few beers in town. I was halfway across the ramp when Phil ran up and pointed toward the parking lot.

"Tom," Phil called. "Look!"

I followed Phil's gaze. Frank and Marie had stepped from their car. A man followed Marie. I waved and was about to run to them, but stopped when the man stepped from behind Marie.

"Go to him, Tom! I told the mission commander what was going on. He said we'd wait. Go!"

The man looked across the ramp. He took a step, then stopped. Marie said something to him and he walked toward me. My heart pounded, and my throat was thick with joy. I choked back tears. My chest was ready to burst, and I trembled with excitement and trepidation. The man stopped a few paces from me. He appeared wary, afraid of his reception. Uncertainty gripped me too. Had he come willingly? Had he come only to please Frank and Marie? Did he even want to see me?

I smiled and my lip curled the way it always did, the same way my mother's lip had curled. My tears were warm and salty.

"Dad?"

"Hello, Tom." His voice choked with emotion. "You look just like your mother. You look just like her."

I ran to my father and took him in my arms. "Dad."

"Oh, Tom. I'm so sorry for everything."

"No, Dad. This is a new beginning. There is nothing to be sorry for."

Chapter Thirty-Four

Tom

I paused at the top of the aircraft ladder to wave to the group who had come to see me off. An odd pressure seized my chest. My heart ached with love for my new family. I waved to Sam. I waved to Frank and Marie, and Phil and Little Lucy. I waved to Aida, who stood with Sam's arm around her shoulder. I waved with the relief that had washed over me as the tension drained away. For the first time in what seemed forever, I was completely at ease. Aida would join me in Hawaii in a few months. Frank and Marie would see us when they visited Hawaii. Sam would join me soon and, in a way, so would my mother. She would become as much a part of my life as Sam through his memories.

I couldn't leave Sasi without explanation and had called her from the hangar earlier in the week. She understood and was sorry I wouldn't return to her. She sincerely wished me every happiness with Aida. She hoped we'd meet in Barcelona someday and have a glass of sangria together. We left it at that.

I settled into my ditching station next to the overwing escape hatch and peered through the window as the aircraft taxied to the runway. I snapped a photo of the five people who meant the most to me.

After the aircraft leveled off, I retrieved my backpack from the cargo area. I took a seat at the galley table, poured a cup of coffee, and removed my leather journal from the pocket of the backpack. I opened to an entry I made when I thought I was leaving Susanna for a year-long tour alone. With the open journal on the table, I smoothed the crease with my finger and read: Susanna's love caressed me with …

... the softness of a mother's lips. Passion gripped me for this beautiful Spanish woman whose green eyes pierced and tugged at my soul with the gravity of a thousand suns. My heart bled when we parted and exploded when we came together. My mind flew away when her arms enfolded me. Enveloped by her breath, her fragrance of orange blossoms, her warmth, my face pressed hard to the translucent white of her neck as I pushed and clutched and struggled to become her. Her searing flame boiled my blood and swelled my desire as we thrust together into regions of unexplored emotion. Peak upon peak we ascended 'til at last we reached the climax of energy, breath catching in our throats, lips pressed together in a passionate release of giving one to the other. I swallowed her moans into me.

Together we sought to live and smile and laugh and love for the few short months ahead, for I would leave Spain soon, and a year would pass before our lips could touch again. The thought saddened us, and we pushed it away, yet it lingered, a dark foreboding on the horizon, an unwelcome intruder bringing an edge of sadness to our joy.

Summer passed, and with it, warm days spent walking on Mediterranean beaches and nights cooled by breezes from the sea as we explored the narrow cobblestoned streets of Barcelona. We danced in discotheques and sipped sangria in bodegas; we shared cones of fried rice and shrimp bought from street vendors; we sat in chapels and listened to the chanting of monks for we both loved beautiful music. My hand always pressed the small of Susanna's back; a mere wisp of a woman, I feared she would fly away on the tail of a wind. Our hands rarely unclasped, and her head rested on my shoulder always. I had never known such joy.

I sat back, my throat tight. The hum and vibration of the aircraft lulled me into a drowsy reverie. I reflected on my relationship with Susanna, the deep love between us that touched others the way Sam and Susanna's had. I thought of my relationships with Aida, Lek, and Sasi. I understood at last that the love between a man and a woman is a love like no other. Each love is its own love, unique, special, personal. This love cannot be shared. Love can be envied, can be called fairy tale, but it cannot be imitated. Love is not black and white, but changes with each sundown and rises anew each day. Love grows deeper as infatuation gives way to passion, the first blush of mature love. And passion becomes intimacy, then sharing and commitment, and finally, companionship, that time of life when husband and wife walk together in loving friendship. Sam did not have the chance to move beyond passion for Susanna. Her death left him grieving for what might have been, not for what he lost. I had not given myself time for love to blossom with Aida when I reached for the fairy tale. But then I met Sasi, who helped me say goodbye to Susanna and returned me to Aida.

Through Aida, I learned that I had not known what love was and therefore had no foundation upon which to build a deep and meaningful relationship with a woman. My love had been pursuit of an imitation love. The futile pursuit had no end, but a continuous striving for fulfillment that brought only emptiness. My love for Susanna was real, enduring, and eternal, nothing could change that, but it was based on the reflection of a love I longed to have myself.

I replaced the letter in the envelope and slipped it into the pocket of my backpack. Settling into the seat, I closed my eyes. A thought occurred to me and I removed the necklace and held it so the light reflected from the medallion, the rubies, and Susanna's ring. I gazed at the precious objects until wetness blurred my vision. The heart bleeds the same in love and grief, and mine bled at that moment. My heart swelled and warmed until I thought I would choke with happiness. I let the tears run as I slipped the necklace into the blue silk pouch and tucked the pouch away. I leaned back in the seat, and as the brilliant, white clouds floated past the window, the weight of two Susannas lifted from my shoulders and my heart flew light again.

Benediction

Aida was always the one, Susanna.
Yes, Tomás.
She has given me the half of my heart I buried with you.
Yes, Tomás. I knew love would come to you again.
I grieved so long, Susanna.
Yes, Tomás. Too long.
Aida makes me feel like you and I are together again.
I am happy for you, Tomás. For you both.
I can't bring you back, Susanna, so I must go on living for both of us.
Yes, Tomás, and you must forget me.
No, Susanna. I won't forget you.
You must forget me if you want to love Aida.
No, Susanna. I can love you both.
How can you love us both, Tomás?
I can love you both because I am not choosing between you.
Because I am dead, Tomás?
No, my dearest love. Because I no longer grieve for you.
I am so glad, Tomás. Now your heart may live again.
My heart may live again because I love again.
What else, Tomás?
Because Aida loves me the way you loved me, Susanna.
How did I love you, Tomás?
You loved me to the depth of my soul with no expectation of anything in return. You were my companion, and whose comforting presence was like the womb that surrounds the unborn child: protective, warm, loving.
Oh, Tomás, that is indeed how I loved you.
Will you always be with me, Susanna?
Of course, Tomás. True love never dies.
I will always love you, Susanna.
I will always love you, Tomás.

The Author

William C. Pennington was born in Ankara, Turkey, to an Air Force father and mother. He grew up in Turkey, California, Holland, and Florida. When his third-grade teacher, Miss Jenkins, asked him on the first day in class where his hometown was, he answered he didn't have a hometown. So it was. The world was Will's hometown. When he later gave his heart to the Navy, Will continued traveling his hometown, serving for twenty-seven years at military bases around the globe. His world-wise youth and service gave him insight into cultures most people encounter only in books and documentaries.

Calling upon his well-traveled background, Will writes of the peoples he lived among and the places he calls home. He maintains a writer's blog, *Writers Envy*, practices his craft earnestly, and fancies reading and writing poetry above all things. A collection of Will's personal essays was published in the anthology *Four Feet Down,* available on Amazon. He resides in Saint Leonard, Maryland, with his wife, Jayne Michiko Ono, two rescued pups, Yukio and Sachiko, and memories of Smoky, Misty, Toby, and Yoshi. You may follow Will on Facebook, Instagram, and Twitter. You may also contact Will at william.c.pennington@writersenvy.com.

Made in the USA
Coppell, TX
19 May 2020